2017

Out of a Dream

Sandy Cove Series Book One

Rosemary Hines

To the One who promised He would redeem the years the locusts ate away. Thank you for rescuing me out of the miry pit of deception and planting my feet on your solid rock of truth.

"I am the way, the truth, and the life. No one comes to the father except through me."

~ Jesus

(John 14:7)

CHAPTER ONE

March
Sandy Cove, Oregon

Michelle Baron's heart raced, pounding in her ears. She panted, gasping for every breath. Her eyes searched for an escape. The passageway was dark and narrow. A faint beam of light flickered at the end. She fought the damp, suffocating air. Footsteps from behind made louder and louder slaps on the pavement. How much farther could her legs carry her?

She felt a hand reach out and grab her shoulder. Spinning, she found herself staring into the face of a middle-aged man. His gray hair was tousled and his wrinkled face looked intense. The seriousness of his expression frightened her. "I'm Marty, Michelle. I can help you."

She shook her head in fear, turned, and ran.

"Michelle....wait...Michelle...."

If only she could get to the light....

"Michelle! Hey, wake up! Are you okay?"

A hand was on her shoulder again. She awoke in a sweat, her eyes darting like a hunted animal. The sound of the wind howling outside added to her disorientation as the rain beat in a steady pattern, like the footsteps which had pursued her.

"It's okay, Michelle." Her husband pulled her toward himself.

She reached for Steve and his embrace enveloped her. Clinging to him in the predawn darkness of their bedroom, she felt like a helpless child rather than a twenty-one-year-old newlywed.

"It was the same, Steve. Just like last week." Michelle shivered. "Where are these dreams coming from?" She clutched him like a life raft, searching his face for answers.

Holding her around the shoulder with one arm, Steve reached over and flipped on the bedside lamp, gently pushing her long, dark hair off her face. "I don't know, babe. I don't know."

As he held her close, her breathing slowed. She began to relax as he cupped her face in his hands. "Maybe you should talk to someone about this. You know, someone professional."

"Like a therapist? Do you think there's something wrong with me, Steve?"

"No, Michelle," he replied with a loving but somewhat patronizing tone. "I just think that maybe a counselor could help you figure this out. I hate to see you going through this night after night."

He arose from the bed and walked into the bathroom, adding under his breath, "Besides, I've got to get more sleep before these big briefings."

When he returned a moment later, he asked, "Did you have these dreams before we got married?"

Michelle shook her head. "Not like this."

"Maybe it has something to do with me or being married."

"It's not you, Steve." She stared off into space, her brow furrowed as she automatically began twisting a small patch of hair at the nape of her neck.

He sat down again beside her, reaching for her hand and gently guiding it away from the small clump of hidden, frayed hair. "I don't remember you having any nightmares on our honeymoon," he said softly.

"Me neither." Michelle looked up into his eyes and smiled slightly. "Like I said, it's not you, Steve. It's not the marriage."

"Well, what do you think it is?"

"I don't know. Maybe it's the move. Maybe I just need to get used to living up here," she replied, fighting off images of her family and friends down in Southern California.

"I thought you were fine with this," he said, lifting her chin with his finger so they were looking eye to eye. "You knew I'd be taking this job before we got married."

"Yeah. It sounded like an adventure at the time…"

"So now you wish we hadn't moved up here?" He looked concerned.

"No." She glanced away, tears beginning to pool in her eyes. "You just don't get it," she said softly.

"You're right, Michelle. But I'm trying." He stood up and walked over to the closet.

Their half-grown kitten, Max, jumped up on the bed beside Michelle. She took him into her arms and stroked his soft, multicolored hair.

Steve started to walk back into the bathroom and then turned. "Hey, do you think these dreams might have something to do with that yoga class you've been taking?"

Michelle bristled, her defenses rising. "No, Steve. Yoga helps you relax and get more centered."

"Just asking. You said there were some hypnosis things they were doing in that class."

"What? The guided imagery?"

"Whatever you want to call it. Didn't you say the teacher had you guys imagining some scene and going toward a light?"

"What's with you and my yoga class?" Michelle asked defensively, her early morning fear turning into aggravation.

"Hey," he replied, "I'm not the enemy here, okay? I'm just trying to help you figure out these dreams."

Steve's pragmatic side frustrated her. Couldn't he understand how lonely she was since they'd moved so far away from her family and friends? He was busy at work all day pursuing a career he loved. She was left at home alone.

"You were the one who suggested I take the spring semester off so that we could get settled. What am I supposed to do while you're at work all day? My yoga class is the only thing I really have to look forward to during the week."

Sighing, Steve walked over to her and placed his hands on her shoulders. "You're right, honey."

His soft reply caught her off guard. Michelle's anger began to melt as she looked into his pale blue eyes. Ever since she met him at the university library, she was attracted to his gentle smile and his weathered and boyishly handsome face. At twenty-six years of age, he seemed so much older and more mature than Michelle and her classmates. But it was his eyes that captured her heart. They were able to gaze into her very soul.

"Let's do something special tonight," he suggested, wrapping his arms around her waist. "I'll try to get off early."

Michelle smiled tentatively and nodded. Giving him a kiss, she turned to grab her robe off the rocking chair and head downstairs to make the coffee.

The cozy cottage decor of their kitchen had a mood-lifting effect on her, and the aroma of freshly brewing coffee soon filled the room. Before she could pour herself a cup, Max cornered her against the counter, rubbing across her legs and purring.

She reached down and ruffled his fur. "What is it, Max? Are you hungry?" she asked, her voice still a bit shaky.

Max mewed in response, his green eyes looking up plaintively into hers. She walked over to the cupboard and pulled out a can of cat food, and he immediately began prancing in circles, as if chiding her to hurry.

After getting him settled with his breakfast, she peeked out the window over the sink to get a first glimpse of the new day. Heavy rain clouds blanketed their neighborhood, overshadowing a thin sliver of light on the horizon.

When they first moved to Sandy Cove in January, Michelle had enjoyed the stormy Oregon weather. California was undergoing a warm winter drought, and she savored the opportunity to keep a fire going in the fireplace and snuggle beside it with Steve when he finally got home from work at night.

By February the constantly dripping sky became monotonous. Now March looked to be much the same.

She flipped on the television and listened as the weatherman predicted a full day of rain with moderate wind. "Oh brother," she said in a low whisper, all joy drained from her voice.

Though Sandy Cove was a quaint, likeable seaside community when warmed in the glow of a sunny day, for much of the year its atmosphere was one of persistent clouds and temperamental storms. Gazing outside, Michelle sighed. The weather matched her mood these days—restless, depressed, uneasy. She punched off the power button, silencing the news.

Opening the bag of wheat bread, she walked over to the toaster and dropped two pieces inside. She checked the setting. Light. Pushing down the lever, she turned to the refrigerator for the butter and jam. *Better hurry or Steve will leave without eating again.*

Michelle set the spreads beside the toaster, poured two cups of coffee, and carried them over to the table. Sitting down, she glanced at the unpaid bills standing in the napkin holder. Going from college coed to married homemaker was not all she'd hoped it would be.

As she listened to the sounds of Steve upstairs and sipped her coffee, she indulged in a moment of reminiscing.

The past ten months were somewhat of a blur. Steve's initial constant attention and affections had quickly won her heart. The thought of marrying a law school graduate and moving to a new town in another state seemed so romantic and exciting as they discussed it at the Italian restaurant the night he proposed.

Their breathtakingly beautiful Christmas wedding was the finishing touch on a fairy-tale romance. Michelle almost felt like she was floating above the congregation as she promised her life to Steve.

"I *should* be happy," she remarked with a sigh.

After all, how many law graduates were offered a junior partnership right out of school? Steve's uncle had been great. Retiring from his law practice in Sandy Cove to pursue his dream of writing legal intrigue novels, he had convinced his partner to bring Steve into the firm as his replacement. Knowing that the move would displace these Southern California natives, he'd also generously loaned them the money for a down payment on their house.

So why wasn't Michelle happy? Somehow she needed to shake the gloom she wore like a tattered shawl. If she could just get to the bottom of her dreams....

"What are you thinking about?" Steve asked as he entered the kitchen.

As if on cue, the toast popped up at the same moment, and Michelle walked over to butter it. "Just stuff."

"Any stuff I need to know?" Steve approached her from behind and wrapped his arms around her waist as he kissed the back of her head.

Wanting to avoid rehashing their earlier conversation, she replied, "Just thinking about the night you proposed to me." She turned and handed him the plate with the buttered toast.

"Ahh, yes. Great lasagna," he replied with a grin.

"Leave it to a guy to remember the food." Michelle's eyes rolled as she gave him a faint smile.

"Well, I'd love to sit here and stroll down memory lane with you, but—"

"—but you've got to get to work," Michelle interrupted, hoping her voice didn't sound resentful.

"You got it, babe!" Steve grabbed a piece of paper towel for his toast. "I'll eat on the way. Could you pour my coffee into this?" He handed her his travel mug that had been sitting on the counter.

She quickly transferred the coffee from the cup on the table into his thermal mug and sealed the lid. "Here you go, sir."

"I'll see *you* tonight," Steve replied, leaning over and giving her a good-bye kiss.

As Michelle got ready to take her shower, she glanced at the unmade bed and shivered as she remembered her early morning episode. She knew that she needed to talk to someone about these dreams. But who?

A warm shower washed away some of her anxiety, and she felt lighter as she slipped into her workout pants. The soft, gray fabric fit comfortably and flattered her tall, slim figure. A pale yellow sweatshirt contrasted with her long, wavy black hair that fell in cascades down the center of her back.

Bending at the waist, Michelle brushed through the waves upside down. When she swung herself upright again, her hair fell perfectly in place creating a thick, shiny frame around her delicate face. Her hazel eyes carefully guided her as she applied lipstick and eyeliner. The final result was stunning.

Many people had told her she should be a model. But walking down a runway or posing for a photo shoot scared her. Her shy nature preferred to hide comfortably in the background. While beauty was one of her God-given strengths, confidence was not. Besides, Michelle had a different career path in mind. She would be a teacher. Someday.

Glancing at her watch, she realized it was about time to leave for yoga. "Monica should be here any minute," she commented to Max, who was rubbing up against her leg.

A moment later the doorbell rang. "Gotta go!" she added, turning and heading downstairs with Max at her heels.

Out of habit, she peeked through the peephole before turning the bolt. There was Monica Nabors, her only friend in Sandy Cove.

Opening the door, she thought about how much Monica reminded her of a friend from elementary school. Her rather plain face possessed a wide smile that rested between two dimples. It was her smile, Michelle decided, that gave her a certain air of familiarity.

"How's it going, girl?" Monica asked.

For just a moment, Michelle flashed back to their initial meeting. It had been at their first yoga class. Plunking herself down on a mat next to her, Monica had thrust out her hand offering her name and a smile.

Regaining her focus, Michelle replied, "Fine. How about you?" She pulled her jacket on and reached for her umbrella.

"Other than Tony driving me crazy, I'm great!"

Michelle laughed as they walked together out to the car. Monica's husband, Tony, worked construction and there were too many days when the weather kept him cooped up at home. According to Monica, those were the days when she was glad to have her job at the drugstore.

"How's that lawyer of yours?" her friend asked, climbing into the driver's seat.

"Actually, I wish I had your problem. Steve's hardly ever home."

Monica nodded and smiled. "Let's trade!" she suggested with a grin. She had a disarming way of making Michelle feel comfortable and special. Though several years older than Michelle, they clicked well as friends.

"I'll think about it."

"Yeah. Right."

"How's Tony's mom?" Michelle asked as they approached the recreation center where the yoga class was held. Currently, Monica's mother-in-law, Beth, was staying with Monica and Tony in the aftermath of her husband's death.

"She's fine. Reads her Bible day and night. I'm not sure what she sees in those old stories, but they seem to comfort her."

Michelle just nodded, thinking about her grandparents and their solid Christian faith.

As they walked into class, Bev Harrison, the instructor, nodded to them with an ethereal smile. Her gaze settled on Michelle. "Are you okay, dear?" she asked, her face showing concern.

Michelle hedged for a moment or two, replying that she was fine. But after Bev persisted in her inquiry, she finally confessed the source of her anxiety.

"Dreams are gifts, Michelle," the teacher explained as Monica listened in. "You just need to understand their hidden messages. I know someone who can help you."

She handed Michelle a purple business card with silver lettering. The New World Bookstore. Starla Stein, Proprietor. The address was a local shopping center. "You'll love Starla." Bev smiled reassuringly and nodded as if to emphasize her point. Then she turned and walked toward the front mat.

"Let me see that card," Monica said, extending her hand. She looked it over and read the address. "This place is in the same strip mall where the drugstore is. I've been wanting to check it out. Maybe we can go this week."

"Okay," Michelle replied, tucking the card into her pocket.

By this time, the rest of the class had arrived. Bev welcomed everyone. As she began her instruction, they assumed their relaxation positions, closed their eyes, and listened to her lulling voice while she guided them down an imaginary path to a peaceful meadow.

Michelle tried to relax, but a nagging sense of anxiety remained. Opening her eyes momentarily, she could see Bev's weathered face, pulled tight by the braid in her waist-length gray hair. Though the older woman's voice sounded peaceful, her body was rigid and her forehead was slightly furrowed. Everyone else seemed relaxed and almost in a trance.

Quietly taking a deep breath, Michelle closed her eyes and forced herself to picture the meadow in her mind.

It was five o'clock when Steve's car pulled into the garage. The creaking sound of the garage door caught

Max's attention, and he began pacing back and forth in the kitchen waiting for Steve to come into the house. Meanwhile, Michelle carefully lifted the pizza from the oven and set it on the counter.

The coffee table in the family room was already set with colorful quilted placemats, two new vanilla scented tapered candles in glass holders, and two crystal goblets. Michelle had started a fire in the fireplace and the room was aglow. Romantic classical guitar music played softly in the background as the rain danced outside the window.

As Steve entered, Max darted over to greet him. Steve nearly lost his footing as the cat ran between his legs. "Whoa there, boy!"

Michelle laughed. "Guess he's been missing you today."

Setting his briefcase down, Steve squatted and scratched Max behind the ears, then stood and wrapped his arms around Michelle's waist. "How was your day, babe?" he asked as he kissed her.

"It was fine. I went to yoga with Monica."

"Oh. That's nice," he replied as he released her and picked up the mail on the table.

"No snide remarks about yoga?" she asked.

"Nope." He looked at her and smiled, then leaned over and gave her another lingering kiss. "Let's eat. That pizza smells great!"

Together they managed to carry the plates, salad, and drinks into the family room, Max on their heels.

"Good job on the fire," he commented, sounding proud of her newly acquired talent for starting a wood burning fire.

She smiled. "Thanks."

They settled down on the floor facing the fireplace, and chatted while they ate. Max made the most of the situation by curling up in a ball next to Steve. His

17

warm, furry body and contented purring completed the family portrait.

After they finished their dinner, Michelle leaned against Steve. His strong, but gentle, arm around her made her feel safe and loved. As she rested her head against his chest, she could hear his heartbeat. The steady, rhythmic sound soothed her and she closed her eyes.

Golden flames in the fireplace were caressing the logs. A sweet fragrance from the vanilla candles mingled with the scent of burning wood. Lilting guitar music drifted through the air.

Neither of them spoke. Michelle felt Steve shift positions. She looked up, her eyes meeting his. Steve slowly bent down and kissed Michelle.

"I love you, babe," he said in a husky voice.

"I love you, too." She reached over and cupped his face in her hands as she returned his kiss. Then wrapping her arms around his neck, she dissolved into his embrace.

It was well after midnight when they finally climbed up the stairs to go to bed. Although she'd been relaxed and happy spending an intimate evening with Steve, Michelle could feel her chest tightening and her heart rate quickening as they left behind their love nest in the family room. With her nightmares becoming a regular occurrence, their bedroom was turning into more of a prison than a haven. She knew that Steve would quickly fall asleep, and she would be left alone, clinging to her covers as if to shield herself from her fears.

Steve took her hand as they walked up the stairs. "Thanks for a great evening," he said, giving her hand a squeeze.

Michelle nodded and squeezed his hand in return, hoping her anxiety didn't show.

Max had long since retired to his favorite spot for the night—on the rocking chair in the corner of their bedroom. She smiled as she glanced at his curled up body.

Steve was first in bed, and she hurried to get into her nightgown. The room felt chilly compared to the warmth of the fireplace they had enjoyed all evening. She slipped under the covers and snuggled up against her man. His warm body felt good, and she tried to relax.

But her mind remained troubled. Just the act of closing her eyes brought up images of the dark tunnel that haunted her dreams.

Tomorrow I'll go see Bev's friend. Maybe she can help me.

The rain pelted against their bedroom window, and Michelle tried to picture a calm meadow in her mind as her nightly fears engulfed her.

CHAPTER TWO

The sky was rapidly darkening as Michelle drove toward town the next morning, determined to get to the bottom of her nightmares after another restless night. She'd tried to call Monica to see if she would go with her, but the phone had gone directly to voicemail.

Heavy, black clouds blanketed the coastline and an onshore wind was driving the storm straight toward Sandy Cove. Michelle glanced down at the passenger seat to reassure herself that her umbrella was in its usual resting place. Since their move, she had learned not to leave home without it. Daily Oregon "liquid sun," as Steve referred to the climate.

Pulling into the parking lot of the mini-mall, she maneuvered her car into the only spot she could see that was anywhere near the bookstore. She flipped open her cell phone and dialed Monica one more time. No answer. Looking toward the bookstore, a familiar anxiety began attaching itself to her heart. Grabbing her umbrella, she forced herself out of the car, locked the doors, and hurried toward her destination.

The cold wind nipped at her face. Any apprehension she felt about approaching someone she didn't know was rapidly replaced by an eagerness to get inside.

Glancing into the window of The New World Bookstore, Michelle caught a glimpse of the statue of a hand holding a crystal globe. It was surrounded by a selection of books poised on black velvet material. Metallic silver and gold confetti stars were sprinkled over the entire display, giving it an ethereal aura. She paused momentarily under the overhang to read the titles.

Natural Health Remedies,
Eastern Thought,
Yoga and Meditation,
Divination, Tarot Cards & Prophecy,
Spiritual Enlightenment,
Dreams & The Subconscious Mind,
New Age Therapies,
Alternative Lifestyles,
Ecology & Environmental Studies,
Women's Issues,
Astrology, Reincarnation & Personal Evolution.

Pulling the door open, Michelle immediately noticed the fragrance of pine-scented incense. She could hear the sounds of flute and lyre music adding to the mystical ambiance of the softly lit bookstore.

No one was at the counter, so she began to wander through the bookshelves and table displays. The store was larger than it appeared from the street, winding back through many rows of interestingly angled shelves and islands.

Rounding one pyramid-shaped display, Michelle noticed an older woman in a long caftan-style dress perusing a large, heavy book. Her long gray hair was pulled back into a loose ponytail held in place by a leather-covered barrette. The woman looked up at her and smiled, wrinkle lines raying out in all directions from her light blue eyes.

"Can I help you with something?" she asked.

"I'm looking for someone named Starla," Michelle replied, glancing down at the business card she was clutching in her hand.

"Look no further. How can I be of service to you?" the woman responded warmly as she stretched out her arms, a collection of gold and silver bangles jingling from her wrists.

Michelle's throat tightened, and she forced herself to swallow before speaking. "I'm in a yoga class taught by Bev Harrison. She told me you might be able to help me with some strange dreams I've been having lately. She said that you interpret dreams."

Her heart started racing. Suddenly she wondered if this whole idea was a mistake. *I should have waited until Monica could come with me*, she thought to herself.

Starla reached out to gently touch Michelle's shoulder. "I'd be happy to help you, dear." She exuded the same kind of friendliness that Bev did. Michelle willed herself to push aside her uneasiness.

"What did you say your name was?"

"Oh... it's Michelle," she stammered. "Sorry. I guess I forgot to introduce myself."

"No reason to be sorry, Michelle," the woman replied reassuringly. "Why don't we sit down by the fire and have a cup of herbal tea? I just made a fresh pot." She took her hand and led her further back into the store.

As they walked through rows of books, Michelle noticed the glow of a potbellied stove in the back corner of the bookstore. A cluster of three bistro tables, placed in a crescent shape, hugged the warm fire. Each table was draped with a tapestry print tablecloth in dark burgundy and gold. On the center table was an ornate Oriental teapot, with steam gently drifting from the spout.

Starla released her hand and gestured to one of the chairs, inviting her to sit down. Disappearing momentarily, she reappeared with two black and gold mugs. Michelle gratefully accepted the soothing green tea poured for her, and still wondering about the wisdom of her decision, began to tell Starla about her dreams.

"The main dream that I keep having is about a tunnel or passageway of some kind. It is always pretty much the same. I am trying to get to the end of the tunnel—to the light at the end. But I can never get there." Michelle raised her eyes, looking hopefully at the woman.

"Hmmm..." Starla mused, staring off into space. "Tunnels are usually signs of transition. Are you going through some changes in your life right now?"

"Well, my husband and I just recently moved up here from California. Steve is an attorney, and he was offered a partnership here in Sandy Cove when his uncle retired from the firm," she said.

"Any other changes? How about spiritual developments?" Starla asked.

"I'm not really into spiritual stuff," she replied. "I did start to take the yoga class a couple of months ago, but I don't know if you consider that to be spiritual."

The woman smiled a knowing smile. "Yoga can be a very spiritual experience, dear. Perhaps your tunnel is the beginning of a journey to a new level of personal evolution."

"What do you mean?" Michelle asked uneasily, reaching up under her hair and beginning to twist the broken strand.

"Personal enlightenment, Michelle. For instance, the light at the end of that tunnel—it could represent your higher self, the part of you that is connected to the wisdom of the universe. As you move toward greater harmony within yourself, you become open to new forces of power and enlightenment." She paused for a moment, and then continued.

"It's called the Universal Consciousness, sort of like a big spiritual Internet that we link up to through the power of our minds." She placed one multi-ringed hand on Michelle's arm, and Michelle released the hair she had been twisting. "Just as you can access a huge amount of information through your computer modem, we are all able to access infinite wisdom by aligning ourselves with the consciousness of God through our higher selves."

Michelle's thoughts reeled as she tried to make sense of what she heard. "But what does all of this have to do with my dreams?"

The woman leaned closer. "Your dreams are telling me that you are moving from a place of childlike simplicity to a higher level of wisdom and enlightenment. You said that you are moving toward a light at the end of the tunnel. I believe that light is the God-consciousness we all seek." She paused and then asked, "Do you have any religious background, Michelle?"

"Well, my grandparents are Christians," she replied. "In fact, my grandfather was a pastor until some health issues require him to retire."

Starla nodded knowingly.

"But we were not raised in any particular faith. My parents thought that we should make up our own minds about our beliefs."

"A wise approach," the caftan-draped woman commended. "Traditional Christianity is so rigid. It lacks the potential for real spiritual exploration and growth."

Michelle thought about her grandparents. "Traditional" was a good word to describe them, but "rigid" seemed a bit harsh. Starla did seem knowledgeable, though.

The next thing she knew, she was being led back through the rows of books to a section about dreams and their meanings. Starla handed her a large dark green volume with gold lettering, *Dreams: A Window into the Spirit*, by Marty Gessler. The author's name caught her eye immediately. She flipped to the back flap of the book jacket to see if there was a photo.

The face of the author stunned her. It seemed remarkably similar to the man who had tried to talk to her in the tunnel during her most recent dream. Marty. What did it all mean?

"Is something wrong?" Starla asked.

"No. No, not really," Michelle stammered. "I just thought that I recognized the author from somewhere."

"It's unlikely, dear," the older woman replied. "Marty Gessler died over twenty years ago. He was really ahead of his time. A genius. His understanding of the dream process is uncanny. It's clear that he was a highly-evolved individual."

"He looks like someone from one of my dreams," Michelle said hesitantly, her focus riveted on the photo.

"Interesting," Starla replied.

Michelle could feel the woman studying her.

"Maybe he's reaching out to you, dear. Your answer might be in this book. Why don't you read it and see?"

Michelle nodded. She cradled the dark green volume to her chest. "I'll take it." Her hands were trembling, and she wanted to go home.

As they approached the register at the front of the store, the door swung open, letting in a gust of cold air and an attractive young man in his early thirties. His features were similar to Steve's—blond hair, blue eyes, and a slim build, but his face was more angular with a square jaw and chiseled nose. Michelle felt her cheeks flush as he made eye contact with her and flashed a smile.

"Trevor!" Starla exclaimed joyfully. "So good to see you, darling! Meet my new friend, Michelle. Michelle, Trevor Wind. Counselor, teacher, and fellow searcher."

"Nice to meet you," Michelle stammered.

"The pleasure is all mine," he replied smoothly.

Michelle dug through her purse nervously, searching for her wallet. She could feel Trevor's eyes on her. *What is the matter with me? I'm acting like a schoolgirl.*

Thanking Starla for her time, she quickly paid for the purchase and started out the door.

"Michelle! Did you get one of these?" Trevor asked, holding out a flyer advertising a class on personal development and spiritual growth. His photo in the center of the layout indicated his position as instructor of the class.

Michelle reached out and took the flyer. "Thanks," she responded with a smile.

"Hope to see you there!" he replied with a wink.

Again Michelle felt her face flush. She turned away and walked out the door. The brisk air stung as she exited. She was still feeling unsettled from her encounter with Trevor. It reminded her a little of the first time she met Steve. That same rush.

Trying to push the whole thing out of her mind, she remembered the reason for her trip to the bookstore and found herself eager to get home and look through her new book. Unlocking the car door and climbing in, she placed it on the passenger seat, buckled her seat belt, and drove out of the parking lot, completely forgetting about an intended stop at the drugstore.

Michelle was surprised to see Steve's car in the garage when she pushed the automatic door opener. What was he doing home in the middle of the day? Grabbing her bag, she hurried inside.

Steve was sprawled on the couch in the family room under the afghan they usually kept draped over the armrest. Max was curled up at his feet, and they were both asleep. The sound of Michelle placing her bag on the table caused Steve to stir. He looked over at her and sighed.

"Are you O.K.?" she asked.

"Not really. I feel like I've been hit by a truck," he said. "It must be that flu bug everyone's been complaining about. I took two aspirins, but I'm still aching all over." He paused then added, "Where have you been? I tried to call your cell, but it went straight to voicemail."

"I had to run a few errands," she replied, mentally kicking herself for forgetting about the drugstore. She pulled her phone out of her purse and flipped it open. A black screen greeted her. "Dead battery. Sorry about that," Michelle said, and then added, "Can I get you something? How about some soup or something to drink?"

Steve smiled weakly, flinching as he tried to prop himself up. "Soup would be great, honey. I just can't seem to get warm."

Apparently Max was not thrilled with Steve's shifting and moaning. He hopped down from the couch and followed Michelle into the kitchen. The sound of the can opener caused an onslaught of pleading meows.

"This isn't tuna, Max," Michelle chided. "You already ate today, remember? Go find your toy."

By mixing some leftover vegetables and rice into a pan with the can of chicken soup, she was able to prepare a hearty lunch for her husband. It smelled good, and she decided to have some herself. She ladled the hot stew-like mixture into large mugs, placed them on a tray with spoons, napkins, a plate of cheese and crackers, and two tall glasses of tea.

Carrying the tray carefully into the family room, she put it down on the coffee table, and then helped Steve get into a comfortable sitting position. They ate together while she told him about Bev's friend, Starla, and The New World Bookstore.

Steve raised his eyebrows as she shared Starla's interpretation of her dreams. "Sounds a little weird to me, Michelle," he warned. "Don't take this stuff too seriously." He rubbed his hands across his eyes. "When I suggested you talk to somebody about your dreams, this wasn't exactly what I had in mind."

"I know. It's just kind of interesting about that Marty guy in my dream the other night and how he looks like the Marty who wrote this dream book."

"Maybe you just think that because of the name. Can you really remember what the guy in your dream looked like?" he asked, sounding skeptical.

"I don't know. Maybe you're right. He just looked kind of familiar when I saw the photo on the book jacket. But it's hard to remember for sure what the guy really looked like in my dream," she admitted.

"Just don't get all weird on me about these crazy dreams, Michelle. They probably don't really mean anything anyway."

She nodded her head, not wanting to get into a heated discussion with him when he wasn't feeling well. He really looked tired and pale. "Why don't you take a nap for a while?" she suggested.

"I think I will." Slipping back down under the afghan, he thanked her for lunch and closed his eyes.

She quietly got up and carried the tray back into the kitchen. After rinsing out the mugs and the pan, she went upstairs to their bedroom where she could get some things done without disturbing Steve.

Flipping open her laptop, she reread a message she'd received earlier in the week from her best friend, Kristin Matthews. As the keys clicked under her fingertips, she poured out her thoughts in reply.

Michelle felt totally safe with Kristin and was able to candidly share all about her strange dreams. Missing Kristin more and more with every line, she yearned to see her friend and sit face-to-face sharing her thoughts and fears. She ended the email urging Kristin to consider coming to Sandy Cove for a visit.

"Now what should I do?" she asked Max, who was curled up on the rocking chair. Thoughts of Seal Beach continued to flood her mind and she decided to call home.

"Yes?" a male voice gruffly answered.

"Dad?" Michelle asked tentatively, unaccustomed to her father answering the phone so brusquely.

"Michelle?" her father's voice softened.

"Hi, Dad. Is everything okay?"

"Fine, honey. Why?"

"You sound different. I barely recognized your voice," she replied.

"Must be the tail end of my cold."

"Maybe. Is everything else okay? Mom said your heart was bothering you. Racing or something."

"Don't you worry about me, kiddo. I'm fit as a fiddle. Really. Let me get your mother. She's been eager to talk to you." There was a brief pause. Then Michelle heard him call out, "Sheila! Michelle's on the phone."

A moment later her mom came on the line. "Hi, honey. How are you?"

Hearing her mother's voice immediately magnified Michelle's homesickness. Though their conversation started out light and casual, within minutes Michelle was telling her how much she missed her.

"I miss you too, Mimi," her mother replied, using her pet name for Michelle. "Is everything okay, honey?" she inquired gently.

"I guess. Steve and I are doing fine, the house is coming together, and I'm learning to find my way around Sandy Cove." Michelle paused, feeling her voice start to shake. "It's just hard being so far away from everyone."

"I know, sweetheart. It's a big adjustment. I've been meaning to try to get away for a week or two and come up to visit like you suggested last month. Do you want me to talk to your dad about it and see what I can work out?"

"That would be great," Michelle replied and then added, "Is he alright, Mom? He sounded kind of funny when he answered the phone."

"He's just got a lot on his mind these days. Hold on a sec, dear," she added. Michelle heard some rustling and then her mom's voice returned. "I wanted to change rooms. Your dad is really touchy lately. There's some kind of lawsuit going on at work, and he's very concerned about it. I don't know the whole story, but you know how your father is."

"Mr. Independent. Yeah, I know, Mom. I wonder if he'd talk to Steve about it."

"Maybe. I'll see if I can get some more information before I come up. If I talk to Steve first, he might be able to give me some pointers to mention to your father."

"Good idea," Michelle replied. "I'm so glad you're going to try to come up and visit, Mom." Her spirit felt lighter just thinking about seeing her mother again.

"Me too," Sheila agreed. "I have a couple of appointments this week, but I could try to fly up next Monday or Tuesday."

"That would be great!" Michelle replied enthusiastically. "Call me back as soon as you've talked it over with Dad."

They wrapped up their conversation with Michelle feeling much better. The sound of Max mewing by the closed bedroom door reminded Michelle of Steve downstairs with the flu. She silently hoped that he would be better before Monday. *I hope I don't get sick, too.*

She picked Max up and cradled him in her arms, nuzzling his soft fur. "Want to read with me?" she asked as she picked up the dream book and carried it to the rocking chair. Max wasn't interested in sharing her lap with the large green volume. He leapt down and strutted across the room to settle next to the heater vent.

Perusing the table of contents, a chapter heading caught Michelle's eye. "Spirit Guides and the Link to Dream Analysis – Find Your Spirit Guide Within". *That sounds interesting,* she thought, flipping the pages to that chapter.

I just might be getting to know you better, Marty, she reflected silently as she thought of the man in her dream.

Michelle's father, John Ackerman, sank into the dark burgundy leather chair in the corner of his den. It was well after midnight and, unable to sleep, he had gotten out of bed to keep from waking Sheila with his tossing and turning. All vitality was drained from his spirit, and he felt desperately alone.

Fear closed in on him with a vise-like grip, and he felt himself being pulled into a black chasm in his mind. Over and over he replayed in his mind the events at the hearing and the incriminating evidence that was being twisted and used against him. Most of the documents had never crossed his desk. Yet there they were, clearly revealing his signature on them.

It had been apparent for months that someone at Mathers, Inc. was trying to discredit him. The numerous, unfounded complaints that he had tried to ignore or brush aside as unimportant were now fitting into this picture like a complex puzzle of deception and defamation. But why? Who would want him out of the company? And why would anyone go to such desperate measures as these forgeries?

Could this be about his former secretary, Marilyn Marlow, and their brief affair?

He sat back in his chair and replayed in his mind those three weeks in Dallas. Marilyn's youth, coupled with her intense passion for John had invaded his well-ordered life at a time when age was robbing him of his sense of virility. But it hadn't taken long for him to come to his senses and terminate the affair.

Duty and responsibility overruled personal pleasure in John's world. It had been difficult to watch her pale green eyes fill with tears at their final parting, and he could still remember the feel of her long, soft hair and firm, well-formed body. But his life was back in Seal Beach with Sheila and the kids. Not in the arms of his secretary.

Marilyn was a vulnerable young lady with a crush on an older man. Surely she wouldn't do something this drastic.

Until this morning, John had been certain that he would eventually be cleared of the charges. His main concern had been the loss of productive time at work and the attorney fees necessary to clear his name. Now he wondered if any amount of time or money could free him from this nightmare.

Gazing pensively around the room, his heavy brown eyes lit on a picture of Sheila taken on the beach a year earlier. Tears welled up, and he felt very small in his large masculine body. He could still remember clearly the day Sheila had agreed to marry him. As he looked at her gentle face in the photograph, he yearned to protect the only real love of his life from this debilitating scandal. But how? He needed time to think.

Slumping back in his chair, he gazed out the window at the streetlight. An almost suffocating sensation of despair overtook him. Reaching down, he opened the bottom drawer of his desk and stared at the gun inside.

CHAPTER THREE

Northwest Airlines Flight #213 from Orange County, California, was descending over the Portland airport. From the air, Michelle's mom, Sheila Ackerman, gazed out of her window as the ground rushed up to meet her.

The sun broke through momentarily and the lush green field and trees bordering the airport were vibrant. Homes dotted the fir-covered rolling hills on the outskirts of town, resembling a miniature village one might put out at Christmas time. The Columbia River looked like a ribbon of blue satin as it meandered below them. Seconds later, the bright rays of the sun were swallowed by thick white and gray clouds reclaiming their spot over the runway.

Sheila's thoughts had been on Michelle since boarding. Their recent phone conversations worried her. Michelle's voice sounded uneasy and anxious the last time they spoke. Sheila couldn't shake the feeling that her daughter was troubled about something.

As they descended toward the runway, she braced herself for the slight jolt of the landing gear touching down. Smiling at the passenger beside her, she breathed a silent prayer of relief. Although she loved the convenience of flying, she never could never get used to the idea of such big monstrosities actually being airborne.

The pilot's voice could be heard over the speakers. "Welcome to Portland, Oregon. It is now ten-thirty and the current temperature is a chilly 48 degrees. Thank you for flying Northwest Airlines. We look forward to serving you again soon."

Sheila shivered at the thought of the crisp air that awaited her outside. She pulled her compact out of her purse to make a quick check of her appearance. After running a small comb through her caramel-colored hair, she reapplied a muted shade of lipstick.

Her peaches-and-cream complexion was only slightly marred by soft lines around the corners of her eyes and across her forehead. The pale blue suit John helped her pick out for her birthday flattered her soft, natural coloring. Snapping the compact shut, Sheila dropped it into her purse and unbuckled her seat belt.

The flight attendant, a middle-aged woman with a pleasant round face, reminded them to check the overhead storage compartments for their personal belongings. Then the passengers began to disembark.

Sheila retrieved her carry-on bag and started up the aisle. She felt slightly claustrophobic as she waited for the passengers in front of her to filter out of their rows. After finally exiting the plane, she took a deep breath and hurried through the walkway to the terminal.

As she approached luggage claim, she could see Michelle waiting, eagerly watching the long stream of passengers flowing into the airport. Businessmen wearing conservative suits and toting briefcases briskly brushed past her, followed by several tourists and a young mother with two small children.

Sheila waved, catching Michelle's eye. A relieved smile lit her daughter's face as she waved back. Eagerly, they wove between people to embrace.

Michelle's hair felt soft and silky against Sheila's cheek. She squeezed her daughter tightly, feeling the tension in Michelle's firm and prolonged embrace. Then she gently drew back and looked into her eyes.

"I've missed you, sweetheart," she said, smiling through tears.

"Oh, Mom. I'm so glad you're here." Michelle placed her arm around her mother's shoulder.

They worked their way through the crowd to the conveyor belt full of luggage. After collecting Sheila's bags, they headed out to the parking lot.

The chilly air penetrated through her linen suit. "Brrr!!" she exclaimed, pulling up her shoulders.

"Do you want my jacket?" Michelle asked. "I've got a sweatshirt on under it."

"Thanks, honey, but I'll be fine. Is your car close?"

"Right over there," Michelle answered, pointing to her car.

They hustled over and loaded the bags into the back, then climbed inside.

"A bit nippy up here," Sheila said, glancing over to drink in another look at her daughter.

"Not like sunny Southern California," Michelle observed.

Sheila could hear the homesickness in her daughter's voice. "It's not so perfect down there, either. If our drought doesn't end soon, they'll start rationing water. We could really use some of your rain."

"You can have it. I'd take a little drought about now."

Sheila reached over and patted Michelle's knee, realizing once again how much she missed having her daughter close to home. But she knew Michelle was probably in Sandy Cove to stay because of Steve's position at the firm. "You'll get used to Sandy Cove, Mimi," she said, hoping her voice sounded reassuring rather than concerned.

Michelle just nodded and smiled at her mom as she pulled out of the parking lot.

As they merged onto the street, Sheila wondered if Michelle would want to stop for lunch on the way back to Sandy Cove. The last time she visited, they'd eaten at Camp 18, a rustic restaurant and gift shop made of knotty pine that was just off of Highway 26.

"Are you hungry, Mom?" her daughter asked, as if reading her mind.

"I'm fine for now. They gave us a snack on the plane," Sheila replied.

"Would you mind if we eat at the house?"

"That would be fine, honey. I'm eager to get into some warmer clothes anyway, and we can relax and visit better there than at a restaurant," Sheila added, settling back into her seat and glancing out the window at the interesting cloud formations.

The drive back to Sandy Cove passed quickly. They had a lot of catching up to do, and one topic easily led to another just as the road transported them from the city to the quiet coastal community. While they visited, Sheila soaked in the beautiful scenery along the tree-lined highway.

First they drove through the wide, open spaces of the Willamette Valley. As the highway narrowed from four lanes to two, they began winding gradually up and through the coastal mountain range. The forest of pines reluctantly parted to allow the road to make its way through its shrouded terrain. Everything seemed so breathtakingly natural in contrast to the man-made confines of suburbia. Occasional encounters with logging trucks reminded her the forest had uses that extended beyond its scenic beauty.

As they drove, Sheila asked about Steve's new job and Michelle's plans to return to school. Michelle seemed proud as she reported her husband's recent success in his first court case, then she told her about Pacific Northwest University where she hoped to complete her teaching credential. She explained that she planned to begin attending classes in the fall.

"That's great, honey," Sheila replied.

"So how's everything with Dad?" Michelle asked next.

"He's okay. I worry about the strain of his long hours, but he's always managed to burn the candle at both ends and come out winning," she said.

Michelle nodded.

As their conversation reached a lull, Sheila closed her eyes and dozed off.

Michelle looked at her mom and thought about their family. Rarely in her parents' thirty years of marriage had they ever really vacationed together as a couple or a family. All of their trips and excursions usually involved business meetings for Michelle's dad.

He was a driven man, determined to succeed in every undertaking. He thrived on endless hours of hard work and was quick to climb the corporate ladder. A self-made man, propelling himself from a lower middle-class youth to a well-established comfortable lifestyle in a Southern California beach community, her dad preached that all things in life were possible for those who believed in themselves and were willing to work hard.

Michelle remembered his stories of his early days as a "gofer" for a small advertising agency, and how he had worked his way up to West Coast manager of Mathers, Inc., a multimillion dollar advertising firm.

Her father had no time for people who were lazy, and he never entertained any notions of spirituality, other than to say religion was a crutch for weak people. "If you want something, you've got to get out there and fight for it!" he repeatedly declared to Michelle and her brother, Tim.

Extremely pragmatic, he often lacked the warmth Michelle craved in their relationship. It wasn't that he didn't love her. He just didn't have time for needless sentimentality.

He gave his family the best money could buy. In his eyes, that was his role as head of the household. Although she appreciated the creature comforts he provided for all of them, she still felt something was missing, especially when she saw other fathers walking on the pier with their kids or joining them for a romp on the beach.

She could picture her father's expression of deep concentration as he huddled over paperwork spread out on his desk or gazed into his computer screen. Every once in a while he would run his fingers through his wavy gray hair and take a deep breath, then resume his work.

There was never any point in trying to get him away from his desk. Any interruption would meet with a short-tempered response. So she and Tim learned to stay away from the study when John was working.

Michelle sighed and turned her attention back to the road. A short time later, she noticed her mother stirring in the passenger seat. "Sorry I dozed off," Sheila said apologetically. "You look like you've been deep in thought."

"Just thinking about Dad," she replied. "I was worried about his heart, but he says he's fine."

"He doesn't really talk to me about it anymore. After the doctor reassured us that his palpitations were nothing serious, he just started ignoring them. But I do wonder about the toll of this recent lawsuit he's involved in. Hopefully Steve can give me some insight from a lawyer's perspective."

Michelle glanced over at her mom. "I'm sure he'd be happy to. Good thing you weren't here last week. He got some nasty flu bug and was pretty sick for a few days.

But he's fine now. Just busy as usual. He been putting in really long days on a case he's working on right now."

"Well, maybe he'll be able to come home early tonight, honey. I'm eager to see him again," her mother countered cheerfully.

"Here's hoping," she replied.

Soon they were pulling into the driveway of the quaint, country style home on Wayburn Way. Michelle noticed her mother's pleased expression as her eyes surveyed their home.

The rainy climate provided a lush yard with beautiful, tall pine trees, a thick carpet of grass, and an English garden of wildflowers. Bordered by a white picket fence, the property had a storybook appearance.

Michelle parked the car in the garage and helped her mother gather her bags. As they walked into the house with their arms full, Max excitedly bolted toward the door to greet them. Sheila almost lost her footing under the anxious romping of the playful kitten.

"Who is this lively fellow?" she asked.

"Oh, I forgot! You two haven't met," Michelle replied, helping her mother put her luggage down. "Mother, this is Max. Max, this is Grandma Sheila," she said with a smile.

"I don't know about this 'Grandma Sheila' bit, but I'm very happy to meet you, Max," Michelle's mother replied, seeming to enjoy the parody on social amenities.

Seemingly satisfied that his duty was done, Max trotted off to the kitchen, and Michelle showed her mother to the guest bedroom. Painted a soft blue with white trim, the waist-high white bead board gave a cottage feel to the room and yellow sunflowers smiled cheerfully from atop the dresser.

"This room is gorgeous, Michelle!" her mother exclaimed. "You did a wonderful job decorating it. Maybe you should switch from teaching to interior design," she teased.

"I'm glad you like it," Michelle replied, beaming. "It's slowly coming together. The living room is my next project."

"With that cozy family room of yours, you really don't need to spend much time in there, but it would be nice to dress it up for company," her mom suggested.

"That's what I'm hoping to do. I've been checking online for furniture sales, but nothing's clicked with me yet."

"It will, dear. Maybe we can go out looking while I'm here. A large, colorful throw rug and a new coffee table would really help to pull the room together," Sheila suggested, adding, "It's handy that you have this semester off to get yourself settled before taking on your student teaching."

"That's the plan!" she replied, hoping she sounded enthusiastic.

Sheila smiled. She reached over and stroked her daughter's hair. "Well, honey, I think I'll get out of this suit and put on something warm and comfortable."

Michelle nodded. "I'll go get the lunch on."

"If you wait just a few minutes, I'll be happy to help you," her mom offered.

"That's okay, Mom. It's pretty simple. You just relax and get settled while I get it going."

While her mother unpacked and changed outfits, Michelle worked in the kitchen. Earlier that day, she'd run over to their favorite bakery to buy a freshly baked vegetable quiche. Retrieving it from the refrigerator, she popped it into the oven to reheat.

Gathering place mats, napkins, and silverware, she went into the dining room and began to set the table. It felt almost like she was playing house and getting ready for a tea party with her mom. Wanting everything to be perfect, she decoratively arranged the place settings around the centerpiece—a floral bouquet from her garden in colors that matched the woven pastel place mats. Next, she went over to the hutch and carefully removed some china luncheon plates, cups, and saucers.

Her mother came out of the guest room wearing jeans and a soft, peach-colored sweatshirt with pale blue and green seashells printed across the front. She looked much more comfortable and at home. Michelle smiled and gestured toward the dining room table. Sheila's expression showed her approval and appreciation of Michelle's efforts to create a cozy atmosphere for their lunch.

"I'm beginning to feel like royalty," her mom said with a smile.

"Make yourself comfortable. Lunch will be ready in just a few minutes," she promised, excusing herself to check on the quiche.

While Michelle was in the kitchen, Sheila relaxed at the table. Meanwhile, Max took advantage of the moment alone with her. He pranced up and proudly dropped a small gray mouse at her feet. She cried out and quickly lifted both feet off the ground. This reaction startled him, and he ran behind the buffet. A second look revealed the synthetic nature of the rodent, and Sheila laughed to herself as she picked up the little toy to examine it more closely.

Calling Max out from behind the buffet, she wiggled the mouse on the floor, causing its tail to flutter furiously. Max was poised to pounce when Michelle walked back into the room carrying a pitcher of iced tea and a glass bowl filled with freshly cut fruit. As if on cue, Max retrieved the mouse and possessively carried it out of the dining room.

Michelle shook her head. "He can be a bit theatrical at times," she explained.

Sheila laughed again and nodded.

"I'll be right back," Michelle said, making her final trek to the kitchen. A moment later she returned with a bubbling hot quiche on a tray. She carefully placed it on the table and sat down.

Sheila reached over and took her daughter's hand, smiling warmly as she looked into her eyes. "I'm so glad to be here, Mimi. It's still hard to picture you married and living in your own home like this. Your dad would be so proud to see all that you have done to make this house a home."

"Thanks, Mom," Michelle responded, giving her hand a squeeze. "I know what you mean about being married and all. Sometimes I can hardly believe it myself."

They spent the rest of their lunch together reminiscing about Michelle's childhood and adolescence. They laughed about the puppet shows Michelle and her younger brother, Tim, used to perform on rainy days.

"That puppet theater would never get put away around here!" Michelle observed, nodding to the rain now falling outside the bay window.

Then she asked, "Remember the fashion shows Kristin and I would have?"

"Do I ever! You would raid my closet and then parade around in all sorts of interesting combinations." Sheila smiled and sighed. "It seems like just yesterday..." her voice trailed off as she stared out the window.

They were quiet for a few moments. The sound of the rain had a hypnotic effect, and they both sat gazing out toward the street. Sometimes just being together was enough. Words weren't necessary. Sheila soaked in the moment.

Glancing over at her daughter, she saw that Michelle's mind was somewhere else. "Penny for your thoughts," she said.

Michelle smiled. "You sound like Grandpa."

Sheila flashed to an image of Michelle as a small child sitting with her grandfather on their porch swing, as he would say those same words to her. "I guess I do," she acknowledged, returning her daughter's smile.

"I was just thinking about Dad again," Michelle continued. "Does Tim spend any time with him?"

"Not much, dear. Tim wants his independence now. He looks at life much differently than your father. Usually when they get together they just end up butting heads." She sighed, replaying in her mind a memory of the two of them fighting.

"Well, maybe when Tim gets settled into a real job, it'll get better between them," Michelle suggested hopefully.

"Maybe," Sheila replied, trying to cover her own concerns about her son. Everyone in their family was surprised when Tim turned his back on college in his eagerness to be independent. It seemed such a shame to throw away a career in architecture to work at a surf shop.

After a pause, she changed the subject. "This lunch was delicious, Mimi."

"Thanks! I'm glad you enjoyed it," Michelle said with a smile.

As they arose and began clearing the lunch plates, Michelle's cell phone rang.

"My mom just flew in from California this morning," she began to explain to the caller. "I was thinking I'd just skip yoga today, but I hate for you to have to miss it. Tony's car is still in the shop?"

"Yeah, for two more days."

Sheila interrupted their conversation. "You go ahead, sweetheart. I could use a little nap, and I'm sure

44

Max will be happy to keep me company until you get back."

Her daughter turned from the phone, placing her hand over the mouthpiece. "Are you sure, Mom? I really hadn't planned on going today."

"I'm positive, Michelle. I got up so early this morning to get to the airport on time, and I really would like to have a little rest before dinner. Max and I will be just fine. Right, kitty?"

Max glanced her way but did not reply.

"Okay, Monica," Michelle said, resuming their conversation. "I'll be there in about an hour."

"Sorry about that, Mom. If my friend didn't need a ride, I'd just skip yoga today."

"It's not a problem at all. You go have fun at your class. I'll just rinse off these dishes and relax."

Michelle went upstairs to get ready to go, and Sheila rinsed off their lunch dishes, and then took her coffee over and sat down on the couch. A few minutes later, Michelle came bounding down the stairs. She started a fire in the fireplace, then she plopped down on a chair and put on her tennis shoes.

"I'll be home around four-thirty," she reassured Sheila. "We're having that chicken casserole you love tonight."

"Sounds great, dear. Have fun at your class."

"Okay, Mom. If you need anything, Max will help you," Michelle said with a wink.

Grabbing her purse and jacket, she was about to leave when she stopped, turned around, and came back for a flyer that was on the coffee table. "See you in a while, Mom," she said.

As she heard Michelle drive away, Sheila noticed a dark, green book on the end table. "*Dreams: A Window into the Spirit* . . . hmmm, that's interesting," she thought aloud. Picking it up, she flipped through the pages.

Intrigue, mixed with wariness, nudged her to begin reading. As the author's mystical perspective on dreams began to unfold, she felt the slightest twinge of anxiety. Her feelings of concern about Michelle resurfaced.

Something was not right.

CHAPTER FOUR

Michelle could see Monica waiting by the front door when she drove up. She waved, and climbed into the passenger seat. "Thanks for picking me up! I really didn't want to miss yoga today. My body feels like it's tied in a million knots," she explained, smiling at Michelle while she massaged her own neck. "Do you think your mom would want to meet Beth? I feel like I'm babysitting her these days and she seems awfully lonely."

"That's a great idea. She'll only be here for a week or so, but I'm sure we could arrange something." Michelle replied. "Hey, I've got stuff to tell you!" she added.

"What?" Monica looked interested.

"I went to see Bev's friend at The New World Bookstore," she began.

"And. . ."

"And she told me lots of stuff about what she thinks my dreams mean, but she also helped me find a great book about it," she said. "It was really weird, Monica, but the guy who wrote the book looks just like someone from one of my dreams."

"Maybe you've seen him on television before, on one of those daytime talk shows or something," Monica suggested.

"Don't think so. He's been dead for over twenty years." Michelle watched her friend's face for a reaction.

"Wow. What do you think it means?"

"I don't know, but the book is really interesting. I'll show it to you next time you come over," she replied.

"Yeah, I'd like to see it. Maybe I can look up some of my dreams, too. Like those ones about the handsome lifeguard asking me if I'd like to join him up in the lifeguard stand..."

"Funny, Monica." Michelle smiled tolerantly. "Oh, I almost forgot! Check this out," she added, handing the flyer to Monica. "The class starts in two weeks."

"Who's this hunk?" Monica asked, pointing at the photo of Trevor Wind.

"He's the instructor."

"What's the class?" Her friend was obviously focusing on Trevor's face instead of the course description.

"Read this," Michelle replied as she pointed to the course description. After a moment she asked, "What do you think?"

Monica was still reading the credits under Trevor's photo. "It sounds interesting. Let's go to the first class and check it out," she suggested with a smile.

Driving down the tree-lined street, Michelle sensed a feeling of kinship deepening between the friends. It was the bond that accompanies those who partner to pioneer forbidden territories. She recalled having this same heady feeling the day she and her brother, Tim, had secretly smoked one of their dad's cigarettes in the backyard tree house. She brushed aside any connection between then and now, reassuring herself that what she and Monica were contemplating was growth-oriented, not rebellious or dangerous.

As they walked into the yoga class, they saw Bev collecting a stack of large, colorful cards and slipping them into a velvet pouch. It was apparent that she and another class participant had been doing something together with the cards.

Seeing Michelle's curiosity, Bev explained, "Tarot cards, Michelle. They can help you make decisions or gain insights into your circumstances. I'll show you sometime, if you'd like."

Michelle nodded innocently in response to the invitation and settled on the mat in front of her. She had never heard of tarot cards before, but the concept of gaining insight appealed to her. Monica joined her on the floor, taking the mat to her right.

Class was about to begin. They smiled at each other, then closed their eyes and assumed their relaxation positions. With legs crossed and hands resting on their knees, they turned their palms upward and joined their middle fingers and thumbs to close the circle of energy flowing through their bodies.

How comfortable I've become with this, Michelle thought to herself, taking a long cleansing breath. She noticed it was getting easier to slip into a state of deep relaxation. Remembering Starla's encouragement about her dreams signaling spiritual transition, Michelle felt a sense of calm mixed with anticipation. "I must be on the right path," she thought.

Sheila was snuggled on the couch by the fire, engrossed in Marty Gessler's book. Multiple references to personal evolution and reincarnation made the author's affiliation with Eastern thought clear. Sheila had always thought that dreams were a reflection of daily issues, concerns, and decisions being played out by the subconscious mind. Gessler was explaining dreams as a part of the spiritual journey each person takes in the process of evolving to harmony and oneness with the universe. He believed that process required multiple lives via reincarnation, and he divided his interpretations into levels of spiritual attainment, encouraging his readers to journal their dreams as a record of their progress from one plane of consciousness to another.

The further she read, the more Sheila battled her concerns about this book. Michelle was an adult now, and Sheila had always prided herself on her detachment from Michelle and Tim's spiritual choices. Along with her husband, she subscribed to the philosophy that each individual must make their own decisions regarding religious beliefs.

Although she fondly remembered the years of Christian teaching and nurturing her parents had provided, her marriage to John had introduced a broader perspective on questions of faith. The Ackerman family was a breed of independent thinkers, and John challenged her faith with his hard-driving questions and atheistic beliefs. Together they'd agreed to expose their children to a wide variety of religious philosophies in order to allow them to make their own choices.

Placing the book back where she had found it, she breathed a silent, generic prayer of protection over her daughter. Though raised under a constant umbrella of prayer, its application eluded Sheila in most of her daily life. However, in times of deep inner turmoil or fear, she could hear her father's gentle voice in the quiet places of her mind.

"Have you prayed about this?" he had frequently asked whenever she'd brought her childhood concerns to him. With his strong hand covering hers, he would calmly and confidently commit the crisis of the moment into the hands of his Lord. Sheila felt such safety and peace after those prayers.

Was I wrong not to instill this in Michelle and Tim? Sheila thought about the many vacations her children had spent with their grandparents and hoped that they had absorbed some of this powerful faith.

After class, Michelle asked Bev about the tarot cards. She was interested in looking at them but Bev said she'd rather explain them while doing a reading for Michelle. Not wanting to leave her mother at home alone for very long, Michelle was hesitant to take the time. Bev reassured her that a few minutes would suffice for a brief reading of the cards.

"What question would you like answered today?" she asked Michelle.

Michelle's mind flashed back to her mother's concern over her dad. "How will my dad's lawsuit be resolved?" she inquired hesitantly.

"Shuffle the cards three times and then cut the deck once to the left and once to the right," Bev instructed as she handed the oversized cards to Michelle.

After complying with those directions, Michelle gave the deck back to Bev. She watched as her teacher carefully placed seven of the cards facedown in a row, starting from the center and working her way out on each side. Bev's wavy gray hair framed her face like a halo and her green eyes sparkled as she smiled at Michelle.

One by one, Bev turned over each card and explained its meaning. The first six cards indicated strong conflict, possible loss of finances or friendships, an unexpected turn of events including some new evidence that could be harmful if misinterpreted, and the need for careful research into various legal technicalities.

The seventh (and centrally placed) card had an eerie appearance. It revealed a standing skeleton holding a scythe as if harvesting wheat. Michelle detected a brief change in Bev's countenance when she turned over that card. Her eyes registered concern, which was quickly replaced by what appeared to be a forced or artificial calm.

"This card represents change, Michelle. It is called the death card, but it usually signals the death of an old way of doing things or a change of path," she explained reassuringly. "Perhaps your father is on the brink of some career changes or philosophical alterations."

Monica broke in. "I'm sure that's it, Michelle. Remember how you said he always wanted to start his own business? Maybe this lawsuit will end his relationship with Mathers, Inc. and open the door for him to follow that dream."

"It would take something pretty divisive to get him to leave Mathers after all these years," Michelle conceded. "But this lawsuit could do it, I guess."

"We should get going," said Monica. "Your mom's waiting."

"We'll have more time for the cards later, Michelle," Bev promised. "Bring your mom to yoga on Thursday. I'd love to meet her."

"Okay. I'll see if she's interested," Michelle replied.

As the girls drove home, Michelle kept thinking about the cards, especially the death card. Bev seemed reassuring about it, but a nagging sense of anxiety left Michelle wondering if the card's meaning hadn't been more ominous than her teacher had shared.

CHAPTER FIVE

In the quiet, little town of Mariposa, California, Michelle's grandparents, Phil and Joan Walker, were enjoying a cup of tea and some homemade biscuits. They lived in a simple A-frame, wooden house painted white with black trim. This was the home they'd shared for fifty years. It was where they had raised their daughter, Sheila.

Phil pastored a small church in this rural community, until a stroke pulled him out of full-time ministry. Having recovered everything but his stamina, and remaining passionate about his faith, he continued to teach a home Bible study twice a month. Both he and his wife helped out around church as much as they could. And he still clung to the idea of possibly returning to a pastoral position someday.

Overall, the years had been kind to these gentle folks. Although Phil's gray hair was thinning and his face was creased, he had a youthful vitality that communicated itself in his countenance and his sparkling blue eyes. Always quick with a joke or a little limerick, he could bring a smile to almost anyone's face.

Joan seemed almost childlike beside him, her tiny five-foot-tall body dwarfed by Phil's tall, lanky frame. Today she was wearing a casual floral dress that complemented her soft white curls and light gray eyes. As she sipped on her tea, she heard Phil sigh.

"What is it, Phil?" she asked noticing her husband's frown.

"I just can't stop thinking about Michelle," he answered. "She's been on my mind all week. I can't help wondering if something is wrong." He ran his fingers through his hair.

"Shall we call them tonight? I think Sheila was planning to fly up to see her this week," Joan added, studying her husband's expression.

"I don't know about calling her. Let's pray and see what the Lord has in mind," he suggested.

They hadn't talked to their granddaughter for a while. She seemed distant in more ways than just geographically since her move to Oregon. The last time they called, Michelle seemed glad to hear from them, but kept the conversation on a very surface level and didn't stay on the phone for long.

Joan understood her husband's reluctance to interfere in their grandchildren's lives. Perhaps someday the close relationship they once had with Michelle would be restored. In the meantime, she agreed with his suggestion to commit the matter to prayer. Clasping their hands together and bowing their heads, Phil interceded on behalf of his granddaughter.

"Lord, you know how much we love Michelle. She has always been such a sensitive and sweet girl. Please guard her, Lord. Watch over her and give her wisdom. Help her to see how much you love her. Show her the path that leads to you. We know that you have a plan for her and we just want to recommit her to you now. Help us know when and how to reach out to her. Give us patience and discernment as you show us your hand working in and through her life. In Jesus' name, amen."

"Amen," echoed Joan as she squeezed her husband's hand. Gratitude swelled in her heart as she silently thanked God for bringing Phil into her life. His strong faith and steadfast relationship with God had carried them through many difficulties and concerns.

Even in moments of intense crisis, his prayers had been a safe haven, separating her from the storm. His kind of faith was what she hoped her children and grandchildren would discover.

She thought about how Sheila's marriage to John had driven a wedge between their daughter and their God. Much as she loved John, Joan continuously prayed that he would see the emptiness of his philosophical ramblings, and that Sheila would be reconciled to her faith. The ramifications of their lack of spiritual leadership had affected both Michelle and Tim. Neither of them seemed to have any solid footing of faith, and she had watched them try to build lives for themselves based on the self-sufficiency and independence John promoted.

Phil reached over and stroked her soft cheek. "God will take care of it, honey."

"I know, Phil." She smiled and sighed.

As Michelle dropped Monica off at her house, they decided to try to set up a lunch date with Sheila and Beth.

"I'll talk to Beth about it and call you in the morning," Monica promised.

"Sounds good. Maybe Thursday would be good. I can pick you guys up if Tony's car is still on the blink."

"So, do we have to sign up for that class at the bookstore?" Monica asked.

"I think we can just get there early the day of the first class and sign up then," she replied.

"Okay, just don't forget I'm going with you."

"Like I'd really forget that!" Michelle replied, rolling her eyes.

After leaving Monica's house, she thought back to the tarot cards and Bev's interpretations. She couldn't shake an uneasy feeling about that death card. Why had it appeared in the center of the spread? What did it really mean? Was her dad okay? These questions swam in her mind as she threaded her way back through Sandy Cove to Wayburn Way, her left hand on the steering wheel while her right hand twisted her hair.

Steve's car pulled in beside hers as she entered the driveway. He smiled and winked at her, and she grinned back. They both drove into the garage and parked, then Steve walked over, holding his right hand behind his back.

"Surprise!" he exclaimed handing Michelle a beautiful bouquet of red roses.

Michelle smiled warmly and kissed him on the cheek. "Thanks, Steve! What's the occasion?" she asked.

"No occasion. I just wanted to bring you something," he replied. "I've been so busy with work and worn out by this cold that I felt like I was neglecting you."

"Well, I haven't really felt neglected, but I appreciate the flowers. Mom will be impressed, too," she said.

"Oh, that's right! Your mom flew in today," Steve jokingly exclaimed as if he had forgotten.

"Funny!" Michelle countered, swatting him on the rear end as she laughed and headed into the house with her roses.

Sheila greeted them from the breakfast nook where she was sipping on another cup of tea, and Steve graciously bent down and kissed her cheek.

"Welcome to our humble abode," he pronounced, gesturing toward the rest of the house.

"Your 'humble abode' is really quite nice," countered Sheila. "And your cat is adorable," she added as Max leapt from the windowsill where he had been trying to catch a fly.

Michelle showed her mother the roses, and they worked together to arrange them in a tall, glass vase. The conversation among the three of them continued pleasantly through the preparation of dinner.

Seated in the dining room, they enjoyed their meal as Sheila asked Steve questions about his new position. He described his firm and his partner, Roger, then proceeded to explain some of the types of cases they handled.

Michelle listened intently as her mom began explaining to Steve about the lawsuit Michelle's dad was involved in with Mathers, Inc.

"There are some funds missing. Quite a bit, actually, and John's being accused of embezzlement," she began. "I didn't know this at the time, but apparently he borrowed some money from the company, just temporarily, when we were making all the payments for your wedding," she explained. "But he paid back the full amount a short time later."

Steve looked concerned, and Michelle could feel her whole body getting tense.

"So then, after that, a series of similar withdrawals mysteriously began, all of them bearing his signature, but made out to cash rather than to himself. He swears that he had nothing to do with the withdrawals, Steve. And he did pay back all the money he borrowed."

"Does he have an attorney?" Michelle asked.

"Yes, but I can tell your father's not happy with the way he's handling the case."

"Does he have any idea who might be trying to frame him?" Steve asked in a professional tone that was not familiar to Michelle. He suddenly sounded so much older.

"Well, he does have several highly competitive co-workers all trying for the same promotion, but it's hard to imagine any of them going to this extreme to vie for the upcoming opening as general manager of the western states." Sheila stared off into space, as if searching her mind for any other possible culprit.

As her mother and Steve continued to talk, Michelle replayed in her mind the episode with the tarot cards and the final unveiling of the death card in the process. A shadow settled over her as they retreated into the living room for the evening. She wanted to talk to her mom and Steve about it, but figured it would only make the situation seem worse than it already was, or cause them to question her judgment in even participating in the card reading. She knew Steve wasn't open to anything that seemed mystical or supernatural. And her mom probably wasn't either. She tried to push it all out of her mind and focus on the television drama they watched until bedtime.

When Michelle awoke the next morning, the sun was streaming into her bedroom window. She quickly looked around for Steve, wondering if he would be late for work. On the nightstand by the bed she spotted a note propped up beside the alarm clock.

Have a great day, Sleeping Beauty! You look so gorgeous when you are asleep. (Pant, Pant) I'll see you tonight.
Love, Prince Charming

"I can't believe I didn't even hear him get up!" Michelle said out loud.

She peeked through the bedroom door to see if she could hear her mom downstairs. Everything seemed quiet, but she knew her mother well enough to know that she was probably up and dressed already. Throwing on her jeans and a sweatshirt, she quickly ran a brush through her hair, then bounded down the stairs.

Sheila was at the kitchen table sipping on her coffee and reading the newspaper. Max looked up from his perch on the stepstool and greeted her as she entered the room.

"Well, you two certainly look content," Michelle commented.

Her mom smiled. "Good morning, dear. Did you sleep well?"

"Too well. I never even heard Steve get up. How about you? Were you comfortable in that new bed?"

"It was great, Michelle. You and Steve have fixed this house up so nicely. I really love it," she replied.

Michelle smiled. "Thanks!" She went over to the counter and poured herself a cup of coffee. Before she could sit down, the house phone rang. It was her father. His voice sounded weary. Barely taking time to greet her, he asked to speak to her mother.

Michelle watched her mom's expression change as she talked to her dad. Sheila's furrowed brow and silent nods revealed the concern she was feeling. Since the conversation she heard was one-sided, Michelle was unable to decipher what they were talking about. But she felt a heaviness settling into her spirit as her own level of concern rose.

Finally, her mother ended the conversation, reassuring him that she would be home as planned on Sunday afternoon. Looking a little lost, she handed the phone back to Michelle.

"Well, Mom? What is it? Is Dad alright?" Michelle asked.

"I don't know, honey. He doesn't sound right to me. This whole lawsuit thing is really getting to him." Her voice was tense and serious. "Maybe I should go home sooner."

"How could anyone believe that Dad would do something like that?" Michelle asked. "He's been with Mathers for years. Surely they know him well enough to know this can't be him."

Sheila turned and looked into her eyes. "I don't know, Mimi. All I know is that your father is afraid. I've never heard him sound like that before. It's really got me worried."

Michelle reached out to her mom, and they wrapped their arms around each other. Sheila had always seemed so strong and optimistic to Michelle. Now the roles were momentarily reversed, and Michelle felt her mother's vulnerability. She held her tightly, trying to comfort and reassure her.

An image of Michelle's dad darted through her mind. It was a disturbing picture of him sitting alone in a prison cell. *That can't happen*, she thought.

CHAPTER SIX

Grandpa Phil was reading his Bible, when suddenly his son-in-law's face appeared clearly in his mind. Whenever someone came into his thoughts like that, Phil believed it was God nudging him to pray. Closing his eyes, he began to intercede for John. Not knowing what to pray, he began by praying for God's presence in John's life. He asked that God would make Himself known to John.

The more Phil prayed, the more concerned he became. Reaching over to the phone on the counter, Phil began to dial the number for Mathers, Inc. Rarely did he ever call John at work. But he could not shake this ominous feeling that John needed him.

The receptionist greeted Phil and told him that John was not feeling well and had taken the day off. Now Phil was even more disturbed. It wasn't like John to miss a day of work. He quickly dialed John and Sheila's home number, praying that God would give him wisdom about whatever John was going through.

The phone rang five times before the answering machine responded. Phil felt awkward talking to a machine, but he left a message asking John to return his call. Again he committed John's life into God's hands and then picked up his Bible and walked out the front door. Thumper, their aging golden retriever, pounded his tail on the wooden porch as Phil approached.

Sitting down on the top step, Phil reached over and scratched him behind the ears. Thumper gratefully nudged his owner's hand with his nose. There was comfort in this relationship, and Phil felt his peace returning as he reopened the scriptures and resumed his reading.

Michelle's mother tried to reschedule her flight but was unsuccessful. As the two of them were trying to figure out what to do, Monica called.

"Beth and I are thinking about going shopping for a while and maybe picking up some lunch," she said. "Would you and your mom like to join us?"

Michelle presented the idea to her mother. "What do you think, Mom?"

"It doesn't look like I'm going to be getting a flight any sooner, so I guess we might as well go," she replied. "The diversion will be good for me."

They agreed to meet Monica and Beth at an antique store on Main Street. Michelle finished straightening up the kitchen, and she and her mom headed to town.

The four women roamed through antique and gift shops and enjoyed a casual lunch at The Omelet Maker. Michelle was glad to see how well her mother and Beth seemed to get along. Aside from the under-riding current of concern about Michelle's dad, the day turned out to be a happily memorable one.

Before parting to go their separate ways, Monica asked her about carpooling to yoga the following day. "Would you like to join us?" she asked Sheila.

"I don't want to intrude," Michelle's mother replied.

"It's no intrusion, Mom. We'd be happy to have you along." Although she couldn't really picture her mother in the class, she didn't want her to feel unwelcome.

"Okay. I'll think about it," Sheila said.

Although they also encouraged Beth to join them, she politely bowed out, mentioning her desire to spend some quiet time catching up on her reading.

As Michelle and her mom drove back to the house, Sheila expressed her enjoyment of the day. "I'm pleased that you've found such a nice friend, Michelle. I know it's been an adjustment living so far from all of us," she added.

"Monica's great," Michelle agreed. Then she added, "You seemed to really hit it off with Beth. Isn't she sweet?"

Her mother smiled. "Something about that lady reminds me of my mom. I guess it's her gentleness and the peace she radiates."

"I know what you mean. I really expected her to be more melancholy after the death of her husband. But she really does seem peaceful, doesn't she?" Michelle concurred.

When they arrived home, Michelle was surprised to see that Steve was already there. He had begun making one of his famous pots of chili, and the fragrance in the kitchen smelled delicious. She gave him a hug and chatted with him about their day, while her mother retreated to the bedroom to freshen up. By the time Sheila rejoined them, cornbread was cooking in the oven and Steve was grating cheese to top the chili.

Max paced back and forth impatiently rubbing against Michelle's legs and reminding her that he had not eaten. Steve playfully teased him with a spoonful of chili while Michelle opened a can of chicken liver. Max pranced around delightedly as he smelled his favorite meal, and quickly launched into it as soon as the bowl hit the floor.

Within minutes, Michelle, Steve, and Sheila settled in the dining room to enjoy their chili dinner and chat about their day. Although Michelle wanted to talk to Steve about her father, she resisted the temptation to bring it up, not wanting to risk upsetting her mother again. After dinner, they retreated to the family room to watch some television by the crackling fire.

Steve was channel surfing with the remote control, when Michelle caught a few words about the meaning of dreams. She quickly asked Steve to flip back to the program. It was a documentary on extrasensory perception, dream interpretations, and astral travel. Researchers from the former Soviet Union, the United States, and Europe had spent three years documenting people's experiences in these uncharted areas and were presenting their findings in this report.

Michelle was on the edge of her seat as she listened to story after story of people's intuitive, psychic impressions turning out to be prophetic. One woman interviewed had helped police solve numerous mysterious disappearances of children in a rural community in Ireland. She claimed to have dreams and visions that were able to lead police to an abandoned factory where the children's bodies were discovered.

A middle-aged man with long gray hair talked about how his dreams helped him locate his birth mother, who had not seen him for forty years. Mother and son were shown reuniting at the airport in Boston, with the mother repeatedly thanking him for listening to his dreams and tracking her down.

Several people from the Dream Institute in Amsterdam talked extensively about the untapped power of dreams and the value of learning their meanings and purpose. Emphasizing the positive potential of dreams,

Dr. Harvey, founder of the institute, encouraged viewers to journal their dreams. He mentioned several resources relating to dream interpretation, including Marty Gessler's book.

Michelle glanced over at the end table, spotting the large green volume that she had been unable to explore since her mother's arrival. She silently promised herself to look through it that evening before going to sleep.

The final segment of the presentation centered on the topic of astral projection, a type of out-of-body experience in which a person's spirit is able to travel to any place in the world while leaving his body behind. Testimonies included a woman in her twenties who claimed to have traveled from a southern state in America to Alberta, Canada, to see her dying grandmother. Another woman from New York reported having seen her brother standing at the foot of her bed one night, when in fact his body was fast asleep in his army barracks in Germany. He relayed to her a message about their cousin who was AWOL. No one else in the family learned about the cousin's disappearance until several days later.

The eerie stories and convincing testimonies had an impact on all three of them. They continued to watch until the program ended, then spent quite some time discussing what they had seen.

"This stuff is so interesting," Michelle blurted out, letting her guard down. She was intrigued, while Steve and Sheila seemed leery about the claims that had been made.

"I don't know about some of those stories, Michelle," Steve countered. "They seem pretty far out to me."

It frustrated Michelle that Steve seemed so closed-minded. "Are you saying that they are making this stuff up?" she asked with an edge to her voice, her hand reaching up to twist her hair.

Sheila shifted in her chair, appearing to be uncomfortable with Michelle's confrontational tone.

"All I'm saying is that I'm skeptical. I mean, really, doesn't this all seem kind of weird to you?" he asked, turning toward Sheila.

"I guess I'd have to hear more before I could decide for sure," Sheila hedged. She didn't seem to want to come between Michelle and Steve.

"You guys just don't get it. There's more to this universe than what we can see and touch," Michelle countered defensively.

"Maybe you're right, sweetheart," Sheila replied. She glanced over at Steve as if she was concerned about his possible reaction.

"Well, I'm going to just 'project' my body on up to bed," Steve concluded with a yawn.

"Cute," Michelle replied without smiling.

"Can I help you with the dishes?" Sheila offered, hoping to diffuse the tension by changing the subject.

"I'll take care of them, Mom. But thanks for offering."

Steve said his goodnights and left the room, heading upstairs with Max on his heels.

"Don't be too upset with him," Sheila said softly. "He's not trying to stir you up, Mimi. He's just a little skeptical."

"I know, Mom. But it frustrates me so much when he gets that superior attitude, like he knows everything about everything, and I'm just some gullible kid."

Sheila sighed. She wrapped her arms around her daughter. They embraced for a moment, and then Michelle gently pulled back. "Guess I'll do the dishes and go to bed."

"Okay, honey, but I'm going to at least keep you company in there, even if you won't let me help."

"That would be nice, Mom," Michelle replied with a smile.

While Michelle rinsed off the dishes and loaded them into the dishwasher, Sheila chatted with her about some of their old friends and neighbors. Michelle knew her mom was trying to get her mind off the television show and her aggravation with Steve. *Always the peacemaker,* Michelle thought as she listened to her mom chatter on.

It didn't take long to get the kitchen in order. After they turned off the lights and left the kitchen, Michelle picked up the large volume about dreams from the end table and placed it on the bottom step of the stairs to take up with her when she went to bed.

"Do you need anything before you go to bed?" she asked her mother, noticing the drawn look on Sheila's face.

"I don't think so, dear. All I need now is a good night's sleep." She gave Michelle another hug and headed for the spare bedroom.

Michelle retrieved the dream book from the base of the staircase and climbed up to the master bedroom. She was surprised to find Steve still awake.

"I thought you were tired," she started.

"I am, babe, but I've been thinking about your dad and his case. Maybe Roger will have some suggestions about how to put a trace on those checks."

Michelle began sharing with Steve about the phone call from her father. "Mom looked so worried," she concluded.

"Do you think I should call your dad in the morning? I could tell him I'm looking into some possible ways to help him."

"Why don't you talk to Roger first and then decide," Michelle suggested, touched by Steve's obvious concern and desire to help. Roger was the senior partner in the firm and a wealth of information for Steve.

As Steve sunk down under the covers, Michelle crawled into bed with her book.

"What are you reading?" Steve asked.

"Just a book I picked up at The New World Bookstore." Michelle replied casually, not wanting to get into another debate.

She was grateful when he just replied, "Oh. Well goodnight, babe."

"Goodnight." She gave him a kiss and then turned her attention to her reading.

Alone with her book, she began to explore the fascinating realm of her dreams. After several hours, she slipped down into bed, pulling the covers up over her shoulder and pressing her body up against Steve to absorb some of his warmth. Listening to his rhythmic breathing, she soon dozed off.

Suddenly she was sitting alone beside a wide river. Trees and shrubs lined the banks, reaching toward the steady current. The gray green water was churning as it pushed past her. Overhead, the sky was filling with clouds, and the wind was beginning to cause her to shiver. She pulled her sweater tightly around her. It was the pink and white ballet sweater her father had given her after her first dance recital in eighth grade. The cold air slipped between the fibers of the yarn and pierced her skin.

Wanting to leave and yet sensing that she must stay, she huddled in a tight ball as she drew her knees up to her chest and hugged them. It was essential that she wait in this very spot. Somehow she knew that she must stay there and watch. Rocking back and forth to try to get warm, she glanced up the river and spotted something moving quickly toward her, carried by the current. She rose to her feet and squinted her eyes, straining to see what it was. Soon she could see what appeared to be arms and legs flailing about as if in a desperate struggle.

As the form neared her, Michelle recognized her father's face and saw the look of helplessness in his eyes. She called out to him but he could not hear her. His head bobbed under the water then resurfaced. She called again but her voice was lost in the wind. Frantically looking for something to throw out to him, she grabbed a branch on the ground and ran into the edge of the current. For a moment, it looked as if he would grab hold of the end, but his fingers slipped. The rapids overtook him, dragging his body farther and farther down the river, until she could see him no more.

Michelle began to sob uncontrollably. "Daddy!" she cried through her tears.

CHAPTER SEVEN

"Michelle...Hey, wake up!" a distant voice commanded. It was Steve and he was leaning over her, gently shaking her shoulder to break the hold of her nightmare.

Michelle turned and looked at him with a disoriented stare. It took her a moment to awaken fully and realize that what she had seen was a dream. It all seemed so vivid and real.

Pulling herself into an upright position, she accepted the tissue Steve handed her. She wiped the tears off her cheeks, and then sat there silently thinking about the dream and worrying about her father. She could see that Steve was genuinely concerned about her, but he didn't know what to do. He sat beside her and wrapped one arm around her shoulder, stroking her hair with the other hand.

After a few minutes, she began sharing her dream with him. By now she was certain that each dream had a specific hidden meaning, and that she must remember and analyze them all. The combination of this nightmare about her father and the death card in the reading of the tarot cards by Bev had Michelle convinced that her dad was in serious trouble. She could not erase from her mind Bev's initial disturbed reaction when the death card was uncovered in the center of the reading.

Was her father's life somehow in danger? It seemed melodramatic to imagine someone actually trying to kill him, so she dismissed that option. But what about his heart? Was this lawsuit going to lead to a fatal heart attack? Tears welled up in her eyes as the thought overtook her. "Daddy," she whispered under her breath. She shook her head to stop the thought.

Picking up the dream book, Michelle looked for a section on rivers or drowning.

"What are you doing?" Steve asked. His voice sounded apprehensive and edgy.

"Listen to this, Steve. 'Rivers signify upheaval and possible barriers to success. A person seen in a river will be successful in his situation if he is able to master the current or swim from one side to the other. Someone seen successfully riding the rapids in a raft is bound for new levels of exciting growth in life. On the opposing side, is the victim who is being swallowed by the river. This individual is in a crisis and may be facing imminent danger or even death.'"

She paused and looked at her husband. "Oh, my God. What should we do, Steve?" Michelle searched his face for answers, her hand twisting away at the lone strand of hair.

"Well, first of all, I think we should put your book away and forget this nonsense about interpreting dreams," he answered, reaching over and taking the book from Michelle. Then he gently pulled her hand away from the nape of her neck.

"How do you know that it's nonsense? Think about it. The death card comes up when I ask Bev to read the tarot cards about Dad, and now this dream of him drowning in a river. It all fits together. I'm really worried, Steve."

"Do you really believe in those fortune-telling cards, Michelle?" Steve asked incredulously. "I think this dream is just a result of you worrying about your father's lawsuit. As for those cards, it sounds like a bunch of baloney to me," he concluded firmly, a twinge of exasperation creeping into his voice.

She ignored his tone. "I don't know, Steve. It seems too coincidental to me. If you would have been at class, you would have seen how convincing Bev's reading was. She seemed to know much more about Dad and his situation than she should. I think maybe there is something to this psychic phenomenon stuff."

"Come on, honey," he sighed, giving her a hug. "Let's just forget about this crazy dream and go back to sleep. Your dad is an intelligent, capable man, and I'm sure that this lawsuit is just one of those unpleasant detours in life that will soon be resolved."

"Yeah, maybe...," Michelle responded somewhat unconvincingly. She felt a little irritated with Steve and his apparent indifference to psychic experiences. At the same time, she was glad he was there holding her, and she knew that he really did care about her dad. Hoping he was right, she settled back under the covers and nestled against him.

Michelle awoke early and slipped silently out of bed. She decided to sneak downstairs and fix breakfast for them before her mom and Steve awakened. Max seemed to sense the secrecy of their mission, and he trotted silently beside her.

Once safely in the kitchen, he began rubbing against her legs and purring. She started the coffeepot and began mixing the batter for waffles. After she had the batter for the first waffle in the waffle maker, she opened a can of cat food, thanking Max for waiting patiently, and then set his breakfast on the floor beside the stove.

Next, she heated some maple syrup in the microwave and got down the canister of powdered sugar. Inspired to set out a gourmet meal, she decided to defrost some strawberries and whipped topping.

By the time Steve came into the kitchen, the table was set and a variety of toppings in lovely crystal bowls surrounded a platter of steaming hot waffles.

"Wow! This looks delicious, honey," he said. "Where's your mom?"

"I guess she's not up yet. We can go ahead and eat, and I'll fix her a fresh waffle later."

After enjoying their intimate breakfast together, Steve gathered his paperwork and briefcase for work. Neither of them mentioned her dream or their discussion from the night before. Steve thanked her for breakfast, gave her a kiss good-bye, and left.

While she waited for her mother to get up, Michelle sat sipping her coffee and thinking. She felt drawn to learn more about her dreams and about the interesting, mystical topics she had seen at the bookstore. After last night, she wondered how receptive Steve would be to her participating in the class on personal development and spiritual growth that would begin at the bookstore the following week.

She'd always admired and respected Steve's intelligence and his levelheaded approach to life. Now she wondered if they both might have been missing out on another important dimension.

At three-fifteen that afternoon, Michelle and Sheila were waiting for Monica to arrive to pick them up for the yoga class. Sheila had talked briefly with John that morning. After reassuring her that he was fine, she decided to stop trying to find another flight home and stick with her original plan to leave on Sunday.

The sound of a car pulling into the driveway signaled Monica's arrival, and they quickly exited out the front door. Michelle could see Max watching them leave from his perch at the bay window. She smiled and followed her mother out to the car.

After they arrived and got settled on their yoga mats, Michelle felt a little funny about having her mother there. Bev spent most of the hour doing a variety of breathing and stretching exercises, then taught them two new postures. Michelle's mother had some trouble with some of the moves, but she pressed on and did the best she could.

Near the end of class, Bev mentioned the awakening of Kundalini as the ultimate goal of yoga. Vaguely remembering her using that term at another class, Michelle could not recall what it meant. After class, she asked Bev to explain it again, as Monica and Sheila listened in.

"Kundalini is a serpent goddess who is able to travel up a person's spine during yoga practices and release the body's psychic centers or chakras," Bev stated matter-of-factly. "The final result can lead to a heightened state of enlightenment."

"Oh. Starla has been teaching me more about that. Enlightenment, I mean," Michelle replied. She glanced at Monica and her mother. Their expressions were very different. Monica was intrigued, but her mom seemed troubled.

Sheila felt uneasy as she listened to the yoga teacher's explanation. She could see that Michelle was soaking in every word. The class and Bev's words reminded her of a woman named Christine, who Sheila used to know from PTA. Christine was very immersed in yoga and would close her eyes and take deep breaths whenever something controversial came up at their meetings. Everyone in their circle thought Christine was peculiar. Sheila cringed inwardly when she thought about Michelle getting more involved in this endeavor.

"Is there something troubling you?" Bev asked her.

"No. I'm fine. Just a bit tired, I guess," she replied with a forced smile.

Bev turned her attention back to Michelle. "The advanced training program will begin again in a few weeks. I think you're ready to step up to that level."

Sheila watched her daughter smile in response.

"Why don't you and Monica discuss it and let me know," the teacher suggested.

"Okay," Michelle replied. "We're also thinking about taking a new class at Starla's bookstore."

"BlendTherapy!" Bev smiled. "You'll love it. Trevor teaches it, I believe. There's a strong chord that will connect what you are learning here with what you get in that class."

BlendTherapy? She thought. *I've never heard of such a thing.*

"Really? Good." Michelle didn't seem to notice her mother's concern, but Bev must have picked up on it.

"I love the way you've raised your daughter to be so open," she remarked to Sheila with a warm smile. "You've given her the gift of choosing her own path."

She returned the woman's smile. "It's always been our goal to let our children discover their own beliefs."

"Very commendable. You have an intelligent and sensitive daughter. She'll make wise choices," Bev replied reassuringly.

On the way home in the car, Sheila listened carefully to the conversation between Michelle and Monica. Both girls seemed very enthusiastic and excited about the other class. Apparently, the class was an introduction to a new form of psychology called BlendTherapy. Bev had mentioned a meshing of traditional psychology with a New Age perspective on the spiritual realm of life.

Her daughter appeared hungry for spiritual exploration and understanding, and Monica encouraged her as a willing partner in this venture. Sheila wondered what Michelle's grandparents would think of this. Or for that matter, what she, herself, should think. Although Michelle had always been a levelheaded girl, it was clear that she was about to dive into something that could radically change her life.

CHAPTER EIGHT

Traffic was congested leaving the airport Sunday afternoon. Michelle's mind wandered as she crept along the road, her thoughts replaying the last few days of her visit with her mom. Feelings of homesickness she'd fought for months resurfaced with a wave of emotion as she watched her mother's plane take off.

It had been great spending so much time with her mom. But today, the emptiness she had been trying to deny suddenly overwhelmed her. And something about her mother's parting words left her feeling apprehensive.

"Try to come down this summer, Mimi. And we're hoping you will be home for the holidays, too," she had said as she hugged Michelle and left to board her plane.

It had never dawned on Michelle that she might not see her parents this Christmas. She'd never spent the holiday without them. Although her mother's intention was to sound optimistic and to create a bridge to their next get-together, her choice of words had impacted Michelle in the opposite way. Fears and concerns about her father were feeding her anxieties, and she wondered what it would be like if she never saw either of them again.

"Snap out of it," Michelle chided herself as tears began to fill her eyes. "What is the matter with me?" she wondered aloud. But she just couldn't shake an uncomfortable feeling that nothing was going to be the same again.

John Ackerman kept replaying over and over in his mind the new evidence that could convict him. He felt like a caged animal. His heart began to race and his breathing quickened. Reaching into the drawer he fingered the revolver he had purchased as a protective measure many years ago. He knew that in a moment he could be free from all the anxiety and fear that haunted him during the preliminary hearings.

The last thing he wanted was a long drawn-out trial, followed by a disgraceful conviction and possible imprisonment. Maybe this was the best answer for everyone. It would save Sheila from the humiliation and uncertain financial future that could result from this nightmare.

He carefully lifted the revolver out of its resting place and was turning it over in his hand when the phone rang. Setting the gun back in the drawer, he reached for the receiver. His father-in-law's voice greeted him.

"Hello, John. I've been thinking about you today, and I thought I'd just give you a jingle," Phil said cheerfully.

"Hi, Dad. It's good to hear your voice. I'm glad you called." John replied, closing the drawer. "Sheila is coming back today, but it sure has been lonely around here."

"How's everything going with that lawsuit, Son? Joan and I have been praying for you."

"Thanks. I can use all the help I can get," John admitted. "It's still too early to tell, but I am a little worried."

"Well, you know how we feel, John. God is in control. Consider turning to Him. He could really help you through this," Phil urged.

"Okay. Yeah, I'll think about it. Hey, thanks again for calling, Phil. You may have helped me more than you know," John said sincerely, glancing at the tightly closed drawer.

Phil breathed a silent prayer as he gently replaced the phone receiver. Had he really helped? Would John consider turning his life over to the only One who could save him?

Sheila had much to think about on the plane ride home. She was concerned about John and wondered what state of mind he would be in when she got home. Rivaling her concerns for her husband were those she held for her daughter. A persistent feeling inside kept flagging her that something was wrong, and that Michelle was headed for trouble.

As she sat and thought about these issues, her father's voice spoke gently in her memories.

"Have you prayed about this, Sheila?"

It was almost as if he were sitting beside her. She closed her eyes and leaned back against the seat.

Michelle and Monica chatted and laughed lightheartedly as they approached The New World Bookstore. Like two schoolgirls looking forward to a new year of classes, Michelle could see that her friend was as eager and excited as she was about their first class in BlendTherapy. She felt a wave of gratitude for Monica. Their friendship helped fill the lonely days she struggled through in her new home. She was confident that this new joint pursuit would further bond their friendship.

As they entered the bookstore, the strong smell of incense momentarily overtook them. Starla waved and beckoned them to the back of the room. A small spiral staircase led up to a fairly large attic.

The only furnishings were pillows of all sizes strewn around the room's periphery. Posters on the wall of Buddha, the Dalai Lama, and Jesus lent a spiritual atmosphere. A large tapestry from India depicting the worship of sacred cows dominated one wall. Though the floor space was bountiful, the sloping ceilings gave the room a feeling of coziness.

In the middle of the room was a mat with a tray on it. A large candle, some matches, a stack of booklets, crayons, and a tape player identified this spot as the focal point for the class.

Starla explained that the instructor would be back momentarily. The sound of the bell downstairs indicated that someone had entered the bookstore, and she left Michelle and Monica up in the attic room to greet whoever it might be. Voices, that grew louder as they approached, belonged to three other women and two young men who had also enrolled in the course.

Michelle and Monica introduced themselves to the new arrivals and then all of them found a spot to sit. With pillows propped behind their backs, the students exchanged a few comments and questions as they waited for their instructor. More voices and bodies drifted into the room during the next few minutes. By the time the teacher, Trevor Wind, had emerged from below, twelve eager students awaited, sitting in a circle around the edges of the room.

Trevor's warm smile and tranquil countenance was captivating. He was poised and confident, introducing himself as their new guide into the enlightening realm of BlendTherapy. Everyone seemed riveted as he gave a testimony of his life, raised by a single mother who battled alcoholism and drug addiction.

Michelle tried to imagine what it must have been like, as he spoke of a lonely childhood, a broken marriage, and drug overdose as the key factors that led to his first encounter with BlendTherapy. Locked overnight in a psychiatric ward for observation after his overdose, he spoke of a kind and gentle nurse named Trisha who had compassionately shared with him about his potential to find hope and peace in life. She promised to help him, and upon his release he'd moved into her apartment.

Michelle noticed the sparkle in his eyes when he told them Trisha was like an angel sent from God. He explained that she comforted and encouraged him and began taking him to her classes in BlendTherapy. She said she saw BlendTherapy to be the answer for so many desperate lives she had witnessed during her work as a psychiatric nurse.

He looked around the circle, making eye contact with each of them, as he explained that BlendTherapy treats the whole person—body, mind, and spirit. According to Trisha, nothing else she had encountered had such potential for healing and a fresh start, going so far as to say that several of her patients, who had been in and out of various psychiatric wards, were now fully functioning, productive members of society.

He explained that an intensive one-year training program had convinced him. He was totally transformed. Now his mission was to help others unlock their inner potential. "BlendTherapy is for everyone who desires to grow," he said as he looked around the room again, smiling compassionately at each individual.

Michelle glanced at Monica, and they gave each other the "thumbs up" sign. They were ready.

"Let's begin with a simple exercise," Trevor suggested. "Close your eyes and imagine a symbol for yourself. For example, you might envision a waterfall ever plunging and rushing, never able to rest. Or perhaps you see yourself as a timid deer on the edge of an open meadow, shy but curious." He paused. Silence blanketed the attic room.

Michelle could hear her heart beating as she searched her mind for a symbol.

A few long moments later Trevor continued. "While you are thinking, I am going to place before you a booklet. The first page inside is blank. When you have a clear picture of your symbol, open your eyes and sketch it on that page."

Soft mandolin music drifted through the air from the tape player, as she heard him quietly pass out the booklets and crayons. The rustle of pages told her that various participants had begun drawing in their booklets. When she opened her eyes, she saw that Trevor sat directly across from her and had begun to make his own sketch in a booklet.

She flipped open her workbook and picked up a crayon, beginning to sketch her symbol tentatively. Feeling eyes on her, she glanced up from her drawing and saw that Trevor was studying her. She couldn't help but notice his handsome face and sensitive eyes. It made her blush when he smiled. She quickly looked back down at her booklet and tried to regain her composure as she finished her drawing.

Next Trevor had the students introduce themselves and share their drawings around the circle, one at a time. Some of the illustrations were quite eye-catching, revealing the artistic talents of various students.

When it was her turn to share, Michelle felt embarrassed by her rough, childlike sketch of a kitten looking out a window. However, Trevor seemed pleased.

"Very insightful," he said. "What are you looking for outside of your world?" Smiling in a reassuring way, he moved on to Monica without waiting for Michelle to reply.

After all the students had shared their drawings, Trevor gave them an assignment for the week. He instructed them to begin a journal. Each day they were to reflect for a time on their drawing and ask themselves what the drawing revealed. Any and all thoughts that followed were to be recorded. He thanked them for joining him in the adventure of BlendTherapy and promised to see them all the following week.

As the students gathered up their belongings, Michelle glanced over at Trevor. Two women were talking to him about their prior experiences with therapy. He seemed intently interested in their stories. His compassion was evident, and she was impressed.

Sitting at the desk in her bedroom, Michelle excitedly described her first class in BlendTherapy as she typed an email to her friend, Kristin.

"Trevor is so warm and friendly. He made us all feel at ease right away. You'd love him, Kristin. He just seems to really care about people."

The sound of Steve's car broke her concentration, and she signed off and clicked the send box. Glancing at her watch, she raced downstairs. It was already seven o'clock, and she hadn't even started dinner. Quickly grabbing a box of macaroni and cheese out of the cupboard, she hurried to get a pan of water on the stove, nearly stepping on poor Max as he lamented his lack of dinner.

Steve looked tired and hungry as he entered the room.

"What's up, Max?" he asked as the feline cried and rubbed against his leg.

"He's just hungry," Michelle answered. "I got busy writing an email to Kristin and lost track of the time."

Steve sighed. "Guess we have to wait for dinner, fellow." He scratched Max on the back and gave Michelle a quick peck on the cheek.

She quickly put some cat food in a bowl on the floor and then followed him into the family room. "How was your day, hon?" she asked.

"Too long. How 'bout yours?" Steve collapsed on the couch.

"It was great. Monica and I had our first class in BlendTherapy today."

"Blend what?" Steve asked.

"BlendTherapy. Remember I told you about the flyer I got from the bookstore?" she said, trying to be patient. It was obvious Steve had little interest in this new venture.

"Oh yeah, right. I remember now. So how was it?" Steve rested his head back on the cushions.

She launched into a full-blown description of the class and their homework assignment for the week. "The teacher explained to us how BlendTherapy addresses all the parts of a person—body, mind, and spirit. Then we sat with our eyes closed and thought of a symbol that represented who we are. We drew the pictures of our symbols and discussed them. You should have seen some of the artwork. It was amazing."

Waiting for him to reply, she glanced over and noticed that his eyes were closed and his chest was slowly and rhythmically moving up and down. He was asleep. At first she was crushed by his indifference, but then chided herself for not being more sensitive to his obvious exhaustion. Still, as she walked quietly back into the kitchen, she couldn't help but think about Trevor and the way he focused so intently on her when she spoke.

Shaking her head in an attempt to shake away that thought, she set about completing their simple dinner as she chatted with Max. When the meal was almost complete, she walked into the family room and looked at Steve asleep on the couch. Unsure whether or not to awaken him, her dilemma was solved when Max rocketed himself onto Steve's chest and abruptly ended his nap.

He seemed a bit disoriented then somewhat embarrassed when he realized he'd fallen asleep. "I'm sorry, Michelle. I guess I'm more beat than I thought," he apologized.

She forced a smile and reassured him she understood. "Dinner will be on the table in just a minute," she added.

Their meal was quieter than usual, and Michelle could tell that Steve had a lot on his mind. She caught herself smiling partway through the meal as she remembered Trevor's question about what she was looking for. Blushing, she looked over at Steve, but he was lost in his own thoughts. She sighed and got up to do the dishes. Steve scooped Max up and headed back to the couch to relax.

Over and over in her mind, Michelle replayed the class, seeing Trevor's friendly smile and his compassionate eyes. A voice inside told her that these thoughts were dangerous, but she was mesmerized by her teacher's charm.

That night Michelle had another one of her dreams.

A black tunnel. Cold and alone. She strained her eyes to see the end of the darkness. Where is the escape? The blackness seemed to swallow her, her heart beating furiously. Trying to scream, she found herself unable to make a sound. Running. Breathing. Crying. Now someone was following her. His voice called out, "Michelle, it's me. You're safe. I'll help you."

Michelle turned. She fell into his strong arms. The tunnel dissolved and they were standing in a field of wheat. The soothing sound of his heartbeat calmed her as she rested her head against his chest. Looking up into Steve's eyes she realized something was different.

This wasn't Steve. But it was. It felt like Steve; she recognized the feel of his body against hers. But the face, the face belonged to Trevor. It was Trevor's aqua eyes that reassured her.

Michelle awoke with a start. She looked over at Steve, asleep beside her, and was flooded with a myriad of emotions. Unable to free herself from images of Trevor, her guilt escalated.

I love Steve, she reminded herself silently.

A moment later, he rolled over and snuggled against her. She could feel her racing heart begin to slow, but her mind spun with confusion.

CHAPTER NINE

The sound of the shower pulled Michelle from her sleep. Somehow she had missed the alarm clock again and was surprised that Steve was already getting ready for work. She sat up and thought about her day ahead. Then her dream came filtering back into her consciousness.

"I'll have to see what Mr. Gessler thinks about that one!" she murmured to herself as she arose and got dressed.

She was just about to race downstairs to get Steve some breakfast when he collided with her between the closet and the bathroom. "Sorry," he said without even looking at her. "Do you know where my gray tie is? It's not on the rack."

"I think I dropped it off at the cleaners with your shirts."

"Bummer." He rifled impatiently through the ties that remained.

Michelle could see he was not in the best mood. "Here. Wear this striped one. It'll look fine with that shirt," she offered, handing him one of the ties her mother had sent him for his birthday.

"Yeah, okay," he replied, quickly snatching it from her hand and heading for the mirror.

"Do you want me to fix you some toast?" she asked.

"Not today. I'm late already." He whizzed past her and down the stairs.

"No hug?" Michelle asked the empty space he left behind. She'd hoped she'd be able to spend a few minutes with him, especially after last night. But his job was becoming increasingly demanding, and his responsible nature drove him to extend his hours at both ends of most days. If there was one thing she'd learned about her husband, it was that he detested leaving unfinished business. The way he left so abruptly meant he would probably be getting home late again tonight.

She knew Steve's job had the potential to bring them great material wealth and status. In addition, he clearly loved what he did. She was proud of his new position as a junior partner, and she was happy that he was thriving in an area of personal interest to him. But she yearned for the early days of their relationship when he seemed like he couldn't get enough of her, when she was his focus and passion.

Michelle looked in the mirror. Running a brush through her hair, she quickly applied some makeup. Meanwhile, Max was putting on his own act of impatience, rubbing against her legs with all of his weight and crying like he hadn't eaten for a week.

"Okay. Okay. I hear you. Just give me a second," she countered, finishing her mascara and nearly tripping over him as she turned to leave the bathroom. "Watch out, you little rascal," she chided, scooping him up and carrying him down to the kitchen.

After feeding Max and making her coffee and toast, she sat down at the breakfast nook with her journal. The start of each new day was always the hardest part for her. Knowing that she wouldn't see Steve for at least ten hours and not sure how she'd fill her empty day, she felt particularly displaced and homesick.

Trying to distract herself, she began a one-way conversation with Max. "See the kitten, Max?" she asked, pointing to her drawing from class. "That's me, looking out the window." She paused, the gloom threatening to return. "Why am I doing that, you ask? Probably looking for my long lost husband."

Max looked up at her and purred, content with his full belly and oblivious to her struggle.

"Well, you're a big help, pal," she sighed. "Trevor said to write down everything that comes to my mind when I look at this drawing. Guess I should be recording these thoughts." She picked up a pencil and began to write:

I'm looking for companionship, that close bond of family and friends I miss from California. I'm looking for adventure and meaning. I'm looking for opportunities to grow.

Her cell phone rang and startled her from her journaling. It was Starla from The New World Bookstore.

"Greetings, Michelle! Starla, here."

"Hi, Starla."

"I thought I'd give you a ring and tell you about a few new books that just arrived."

"Oh, yeah? Tell me what you got," Michelle said.

"Some great new titles by several of Gessler's associates. They're out in paperback."

"Really? Maybe I'll come by and have a look," she responded.

"Are you okay, dear? You sound kind of down," Starla said.

She hesitated. "I'm fine. Just a little lonely. My husband's working really long hours right now, and it's kind of hard being so far from family and friends."

"Well, why don't you just come on down and spend the morning with me? I've got a fresh pot of herbal tea brewing, and we can sit by the fire and rummage through some of these new gems," the woman offered.

"Sounds tempting."

"Then it's settled!" Starla exclaimed. "Come as soon as you can. Ta Ta!" and she hung up.

"Well, I guess I'm going to the bookstore, Max," she announced as she stood to her feet and began tidying up the kitchen. As if he had been dismissed, Max solemnly retreated to the family room.

Michelle sat in the comfortable overstuffed chair sipping her tea, as Starla carried a small stack of books toward her. Starla's motherly approach eased some of her homesickness and made her feel comfortable. The tea was deliciously spiced with cinnamon and honey, and the cozy fireplace warmed another gray day, adding to the friendly atmosphere. Michelle was glad she'd decided to come.

The New World Bookstore was becoming her favorite retreat. In addition to a sense of comfort and companionship, she could also feel adventure in the air as she dug into the books before her. Starla was right that this was so much more expansive than her upbringing.

The closest thing to spiritual matters she'd experienced was the Christianity of her grandparents. But theirs was a fundamental faith, and aside from prayer, there didn't seem to be anything mystical about it. Mostly it just appeared comfortable and traditional, not exciting and adventurous. Grandma and Grandpa were very sincere, and she adored them, but they didn't seem particularly curious or open-minded about expanding their horizons.

The down-home approach of her grandparents sharply conflicted with her father's intellectualism and self-sufficiency. He seemed more willing to be open in some ways, yet he resisted anything that removed ultimate control of his destiny from his own hands. He enjoyed discussing topics such as parapsychology and self-hypnosis but remained staunchly opposed to what he termed as "blind faith" in an invisible God. It was almost like he was his own god and needed no other.

Now Michelle wanted to discover her own truth. She reveled in the freedom she had to sift through books and share ideas with Starla. The New Age material lining the walls and shelves of the bookstore beckoned to her. She yearned to explore broader horizons and discover all of her options. Somehow there must be a way to blend the self-sufficient, intellectual approach of her father and the inner peace of her grandparents with these New Age metaphysics and spirituality.

Starla eagerly agreed and seemed to love sharing her own philosophies of personal evolution. This linked Michelle with her newest acquaintance and helped her to feel a part of the bookstore patrons.

After several hours of visiting and poring over a variety of books, she decided she should get going and do some of her errands. As she was about to leave, Trevor walked in. He greeted Starla with a gentle embrace, and then gave Michelle a brotherly hug as he draped one arm around her shoulders.

"How's my favorite kitten?" he asked with a twinkle in his eye.

Michelle could barely respond as she fought the blush that was creeping up her cheeks. After mumbling something about having to run, she eased her way toward the door, thanking Starla before slipping out. Even as she walked to her car, she felt Trevor's eyes following her. Why was she so unnerved by him?

It was nearly ten o'clock by the time Steve finally got home that evening. When he texted earlier to say that he would not be home for dinner, she'd fixed herself a bowl of soup and decided to research her dream about Trevor. As she scanned the index of Gessler's book, she found some references to mistaken identities. This led to a section that described what she had experienced in the dream when Steve had become Trevor. She carefully read the passage.

"A change of identity from one key figure to another indicates confusion about present relationships and a sensitivity to personality vibrations. Often these images indicate inner desires and unsatisfied drives. The dreamer wants to believe that the relationships are stable but recognizes the fluctuating chemistries and is simultaneously drawn to the opposing figure in ways he or she may deem consciously unacceptable.

"These dreams rarely occur in individuals who are truly content and secure in their relationships. Thus, such a dream indicates the need to reevaluate current situations and perhaps redefine personal boundaries within the relationships in the dream. This may mean an expanded view on interpersonal relationships to allow the exploration of the opposing party.

"It is possible there has been a cosmic invitation extended to the dreamer and some past values or morals are hindering the development of this relationship. Such unhealthy restraints usually result in repeated episodes of the same dream in various settings until the dreamer either yields to the invitation and develops a meaningful bond with the opposing figure, or forces subconscious suppression."

Michelle was trying to sort through all this. Was
Gessler saying that she needed to explore some kind of
relationship with Trevor, or she would keep having these
dreams? And what was this part about a cosmic invitation
and reading personality vibrations? It seemed to indicate
that Trevor might be sending her some kind of signals.
Unable to deny her feelings of attraction toward him, she
was wrestling with guilt and forbidden desire when Steve
walked through the door.

"Hi, sweetheart," he said softly, exhaustion
written all over his face.

She could feel her color change as she quickly
closed the book and rose to greet her husband. "Hi,
Steve. How'd it go?"

"We're making progress. Hopefully we'll have this
case wrapped up and ready to present by next week. Sorry
about dinner."

Michelle gave him a hug. "No problem. Max and
I spent the evening reading," she replied, hoping he
wouldn't ask about her book. She offered to fix him some
soup and he gratefully accepted.

After dinner, Steve went upstairs to go to bed
complaining of a headache. She picked up her book, and
opening it to the marked page, she began to reread the
section. *I wonder if I am putting unhealthy restraints on my
relationship with Trevor*, she wondered. Just thinking about
him caused her face to flush.

CHAPTER TEN

The sun was shining the next morning as Michelle brushed the sleep from her eyes and stretched. A feeling of warmth caressed her as she smiled and soaked in the beautiful colors of the rainbow glittering and dancing on her walls. Starla had given her a large teardrop crystal to hang in her window, and the sun was finally teasing the radiant colors from its hidden potential.

A note on the counter by the coffee maker told Michelle that Steve would be working late again, but that he promised a great time together that weekend—perhaps a dinner at the elegant Cliffhanger restaurant that overlooked the sea.

Michelle decided that she would spend the day outdoors enjoying the clear blue skies and the brisk air. After breakfast, she dressed in old jeans and a sweatshirt, packed a few snacks, her books, and a Thermos of coffee, and headed for the beach. She delighted in the idea of a long walk by the water followed by some quiet time reading and meditating in her beach chair.

It was a short drive to her favorite spot along the shoreline. She parked her car, collected her goods, and walked across the sand toward the water. Just looking out over the sparkling blue-green water brought a smile to her face and a deep sigh from her heart.

How she loved and savored the sunshine, now that she lived in such a bleak and rainy climate. The ocean looked so majestic as large waves pounded against the rugged rocks. She could feel and smell the saltwater in the air. There wasn't a cloud in sight, and the beach was deserted.

She set up her chair and arranged her bags and books on the towel. Then she stood tall and stretched as if reaching up to touch the very rays of the sun. Her spirit had not felt this light in quite a while. Kicking off her shoes and peeling away her sweat socks, Michelle headed toward the water's edge. She loved the feel of the sand beneath her bare feet. It was cool, not warm like the sandy beaches in Southern California, but the soft, powdery texture underfoot made her somehow feel more connected to the earth itself.

Strolling along the wet sand near the breakers, her thoughts flowed freely, her mind wandering back to the happy days of childhood playing and making sand castles with her brother.

She thought about the first time she'd walked the beach with Steve. Three days after their initial encounter in the university library, he had invited her for a picnic on the sand. The way he thought of every detail, down to the checkered cloth napkins lining the spacious wicker basket, really impressed her. They had eaten and talked, walking along the shoreline sharing casual and intimate details about each other's lives until dusk. She'd hated to leave that private space and time.

Since her early teen years, the beach was her favorite retreat when she needed to think. Watching the waves faithfully follow one after the other in a rhythm that only nature could orchestrate, and gazing out into the seemingly eternal expanses of open sea, gave her a broadened perspective on whatever issues or problems she was facing.

Today was a perfect day to reconnect with the beach. An occasional seagull circled overhead while she walked, but Michelle was oblivious to anything or anyone other than herself, the waves, and her ocean of thoughts. She sensed a deep, spiritual connection to the universe as she became one with the sand, the salty breezes, and the warm sun.

This must be what Starla was talking about the other day. A oneness with the cosmos. An ability to tap into that universal consciousness available to those evolved enough to recognize it. She felt a surge of euphoria. *It's a higher understanding of God Himself,* she thought, as she stretched out her arms to embrace the vastness.

Continuing to meander along the shoreline, she reflected on all she had learned. A whole new world was unfolding for her as she continued to pursue her interests in yoga, meditation, and BlendTherapy.

Now she felt more a part of this world, and more a part of the small corner of the universe called Shady Cove. Her friendships with Starla, Monica, and Bev, along with the guidance of her teacher, Trevor, served as the bridge to lead her into this new understanding and perspective. Personal evolution. It was what she had been looking for, especially after giving up so much to move here with Steve.

She could see that she'd gained more than she'd lost. Much more. This move was part of the cosmic plan for her life, to open her to new and better avenues of growth. Michelle never felt more alive, more spiritual.

Spiritual. What did that used to mean to her? Going to church with her grandparents and saying a prayer at bedtime. Now she knew it meant so much more. It meant power. A power that could only be contained by the universe itself. A power that she could tap into through the psychic channels she was learning about in her class and through her reading.

And yet, somewhere in her, the little girl who had soaked up her grandpa's Bible stories seemed a bit sad. Michelle brushed her aside and moved on.

As she turned to walk back to her chair, she noticed someone sitting on a rock close to her little encampment. He smiled and waved to her, and she squinted her eyes to focus on the figure. The cock of his head and his familiar stroll brought a quick identity to her mind. Trevor. What was he doing here? Suddenly all of Michelle's euphoria was replaced by a different kind of adrenaline rush. She could feel her heart rate quicken.

"Hey there, kitten!" Trevor tossed the words into the air. "What a pleasant surprise to find my favorite student in my personal hideaway."

"Trevor," Michelle replied, fighting for composure. "How long have you been sitting there?"

"Long enough to watch you embrace the universe," he replied with a warm, disarming smile.

She felt flustered and a little embarrassed as she thought back to her open-armed gesture.

"You are the sweetest thing to ever grace this beach," he continued. "I love to see that childlike exuberance of yours freely expressed in here. It makes my hideout even more special to me now." His smile melted her. "Hope you don't mind me spying on you. It's like watching a flower unfold its tight bud and smile up at the sun."

Michelle giggled nervously. "You make it all sound so dramatic. I'm not sure an opening flower is a good analogy." She paused and looked away, trying to regain her composure. "Deep inside I'm still that little kitten looking out the window."

"Well, little kitten, mind if I join you for a spell? This day is too beautiful to be wasted indoors, and I can't think of anyone I'd rather spend it with."

Michelle felt a little apprehensive, but her concerns dissolved as she observed his innocent expression and friendly smile. "Sure, why not? I'd love to have some company. It does get rather lonely at home sometimes. Besides, it would give me the chance to talk to you about that conference you were telling us about in class. I'd love to hear more."

So Trevor and Michelle settled on her beach chair and towel, shared coffee from the only cup she had brought, and munched on cheese, crackers and apples. Trevor told her all about the Psychic Energy conference he had recently attended in Seattle and about all the pioneers in this field of New Age discoveries.

She heard much more about the healing power of meditation for all kinds of illnesses, including terminal cancer patients who went into complete remission after applying these meditative techniques.

It was all so fascinating, and she found herself leaning toward Trevor and listening in earnest as he described demonstrations and case histories that had been presented at the conference.

"You are really interested in this, aren't you?" he asked.

She nodded.

"Maybe I should take you with me to the next conference. It will be in Idaho in a couple of weeks. Interested?"

She hesitated. "I would love to go, but what about Steve? I don't know what he would think of me taking off for a weekend conference—"

"—with your teacher, no less?" Trevor finished for her. "Surely Steve trusts you, Michelle. Besides, he's gone so much of the time himself. Wouldn't he want you to do something that interests you?"

"Well... let me think about it."

"You're the boss!" Trevor said with a wink. "Hey, how about dinner? Is Steve working late again tonight? We could order some Chinese food and bring it down here to eat while we watch the sunset."

"Dinner? Ummm, well, sure. Yeah, that would be nice. I haven't had Chinese food in ages. I'm sure Steve wouldn't mind that. He knows I hate to eat alone." Michelle could feel a twinge of guilt, but she pushed it aside.

"It's settled, then," he announced as he helped her gather up all her things and carry them back to her car. "I have my bike right here. Are you up for a ride?"

Michelle looked at the beautiful gleaming black motorcycle. It looked like fun. "Okay," she agreed. Trevor popped open a storage compartment and handed her a helmet, then grabbed his from the handlebar.

It wasn't until they were cruising down the highway that she noticed how close to him she was sitting. The vibration of the bike as it cut through the wind invigorated her. She felt like she was flying! Leaning into a turn, she held him tightly for security. He reached back and patted her knee reassuringly, saying something over his shoulder, but his words were lost in the wind.

She relaxed against his back, enjoying the sights of Sandy Cove as they sailed through the sleepy beach community. She could feel his strength and confident control of the bike. Turning her face up toward the clear, sunny sky, she experienced a sensation of exhilaration. Without thinking, she gave Trevor a little squeeze. He looked back with a smile as he pulled up in front of the Primrose Palace.

"Wow! That was fun!" she exclaimed, grinning and running her fingers through her tousled hair.

"I almost lost you on that turn!" he teased and winked.

She laughed and bopped him on the arm. As they walked into the restaurant, she was immediately enveloped in a myriad of delicious aromas. Trevor convinced her they should buy a variety of entrees and share them all. She felt a little guilty having him pay for everything, but this impromptu dinner caught her off guard, and she didn't have any cash.

He didn't seem to mind at all, making some comment about how rare it was for him to be able to share a meal with such a cute little kitten. Twenty minutes later they were back on the bike, bag in hand, returning to the shore.

Steve was thrilled when Roger suggested he take the evening off. "You've been working too hard on this case, Steve. It will still be here on Monday. Go home and spend some time with that lovely wife of yours." Steve didn't need his arm twisted. He organized his paperwork, purposely left his briefcase beside his desk, and headed for home.

The house looked quiet as he drove into the driveway. The garage door yawned slowly open revealing the absence of Michelle's car. "Hmmm, wonder where she could be?" he thought to himself.

Max must have been wondering the same thing. He let his feelings be known as soon as Steve stepped into the kitchen. Max was clearly hungry, and Steve was his only hope.

"Give me a second, boy," Steve chided. He put the mail on the kitchen table and noticed the cutting board on the counter with an empty cheese wrapper and an apple core. His note from the morning explaining that he would be working late was still by the coffeemaker, but there was no note from Michelle to explain her absence.

He picked up his cell phone and punched in her number. A few seconds later, he heard the familiar chime of Michelle's phone coming from upstairs. He found it plugged into the charger by their bed. "Great," he muttered. "Guess it's not a dead battery this time," he informed Max with a note of sarcasm. "Okay pal, let's get you some food." Max agreed wholeheartedly and pranced behind him to the pantry for his meal.

Steve sat down and started to read the mail while the cat inhaled his Liver Delight. Then Steve's stomach started growling. "What am I going to eat, Max?" he wondered aloud.

Max did not even look up from his bowl, not the least bit concerned about his owner's dilemma.

After a few minutes, Steve's stomach got the best of him and he decided to make himself some dinner. He found a frozen meal in the freezer and put it in the microwave. Glancing at the clock, he noticed it was after six o'clock. He wasn't sure if he should be worried about Michelle or not. It wasn't like her to be gone this time of day, but she had been spending a lot of time at that bookstore. Maybe she'd decided to grab a bite to eat with her friend, Starla.

Although Steve was disappointed she wasn't home, he could hardly blame her since he'd told her he would be home late. He ate his dinner in front of the television, watching the news with Max curled up beside him on the couch.

"Thanks for dinner, Trevor," Michelle said sincerely. "It was fun talking with you and getting to ride your motorcycle."

"The pleasure was mine," he replied smoothly, and then smiled his angular grin. "I'll see you at class next week!"

"Okay!" she agreed, adding, "I'll talk to Steve about that conference in Idaho."

"You do that," he encouraged. "You'll be amazed to see what is happening in the scientific community. I know you'd be fascinated. This marriage between science and spirit has been a long time coming." He started to walk away and then turned back. "Drive carefully," he added protectively as she climbed into her car. She smiled and waved as she pulled away from the curb.

He's a great guy. I'm glad we're becoming friends.

She was surprised and disconcerted when she arrived home and saw Steve's car in the garage. "I wonder what time he got home?" she asked herself aloud.

When she walked into the kitchen, she heard him call out, "Hey, babe! Is that you?"

"Hi, honey!" she answered following his voice into the family room and giving him a kiss. "What are you doing home?"

"Roger gave me the evening off, so I decided to surprise you. I guess I was the one to be surprised. Where have you been?" he asked with a slight edge to his voice.

"I had dinner with a friend I ran into at the beach," she replied.

"Anyone I know?"

"Just a friend from my class at the bookstore."

"Oh," he said, distracted by something on TV.

She breathed a sigh of relief when it was clear he wasn't going to ask any more questions. In spite of the fact that her time with Trevor had been innocent enough, something made her feel uncomfortable about Steve finding out. She decided to wait to talk to him about the conference in Idaho.

Michelle's grandmother sat up in bed. Glancing over at her husband sleeping peacefully beside her, she noticed the digital clock on the night stand said 2:00. Something was troubling her deep in her spirit. It was Michelle. She was in some kind of trouble. Joan could not explain it, but she knew. She could feel it in her bones.

Dear Lord, what is it? she whispered in the recesses of her mind. When no clear answer came, she did the only thing she knew to do—she prayed. Hugging the comforter to her chest as if she were cradling Michelle to her heart, she pleaded with God to watch over her precious granddaughter and to bring her safely through whatever was happening.

A few stray tears escaped the corners of her eyes as she thought about the first time she held Michelle in her arms. Such a tiny newborn with pink cheeks and a shock of dark wavy hair. She remembered the look in her daughter's eyes. Sheila was in awe as she gazed at her adorable new daughter, and John had been so proud that his whole countenance was aglow!

Please, Lord. You know what Michelle needs. Help her, Father. Give her strength and wisdom. And please keep her safe! Joan prayed fervently in her spirit.

CHAPTER ELEVEN

"Teacher's pet!" Monica teased as she and Michelle climbed into her car after class.

"What are you talking about?" Michelle asked defensively.

"You know very well what I'm talking about. Relax, Michelle. I'm just jealous because Trevor is so enamored with you."

Michelle could feel her color changing. "I think you're imagining things," she said, hoping to brush off the whole issue.

"Well, maybe I am, but he sure seems to focus on you more than any of the rest of us," Monica replied. "Don't you notice how he always looks at you first when we discuss something, and how he loves to use you as an example during his demonstrations?"

Michelle shrugged her shoulders and twisted her hair. Monica was her best friend in Sandy Cove and she wanted to tell her about her dinner at the beach with Trevor, but a part of her felt so guilty about it, even though she knew she hadn't done anything wrong.

Thankfully, Monica decided to change the subject. "How about a hot fudge sundae at The Igloo?" she suggested.

"Now you're talking," Michelle replied, smiling with relief.

Michelle checked the answering machine on her landline when she got home. There were two calls. One was from her father. It was a little strange. Something about a business trip and to expect something in the mail from him. He closed with his usual "hugs ya lots, kiddo!" sign off, but it rang a bit hollow in his weary voice. She made a mental note to call home that evening.

The next message was from Trevor. "I got the info in the mail about Idaho. Call me."

Short and sweet. Michelle looked in the full-length mirror and asked herself why she always got so flustered at the sound of his voice or the mention of his name. She was glad that she'd gotten the message before Steve got home. Punching the erase button, she smiled at Trevor's attention. He made her feel special, especially with Steve so busy at work all the time.

"After all, it's perfectly harmless," she reassured herself as she gazed at the wedding photo on the end table. "Steve is around women at work all the time. It's no big deal."

She picked up the phone and returned Trevor's call. He seemed distant at first, but then rallied with his usual warmth when she identified herself.

"Would you like to meet to go over this brochure? Sorry I didn't get it in time to bring to class, or I could have just given it to you there," he explained.

"I don't know, Trevor. I just got home, and I've got laundry and dinner to think about."

"In the vast expanse of human events, is laundry and dinner really that important?" he teased. "Seriously though, I think you should look this over and discuss it with Steve. The conference is filling up quickly, and I'd hate for you to miss it."

"Yeah, I guess you're right. Well, let me throw in a load of laundry and put the chicken out to defrost. Can I meet you somewhere in about twenty minutes?"

"How about The Igloo?" Trevor suggested.

"I just got back from there with Monica," she replied.

"Great minds think alike," he quipped. "Then let's make it the Coffee Stop."

"OK, I'll be there in about twenty minutes," she said with a smile.

"See ya, kitten!" Trevor replied, and he hung up before Michelle could tell him not to call her that. Somehow it seemed too intimate. Oh well, she'd tell him when they met.

John picked up the pen and signed his name. He read over the letter one more time to make sure it said those important things that were on his heart.

Dear Michelle,

Hi, honey. I wanted to write this letter to you to explain some things. I'm going away for a while on business, and I'm not sure when I'll be home. But before I go, it's important to me that you know how special you are. There was never a happier day in my life than the day you were born. I mean it, Mimi. Holding you in my arms while you squinted and wiggled was a magic moment. I'll cherish it forever.

This is a very difficult time for me. Many things are happening that I do not understand. It's too complicated to explain to you, and I don't want to burden you with my problems. Just know that everything will be all right somehow. But I must get away to think and sort it all out.

While I'm gone, please keep in touch with your mother. Tim tries to get together with her for lunch once or twice a month, but you know how busy your brother gets. Besides, your mom really misses having you close. Just try to call her as often as you can. I know I can count on you, sweetheart.

Please know how much I love you, Michelle. It's hard to be a dad sometimes. There are so many things you want to say, but the words get lost. Anyway, for all the times I meant to say it and didn't, I love you with all my heart.

Hugs ya lots, kiddo!
Dad

John smiled sadly. He folded the letter neatly and inserted it into the waiting envelope. Sealing it and giving it a gentle kiss as he stared off into space, he began to walk mechanically out to the mailbox.

Michelle and Trevor sat across from each other at a tiny table for two. Michelle was looking over the brochure for the conference while Trevor studied her. "Has anyone ever told you that you have the most mysterious eyes?" he asked.

"Knock it off, Trevor," Michelle giggled, her heart racing. "You're embarrassing me." She started to reach up to twist her hair, but caught herself and brought her hand back down.

"No, I mean it. There are many secrets behind those windows into your soul. I'd like to explore them."

"Well, for now, how about if we explore this brochure you brought about the conference," she countered.

"Okay, okay. Have your way, Mystery Lady," he sighed with a twinkle in his eye.

They spent the better part of an hour reading about and discussing the various seminars advertised in the multipage glossy brochure. The ones most intriguing to Michelle included: Dream Analysis; Meditation and Wellness; Numerology; Yoga and the Psyche; and Holistic Evolution.

Trevor suggested that she also consider one particularly fascinating workshop on higher consciousness being conducted by a well-known guru of BlendTherapy and a lecture on reincarnation given by a Hindu professor from the university in New Delhi.

Michelle listened carefully to all that he said. She was fascinated by this new world that was being presented to her. For a time, she forgot her uneasiness with him and allowed herself to relax. His enthusiasm was contagious, and she was glad she had him as her guide. Surely Trevor knew more about all this than her, and she should follow his lead.

A question that had been tucked away in the back of her mind resurfaced. "So what ever happened with you and Trisha?" she asked.

Trevor looked off into space for a moment. Then he returned his gaze to Michelle. "She went her way and I went mine. We weren't destined for a long-term relationship, but our time together was magical. I owe her my life."

"Do you ever talk to her?"

"Only if I run into her at a conference or seminar. She speaks at some of the healing workshops." He looked into her eyes and added, "You remind me a little of her."

Michelle saw a sorrow, a longing in his expression. She asked, "Do you think you'll ever get married, Trevor?"

"Me? No. Not likely." He smiled a crooked grin and winked at her. "I'm not the marrying type, kitten." He glanced down at her wedding band. "It's great for a small percentage of people who find their soul mates, but for the most part, I think it's an outdated institution. The people I respect and spend most of my time with are not into those kinds of trappings. Live and love and move on."

Michelle glanced away and caught sight of the clock on the wall. "Speaking of moving on, I'd better get going."

Trevor smiled with that same longing she'd seen before in his eyes. He patted her hand before rising to pay the bill.

"Oh, no you don't," she smiled. "This one's on me."

He graciously accepted her gesture and then accompanied her out to the parking lot. As he climbed onto his motorcycle, Michelle thought about how comfortable she was finally beginning to feel with him. Still, a part of her was uncertain how Steve would view this new friendship. They'd never really discussed friendships with the opposite sex.

Although she wanted to clear the air and make sure he wouldn't have any bad feelings about her friendship with Trevor, she wasn't ready to talk to him about it yet. She wasn't willing to take the risk of having him ask her to break off ties with him. Trevor was more than a friend. He was her mentor. And he made her feel special.

Dinner was ready and the table nicely set when Steve walked in the door. He relished the fragrance of the meal and the warmth of the candlelight as he slipped off his shoes and went looking for his bride.

He found Michelle up in the bedroom changing into a beautiful, soft, lavender-colored velour lounge outfit. It accented her shiny, dark hair and made her look so inviting. He held her chin between his thumb and forefinger and kissed her gently.

She responded with a warm smile and a loving embrace. His fondness for her grew each day and seemed to subtly replace that exhilarating "mad about you" feeling with a deeper kind of stable love and affection.

"How was your day, babe?" she asked affectionately.

"Okay. How 'bout yours?"

"It was good, but I got a weird call from my dad. He seemed really down."

"Were you able to cheer him up any?" he asked, pulling his tie loose and beginning to change from his suit into jeans and a sweatshirt.

"No. I didn't actually talk to him. He left a message on the machine while I was out," she explained. "Monica and I went to yoga together and then had a sundae at The Igloo."

"That's nice," he said, glancing in the mirror and running his fingers through his hair. "Speaking of food, what's for dinner?"

"My grandma's chicken potpie. You'll love it," she promised. "It should be ready in about ten minutes. I'd better get down there and check on it."

Steve retreated to the family room to watch the news while Michelle finished the dinner preparations. It really did turn out to be a delicious feast—flaky piecrust filled with steaming chicken and vegetables in a creamy sauce, a sumptuous Caesar salad with freshly grated Parmesan cheese and giant croutons, and small bowls of canned peaches in heavy syrup.

They enjoyed a quiet dinner together in front of the television, and then Steve collapsed on the couch with a catalog about fishing equipment that had arrived that day in the mail. He flipped through the pages, dreaming of a vacation on a quiet lake somewhere, while Michelle cleared the table and loaded the dishwasher.

It seemed like Michelle was doing more and more of the after dinner chores by herself these days. Steve wandered into the kitchen, came up behind her, and wrapped his arms around her waist.

She turned and kissed him on the cheek. "That was a nice surprise," she murmured softly.

"I love you, babe," he said. "Let's sneak away somewhere together. Just the two of us."

"Sounds great! What do you have in mind?"

"How about a weekend at a bed and breakfast on the lake?" he asked.

"Are you serious?" She looked excited about the idea.

"Serious."

"Wow! I'd love that, honey. When do you think you could get away? And what will we do with Max?"

"Max will be fine for a weekend. Maybe Monica can keep an eye on him. I should be done with this case in about three more weeks. How about the weekend of the twelfth?"

Michelle's expression changed. "Well, actually, I was thinking about going to a conference that weekend with some people from my class," she stammered.

"Really? You never mentioned it to me."

"I'm sorry. It just came up this week," she explained, adding, "I don't have to go. It's not a big deal."

"Listen, Michelle, if this conference is something you want to attend, it's fine. Really. We could go to the lake the following weekend. I'll make it work."

"Are you sure, Steve?" she asked him.

"Positive. You gave up a lot to move here with me. If this class and conference are important and interesting to you, then I think you should go," he answered decisively.

"Okay. Well, thanks for understanding. We'll plan for the lake the weekend of the nineteenth then."

"Good. I'll talk to Roger and try to get a half day off on Friday so we can leave early." He could already picture relaxing at the lake with his beautiful wife and a fishing pole.

"I love you, Steve," Michelle said, pulling him close.

"Love you too, babe," he replied, returning her embrace.

Michelle put the last glass in the dishwasher and turned it on. The hum of the machine had a reassuring sound to it. Another day done. And she was set to go to the conference! Michelle wandered upstairs with Steve, completely forgetting to return her father's call.

Sheila awoke around midnight and noticed that John was not in bed. She pulled on her robe and felt around for her slippers. Walking out into the hallway, she could see a light on in the den. She found John asleep in his leather chair, looking years older than she remembered. On his lap was the file with the court documents. Gently she eased it out from under his hands and placed it on the table beside the lamp.

He stirred slightly, and she encouraged him to his feet, guiding him to bed. She was worried. Really worried. John was always so strong and in control. Now he seemed hopelessly lost and afraid.

What could she do? How could she help this man with whom she had shared more than thirty years? There must be some way out of this legal and emotional mess, some way to bring back the man she knew and loved.

It did not help that Mathers had forced John into a leave of absence until the case was resolved. Now he spent every waking hour focused on trying to solve the puzzle of who was framing him. She could see the tremendous toll it was taking on him. After all, John took pride in his self-sufficient nature. Now that was crumbling, too.

After settling him into bed, Sheila did something she had not done in years. She prayed.

CHAPTER TWELVE

"Hey, Michelle! Do we have a Bible around here somewhere?" Steve called to her from the garage.

"A what?" Michelle asked, poking her head through the kitchen door, a cup of coffee in her hand.

"A Bible. You know. The 'good book'?" he teased as he continued to dig through a box of books.

"Gosh, Steve. I don't know. I haven't seen my Bible since we moved," she admitted.

"What about that old one I had? You know, the one with the blue cover?"

"I haven't seen either of them, hon. Why do you need a Bible?" she asked curiously.

"Well I had an unexpected visitor at work yesterday. Ben Johnson. I used to play football with him in high school," he began.

"In high school? How did he find you up here?" Michelle wondered.

"Actually, he wasn't looking for me. He just spotted my name on my shingle in front of the office and took a wild chance it might be me."

"Wow! Small world!"

"Yeah, that's what I thought."

"So what does this have to do with finding a Bible?" she asked.

"Well, I'll tell you the story." He sat down on another box, and Michelle leaned back against the door.

"Ben was the star quarterback at Claremont High. Great athlete, but a real jerk of a guy. Thought he was God's gift to planet Earth. Strutted around school like he owned the place. Most of the guys respected him for his athletic abilities, but hated him for his arrogance. The girls seemed blinded to his weaknesses, and he always had some cheerleader hanging on his arm. His date for the senior prom was the homecoming queen."

"Oh, one of those," Michelle nodded knowingly.

"Anyway, the last time I saw Ben was after freshman year at college. We ran into each other at McDonalds. He didn't seem the same. Said he didn't like college much, but his parents insisted on him finishing."

"What. He couldn't live without his harem?" she asked sarcastically.

"Actually, yeah. You're right in a sense. He couldn't adjust to not being the big man on campus."

"I've heard of that kind of thing before," she remarked, sitting down on another box to listen to the rest of the story.

"Well, anyway, you would not have recognized Ben yesterday. He was a totally different guy."

"How do you mean?"

"It's kind of hard to explain. He just seems so much more mature. Friendly. Down to earth. Like a regular guy," Steve grasped for words.

"We went out to lunch together," he continued, "and had a great visit. He started telling me about his wife, Kelly, and then—get this Michelle—he told me he is setting out to be a pastor. Can you beat that? Ben got religion. He started sharing with me about this Bible study on campus, and how he met Kelly there. Then he said some stuff about the Spirit of God doing a work in his heart.

"I know it sounds weird, but he was dead serious. He said that his life was completely changed. Now he's looking to start some kind of church up here. I guess he and Kelly have wanted to move to Oregon to get away from the rat race down south."

"Wow," Michelle replied.

"Yeah. Anyway, he asked me about my life. I told him about you, and how I ended up with the most gorgeous girl in all of California." He looked into her eyes and smiled.

She gave him a loving and patient look. "So what else did you guys talk about?"

"Well, then—this is where the Bible comes in—Ben started to tell me some stuff he had been studying about end times."

"What's that mean?" Michelle asked, looking suspicious.

"I don't know all of it, but from what I gather he was talking about the end of the world or something."

"Sounds pretty strange to me, honey," Michelle countered.

"I know what you mean. Those were my first thoughts, too. But then he started showing me a few things in the newspaper and telling me about how they were fulfillments of Bible prophecies. He had scriptures for every one of them. It was actually pretty fascinating.

"So anyway, he kind of challenged me to look into it. Said he would help me if I was interested. He's coming back to the office to meet me for lunch on Monday. That's why I need to find a Bible. I want to look up all this stuff he is talking about," he concluded.

"Okay, well I'll help you look if you want me to. Just be careful. Some of these religious fanatics are pretty convincing," she warned.

Steve smiled. "That's an interesting comment coming from someone who's exploring some pretty far-out stuff. But thanks for your concern, babe. I think I can handle this. Remember, I'm a lawyer. I don't fall for stories without checking out all the evidence."

He could see her countenance turning defensive. "Hey, I didn't mean anything by that. Come here." He patted his knee and she sat down on his lap. "I appreciate your concern, honey. I know there are some wackos out there, and I promise to keep my guard up, okay?"

She leaned against him, seemingly satisfied by his apology. "Okay."

Michelle stood up and opened a box beside the one he was sitting on. "Let's look through this one. It's from my old closet at my parents' house. Maybe my Bible is in here."

Sure enough, near the bottom of the box, under her yearbooks from junior high and high school, was an old leather-bound Bible. The inscription inside read, "To our darling granddaughter, Michelle. You are a special blessing sent from God. Happy Thirteenth Birthday! Love, Grandpa Phil and Grandma Joan."

Steve noticed Michelle's expression change to an almost sad look. "What is it?" he asked.

"I remember when I got this. I was so excited to become a teenager at last. By the time I got this, I'd long ago outgrown listening to Bible stories on my grandpa's lap. I remember politely thanking them, but I think they could tell I was not really that interested in reading it. I feel bad remembering the look of disappointment on my grandmother's face. She must have thought I'd be really excited to get it."

Steve nodded. "This is real leather," he observed. "These things are pretty expensive, I think."

"Yeah, I guess they must be. Well, anyway, now you have one for Monday. Just don't lose it, okay? It has sentimental value," she added.

"No problem, babe. I'll be careful with it. Hey look! We should enter our wedding date on this line here.

There are also places where we can list the births of our babies."

"Don't you think you're getting a little ahead of yourself?" she replied. "Remember, I still have college to finish before we work on *that* project!"

He smiled. "I know, I know. But it sure sounds like fun!" He winked at her and watched her blush. *Man, I'm lucky to have such a gorgeous wife.*

"You're a pervert, Steve. Maybe you should just start reading that Bible," she quipped. She stood up, tossed her hair back, and walked into the house.

Later that evening, Michelle spotted the old Bible on the counter. Steve was out jogging, and she decided to glance through the pages. It felt heavy and important in her hands. The smell of the burgundy leather and the feel of the tissue thin pages seemed distantly familiar.

She was just starting to read the first chapter in Genesis when the phone rang. It was just some salesman for the local newspaper, but it diverted her attention from the Bible, and she ended up deciding to take a hot bubble bath. Sinking down into the suds, she looked over the brochure for the conference. It still amazed her that she was actually going.

"Are you beginning to see what I mean?" Ben asked Steve as he stirred the cream in his coffee. "Like the Eurodollar. See how that fits in with the idea of a global economy? And what about those identification cards they are using at the PX near where I live. They even call it the 'Marc'. A different spelling, but sure seems like a step toward the Mark of the Beast in scripture. You know, no buying or selling without it? Now the military's concern is what to do if someone loses their Marc. It's just natural they would proceed to the next step of a microchip implant."

"Whoa! You're moving pretty fast here," Steve countered.

"Sorry. I guess I get a little carried away. It's just so clear to me. And so exciting." Ben shifted his stocky body, running his fingers through his wavy, chestnut hair. He was still quite handsome, in a muscular sort of way. Steve noticed the continuous shaking of Ben's right leg, but Ben seemed oblivious to the motion.

"If you ask me, it sounds a little unnerving," Steve replied.

"Listen, Steve. This is stuff you need to know. How about if you and I conduct a little informal research together over lunch each day while I'm in town. I'll only be here for about two more weeks, but we could cover a lot of material if you're interested. What do you say?" he asked, his pale blue eyes fixed on him.

"Okay. You've got yourself a study partner," Steve agreed. He'd never realized that biblical prophecy could be so relevant to current events. His interest was definitely piqued. Maybe the Bible was more than a history book. Maybe it really did have some significance today. The investigative attorney in him was intrigued.

Ben smiled warmly and extended his hand to Steve as he rose from his seat.

As Ben drove away, he thought about his time with Steve. Maybe God sent him here for more than just finding a church site. He could hardly wait to call his wife,

Kelly, and tell her about meeting up with Steve Baron in Sandy Cove.

Knowing her, she'd probably say, "No coincidences in God's kingdom." He smiled as he pictured her face. It was hard being separated from his wife like this, even if it was only for a couple of weeks. But it was clear he was supposed to be here.

Trevor was obviously pleased when Michelle told him she could go to the conference. He proposed that they try to book side-by-side rooms at the hotel since it was such a large complex. She agreed, and they called for the reservations. It was not a problem. There were two rooms on the west wing that overlooked the lush courtyard. Michelle felt a little uneasy, but reminded herself that they *were* separate rooms.

"What should I bring with me?" she asked him.

"An open mind and spirit," he replied with a smile.

"You know what I mean, Trevor. Should I bring a notebook or laptop? Also what about clothes?"

"Yeah, you should probably bring clothes," he teased. Michelle threw up her hands in exasperation.

"Okay, okay. Yes, bring a notebook. You won't need a laptop. I'd suggest warm clothes. It can get pretty cold out there."

"Casual or business attire?" she asked.

"Definitely casual. You won't see any stuffy suits or anything like that at this conference."

"Then jeans and sweats are okay?"

"Perfect. Just bring a jacket," he said. Then he added, "I'm really glad you're going, Michelle. You will love this!"

They continued planning and made reservations for their airline tickets. Michelle felt a little guilty spending so much money for a weekend she wouldn't even be spending with Steve. But he had reassured her that money was not an issue and she was to go and enjoy herself. He'd invited Ben to stay at their house while she was gone to save him some money on a hotel room and to give them the weekend to continue their studying.

Michelle was glad he was having such a good time researching all this with Ben, but she was also a little uneasy. This Bible stuff did not seem to blend very well with the direction she was taking spiritually. She made a mental note to discuss it with Trevor while they were at the conference.

Steve cradled Michelle in his arms while they were lying on the bed. "I'm gonna miss you, babe."

"I'll miss you too. But it's just for the weekend," she replied.

"Well, call me as soon as you get there, so I know you arrived safely."

"I know. And call Saturday morning and Saturday night and Sunday morning."

"Are you making fun of me, Miss Jet Set?" he asked jokingly.

"No, Steve. I think it's sweet. And I will call. Promise." She sighed and snuggled against her husband's chest. Her mind was reeling with so many thoughts, but for now she just wanted to cuddle and enjoy this time with Steve.

Trevor sat in his living room smiling to himself. He was really excited about the conference, especially about introducing his new protégé to the fascinating concepts and testimonies he knew they would experience there.

He thought back to their dinner together. *What a beauty she is. I can imagine what her skin must feel like.*

His mind replayed their time together on the motorcycle with her body pressed firmly against his and her arms wrapped around him. He smiled, nodding to himself. *We're going to have a great weekend.*

CHAPTER THIRTEEN

Steve maneuvered his sports car through a maze of other cars, taxis, and shuttles to the passenger unloading curb beside the Pacific West Airlines terminal. Attendants with rolling luggage carts were standing along the sidewalk, ready to tag and take luggage. Steve popped the trunk and leaned over to kiss Michelle.

"Are you sure you want me to drop you off here? I really don't mind paying the parking, babe," he said.

"This is fine, Steve. It's not like I'm leaving for a month. I only have that one little rolling carry-on bag. I'm sure I can manage from here. Besides, I don't want you to be late for your golf date!" she teased as she looked into his eyes and ruffled his hair.

"Okay, well if you're sure. I'll miss you, babe. Don't forget to call tonight as soon as you get settled," he reminded her.

"I will. Promise." She smiled as she held up her cell phone.

Steve got out of the driver's seat and went around to the back of the car. He lifted out her small bag and placed it upright on the ground. She pulled up the handle, locking it in place. Then she turned to Steve, embraced and kissed him, told him to behave himself while she was gone, and started walking into the terminal, turning at the sliding door for a final wave.

Once Michelle was out of sight, Steve climbed back in and drove off, heading for Fairview Country

Club. To celebrate the successful conclusion of his case, Durand Simmonds had extended an invitation to Steve and Roger to join him on the course for the afternoon. One of the perks of working for wealthy clients! Steve was looking forward to a few relaxing hours golfing, followed by a weekend of study with Ben concerning the books of Daniel and Revelation.

Although he hated to admit it, a part of him was glad that Michelle was happily occupied for the next couple of days. These Bible studies were becoming more and more fascinating to him, but there was no way he would have allowed himself a whole weekend of study if she had been home. Besides, it had been a long time since he had the freedom of bachelorhood.

As luck would have it, the sun was shining and a gentle breeze was softly blowing. "Couldn't ask for a better day for golf," he thought aloud as he pulled his car up the winding road to the guarded gate.

Tall trees lined the entrance and pink, purple, and white impatiens overflowed the brick planters, giving the grounds an elegant, well-kept appearance. A sprawling clubhouse with massive windows was planted inside the gate immediately to the left.

Steve sucked in a deep breath of the freshly washed air and smiled. He momentarily wondered if he would ever be successful enough to own a membership in a club like Fairview. For now he was satisfied with the chance to spend his afternoon there.

Trevor was already inside the airport waiting. Michelle spotted him approaching their departure gate and waved, relieved to see him already there. He smiled and waved back.

As she got closer to him, she saw he had a small backpack on his back and a duffel bag in his hand. His teal shirt accentuated his sparkling eyes, and his smile was disarming.

Again, she felt that rush. *Get a grip!* she chided herself silently as she walked towards him.

"The plane's delayed for fifteen minutes. Want to grab a cup of coffee?" he suggested.

"Sounds great. I didn't get a chance to finish mine this morning. Too many things to do before I left."

They strolled over to the coffee stand. The fragrance of freshly brewed coffee smelled delicious. She ordered a mocha hazelnut blend and Trevor opted for his favorite French roast. Carrying their coffees over to the gate, they settled down to wait for boarding.

Trevor had pulled off the Internet some updated information about the seminars at the conference, so he showed her the printouts. She was disappointed that the Dream Interpretation workshop had been cancelled, but he reassured her there were more than enough interesting seminars and workshops available for her to attend during the weekend. Besides she already had Gessler's book. It was the best dream work available.

Within ten minutes the airline attendants were announcing boarding for their flight. Trevor explained that he had gotten to the airport early to request two seats together, one of them by the window.

"It's such a beautiful day, I thought you might enjoy looking out," he explained.

Michelle was touched and thanked him for his thoughtfulness.

"Anything for my favorite kitten," he responded.

She began to tell him not to call her that, when his cell phone interrupted them. While he finished his conversation, they reached the boarding attendant.

Handing her their tickets and identification, they began walking the ramp onto the plane.

Once they boarded, Trevor adeptly placed her carry-on and his duffel bag in the overhead compartment. His backpack had conference information in it, so they decided to keep it at their feet to go through during the flight.

As if to make up for lost time, the plane began its taxi down the runway almost immediately. Michelle peered out the window at the airport drifting past her and thought about Steve for a minute.

Her anxiety rose momentarily as her mind played a game. *What if we never make it there? What if the plane crashes and I never see Steve again.* She started questioning the whole trip. Why was she doing this? It was crazy taking off with Trevor for a weekend in Idaho. What was she thinking?

She was brought back to her senses when the flight attendant tapped her on the shoulder and reminded her to buckle her seat belt.

Trevor reached over and patted her hand on the armrest. He seemed to be able to read her mind. "Relax. Everything will be fine."

Michelle took a deep breath, used her yoga techniques to find her center, and quieted her inner tremors. *I'll be fine,* she reiterated silently to herself.

Once the plane achieved cruising altitude, Trevor and Michelle unbuckled their seat belts and began reading through the conference material again. Michelle could feel Trevor's arm pressing up against hers as they leaned together to share the information. Her pulse quickened.

Soon the flight attendant was serving them beverages and snacks. Michelle decided to have a glass of wine to help her unwind and relax. After a few sips, her tension melted away. Trevor told her a funny story about his first flight across country, and she found herself engulfed in laughter. He had quite a sense of humor and really knew how to tell a tale. It was very entertaining, and further loosened any grip of anxiety.

On one of the new printouts he'd brought from the Internet, Michelle noticed a course that caught her eye: Ancient Scriptures and Prophets of Old.

"What is that about?" she asked him, pointing to the title. He skimmed through the description and then summarized it for her.

"It is about books like the Bible, the Koran, and the Talmud—an overview of the teachings of ancient prophets such as Buddha, Mohammed, Moses, and Jesus. It explains the common thread of these teachings and how they mesh together to explain the path to God. Sounds interesting," he concluded.

"What do you think of the Bible, Trevor? My husband is really getting into a study about it with some friend of his," she said.

"Well, I think the Bible is a valuable history of spiritual evolution in the Jewish world. It gives us some insight into how we all evolve. Take Jesus, for example. Now there's a guy who was far beyond His contemporary society. They knew nothing about spiritual evolution, so they actually thought He was God Himself.

"Now, of course, we know better. He was just living at a higher level of consciousness—able to tap into that universal power or divinity we are all able to attain, whether in this lifetime or a subsequent one," he concluded.

"Wow, I never thought of Jesus that way. I told you my grandparents are Christians, and they taught me to see Him just as you described the people of biblical times—like God Himself, or a part of God, or something."

"I understand, Michelle. My mom was a Christian, and I remember how she used to pray with me and teach me Bible stories before my father took off with her best friend. I used to kneel by my bed and pray to Jesus to bring my dad home. But, of course, that never happened. As I watched my mom start drinking and meddling in drugs, I realized that either Jesus was a fraud or was misunderstood.

"Now I see that Christians are just stuck at a level of perception that doesn't allow them to see the bigger picture. As well meaning as they may be, they are simply too narrow in their thinking. And they try to fit Jesus into a mold that He was never meant to fill." He paused and seemed to search her face.

"But what about my grandparents? He fills that mold for them."

"Perhaps this is not the lifetime for your grandparents to understand God-consciousness. This may be their current state of personal evolution. The next life may be different for them, or maybe you will be the one to open their eyes," he suggested.

"So you don't buy the 'one way to heaven' theory?" she asked with a smile.

"No way, kitten. There are too many people lost if that is true."

This time it didn't bother her that he had called her kitten. His sincerity and obvious compassion for people of many faiths was apparent. And now she understood that his affectionate name for her was somehow a symbol of that global love.

Before she went to bed that night, she suddenly remembered to call Steve. He sounded really tired, mentioning a stressful meeting with a client that had followed his golf game. They didn't talk long. Michelle felt guilty thinking of the playful fun she was having here at the conference while he was wrestling with issues at work.

Still, it was nice to have some time to explore her new beliefs, and what better place than at a weekend seminar with her teacher?

CHAPTER FOURTEEN

Running, running, running. The familiar black tunnel and the icy fingers of anxiety gripping her heart. Faces appeared along the steel walls. They were stretched tight with agony. Arms and fingers were reaching out to her, trying to grab her as she ran. The light was far down the tunnel. It seemed to move further away with every step.

Ducking and dodging the outstretched hands, Michelle began to sob. She saw a man appear ahead of her. Steve? No, it was Trevor. Michelle called his name as she cried. One of the hands caught her by the hair. She screamed and yelled, "Trevor, help me!" From somewhere in the darkness, a pounding on the walls of the tunnel released the grip on her hair.

Lunging forward, Michelle sat up in bed. Her face was streaked with tears and she was shaking violently. A persistent pounding sound brought her to her senses. Someone was knocking on her door.

"Michelle! Are you okay? It's me, Trevor. Let me in."

She fumbled for her robe and pulled it tightly around her as she walked over to the door. She was wiping the tears from her face with her sleeve. Sliding the chain off the lock and opening the door, she stood there trembling. He carefully guided her back into the room and shut the door behind them.

"I heard you calling me and came as quickly as I could. What happened? Are you all right?" he asked as he gently led her to the edge of the bed. Sitting down beside her, he looked into her eyes.

Michelle's heart was still racing as she struggled to recover from the terror of the dream. Trevor's gentleness melted her, and she began to cry again. He held her in his arms and stroked her hair.

"It's okay, kitten. Everything's okay," he soothed.

Finally Michelle regained her composure enough to sit up on her own. She glanced at him to see his expression, afraid that he would think she was nuts. But all she saw was genuine concern and an aura of love that was so appealing.

Slowly she began to tell him about her dreams and how they haunted her. She apologized for waking him and told him that she had been calling him in her sleep because she was hoping he could rescue her from the tunnel.

Trevor showed his understanding by the warmth of his countenance. After she was finished telling the story, he pulled her into his arms again.

"I'm so sorry you are going through this, Michelle. Such a beautiful soul to be so tormented. I will help you get free of this karma," he said, pausing for a moment as if in deep thought.

"Think of it this way. You are like a butterfly still trapped in the cocoon. You know you must escape it, but you can't find your way out. I will teach you how to break free and fly."

She wanted to believe him. "How, Trevor? How do I break free?"

"We'll start by a simple meditative technique." He propped some pillows against the headboard. "Here, sit back against these pillows and close your eyes."

Michelle obeyed.

"Feel your arms close against your body, Michelle. These are your wings. Visualize the pure white cocoon surrounding you. This is your past. It is trying to hold you back.

"Do you see the small opening at the top? There is a light coming into your world. To make your wings strong enough to fly, you must resist the past. Feel your arms trying to push outward. Push hard, Michelle. Now allow them to move a tiny bit outward.

"Look up. The opening is growing a little bigger. Feel the sweet fresh air coming in from above. Now push again with your wings. You can move them further now. Yes. That's right. Good girl. The opening is big enough now for plenty of air to get in.

"Take a deep breath, Michelle. Let it fill your chest with the opportunity to grow and change. Do you feel it? Feel the power, Michelle. Let it all in."

Michelle's eyes were still closed, but her face was very relaxed. She breathed deeply and smiled. Suddenly she felt her arms lifting upward as if in worship. Fully extended over her head, she spread her fingers to the sky. Trevor was silently watching the transformation, nodding and smiling.

"I feel free," she murmured softly.

Trevor did not break into her thoughts. He sat quietly, and she could feel him watching and waiting.

A few moments later, Michelle slowly opened her eyes. She grinned, sighed, and squeezed Trevor's hand.

"Thank you, my dear friend," she said sincerely.

"No, thank you for letting me be a part of your unveiling!" He smiled in return.

"I don't want to go back to bed now," Michelle said reveling in her lightheaded feeling of release.

"Me neither," Trevor responded. "Let's go out for breakfast!" he suggested.

"At three o'clock in the morning?" Michelle asked with a smile.

"Yep. You get dressed, and I'll be back in a few minutes."

"Okay, if you insist!" she replied, laughing.

His smile and caress of her cheek gave her the answer to that.

After he left, she quickly got dressed and brushed out her hair. "I can't believe he saw me looking like this," she sighed, gazing into the mirror. No other man but Steve had ever seen her first thing out of bed. Then she smiled, twirled around, and said, "But I've never felt more alive!"

Trevor really understood her. He knew what to do. He would help her break out of these nightmares. Michelle was certain now that she was meant to be here this weekend with him.

It was Saturday afternoon. The morning had flown by, consumed with two fascinating lectures on parapsychology. Winding their way through the crowded displays that filled the grand ballroom, Trevor instinctively reached back and took her hand. The touch of his hand was now familiar and comfortable to Michelle. She held on and let him lead her through the maze of booths.

"Michelle!" a voice called out to her. She turned to look and spotted Starla waving from a display of books across the aisle. Trevor also saw Starla and diverted their path to stop by to say hello.

"I'm surprised to see you here," Michelle said, suddenly a bit flustered that someone saw her there with Trevor.

"Been coming to this conference every year for ten years now!" Starla explained with a smile. "It's a great opportunity for me to meet the people on the leading edge and to sell some of my books at the same time."

"You look great, honey," she continued as she looked at Michelle. "Different somehow. Freer or something."

Trevor and Michelle caught each other's eyes and exchanged smiles.

"Trevor is helping me get out of my cocoon," Michelle explained.

Starla nodded knowingly. "He's a good guide, Michelle."

"I know," she answered with a blush.

"Well, have a great time! Drop by the shop next week and tell me about the seminars you attended."

"I will," Michelle promised.

"See you later, Starla," Trevor said as they waved and walked off.

"That woman is amazing," he said to Michelle once they were out of earshot. "She's almost like a spiritual mom to me. What an encouragement to see someone who is past midlife and still has such an interest in growing to higher levels of consciousness. Most women her age are so trapped by the past that they can't understand any of this."

"I know what you mean. My mom would think I was crazy if she saw what I'm doing this weekend. I guess that's one of the benefits of being an adult—'Mom' doesn't have to approve of your activities," she replied, as she giggled and smiled.

Down in Seal Beach, Sheila was pacing back and forth in the kitchen of her home. She kept rereading the note from John.

Honey,
I've got to get away for a few days. I'm not sure where I'll be or
when I'll be back. There's too much to sort through. I need to be
alone. Everything will be okay. I promise. Just give me some time.
Please don't call anyone at work. If they try to reach me, tell them I
had urgent family business out of town.
All my love,
John

Where did he go? Was he okay? She was really
worried. This was not like her husband. She decided to
call Michelle.

Steve answered the phone. The expression on his
face changed from friendly to concerned as he listened to
her voice. Ben could tell that something was definitely
wrong. He could gather from the conversation that it was
Michelle's mom and that something was wrong with
Michelle's dad. While Steve tried to sort through the
details, Ben prayed.

"Did you try Michelle's cell phone?" Steve asked.
"She's not here this weekend. She's at a conference with
some friends from that class she's been taking at the
bookstore."

After a pause he added, "Yeah. She probably let
the battery run out or left it back in her room. Let me get
the hotel phone number for you. Hold on a sec."

Steve fumbled through the papers on the counter.
"Here it is." He recited the number at the hotel and then
asked if there was anything else he could do. Finally, he
asked her to call back if she heard anything.

"My father-in-law has taken off somewhere," Steve began to explain. He told Ben about the lawsuit and about how concerned everyone had been. "That's why I was so surprised to see this in the mailbox this morning," he said as he held up the envelope for Michelle from her father. "Michelle and her dad talk fairly often on the phone, but they don't correspond by mail."

"I think we should pray," Ben suggested. Steve said that he didn't really know how to pray but that he would listen while Ben prayed.

"Lord," Ben said with a combination of reverence and affection, "Michelle's dad is in some kind of trouble. I pray that you would be with him on this journey. Go before him, God, and draw him close to you. Teach him the wonders of your love and the safety of your arms. Show him a way through this mess and give him wisdom. Do whatever it takes, Lord, to bring him into the kind of faith he needs today. I lift him up to you, entrusting him into your able hands, in Jesus' name. Amen."

Steve didn't know what to say. He felt such a peace listening to Ben pray. It was almost as if God Himself was in the room with them. Somewhere inside he knew that he wanted what Ben had. He wanted that peace for himself.

Michelle was having a great time. The seminars were more interesting than she had imagined, and she was soaking it all in. She had bags full of brochures, books, and a myriad of other New Age trinkets in her room. She realized that she could spend hundreds of dollars at the booths in the ballroom. There was so much to learn and so many interesting things to try.

It was almost midnight, and she and Trevor were strolling back to their rooms, his arm slung over her shoulder.

"What a day," he sighed.

"The best!" Michelle agreed.

"I hate to go back to my room by myself, but I'm beat," Trevor admitted. He turned and hugged Michelle. His arms felt so good to her. She reached around him and embraced him. After a moment, she felt uneasy and pulled away.

"You okay?" he asked, lifting her chin with his index finger and looking into her eyes.

"Yeah. Just a little tired, too, I guess," Michelle replied with a smile.

"Well, call me if you need me," he said with a wink.

"Thanks, Trevor."

"My pleasure, little butterfly," he said softly.

Michelle stretched out her arms like wings, gently breaking away and "flew" toward the door to her room.

"See you in the morning!" she promised as she slipped inside.

"Looking forward to it." Trevor winked again.

Michelle closed the door behind her, leaned back against it, and smiled a contented smile. She felt great. Trevor was really helping her. "Just what the doctor ordered!" she whispered to herself as she walked over toward the bed.

Lost in her daydreams, Michelle did not notice the message light blinking on the phone. She enjoyed a nice hot shower and then crawled into bed, drifting off to sleep almost immediately.

Sheila was beside herself with worry. Why didn't Michelle return her calls? She needed to talk to her and figure out what to do. Should she go after John? Try to find him somehow? Or should she leave him alone like he was wanting? A nagging fear surrounded her. Something was very wrong, and she was certain John was in some kind of danger.

Finally, she sat down in utter exhaustion and picked up the telephone. She felt terrible calling so late, but she didn't know what else to do. After four rings a familiar voice answered.

"Dad?" Sheila responded, "I need to talk to you."

CHAPTER FIFTEEN

Sheila's mom, Joan, sat up in bed and listened while her husband tried to calm their daughter. It was clear from what she could hear that John had disappeared. She thought about her daughter, Sheila, a woman with grown children of her own, and couldn't help but picture a little girl in pigtails perched on her daddy's lap. Where had the years gone? And how had her precious baby girl strayed so far from the faith that sustained them?

Maybe this crisis was part of God's plan. Perhaps He was allowing this trial in Sheila's life to draw her back into His arms.

"Dad sure sounds strong, Sheila thought, her anxiety ebbing as she listened to his calming voice.

He spoke reassuringly to her, and then drew her gently into a prayer. As he prayed for John's safety, she felt a warm sense of peace replace the fear gripping her. She closed her eyes, and she could almost feel her father's protective embrace as she listened to his steady, clear voice committing her husband into God's hands.

How she wished that she could find that solid faith she once knew as a small child. She wanted to turn away from all the complexities of life and crawl back into that little girl's body and life.

It seemed as if life was suffocating her with worry. Between her husband's lawsuit, his subsequent disappearance, and concerns about Michelle and Tim, she spent most of her waking moments in anxiety. This brief time of prayer with her father was like a refreshing oasis in the desert of darkness.

"Thanks, Dad," she said softly, as his prayer ended. "I knew I could count on you."

"Do you want to come home for a few days, sweetheart?" her father asked.

"I don't know what I'm going to do yet. Let me think about it." She hesitated. "Maybe that would be the best thing for me now. I'll call you back, OK?"

"OK, honey," he replied. "Love you, sweetheart."

"You too, Dad."

Phil hung up the phone and wrapped his arms around Joan. They rocked each other and prayed together for their sweet daughter and her troubled husband.

John looked around the simply furnished accommodations at the Redwood Lodge and sighed. The lacquered log structure gave his room a rustic atmosphere. A turquoise vinyl armchair was stationed in the corner, a double bed with a tapestry bedspread that dated back to the seventies dominated the small quarters, and a rickety round table with two chairs looked out the one small window. Facing the bed was a 19-inch television bearing the only sign of high-tech living—a remote control.

Here he was in the middle of nowhere at a cheap motel, running from the world. John placed his suitcase on the floor, sat down on the foot of the bed, and dropped his head into his hands.

"How did I get myself into this mess?" he wondered sadly. "And how do I get out?"

Rubbing his scalp to attempt to soothe his throbbing head, he slowly sat up and scooted back to rest against the pillows at the headboard. Glancing at the phone he considered calling Sheila. Maybe just talking to her would help.

"No, I can't drag her into this anymore," he told himself.

Instead of picking up the phone, John reached for the television remote control. He flipped it on and began to surf the channels. Flitting from one talk show to another, he finally let fatigue take over and drifted off to sleep, the television droning on in the background of his mind.

Michelle woke up in her hotel room feeling rested and refreshed. The sunlight streamed in through the window as she parted the heavy drapes. "What a perfect day!" she exclaimed. Stretching and smiling, her reverie was broken by a knock at the door.

"Are you up, Michelle?" Trevor's familiar voice called from the hallway.

She opened the door a crack and peered out. "Hey, you!" she giggled. "I just got up."

"You sure look beautiful when you get up!" he said with a smile.

"Funny, Trevor. Come back in about twenty minutes," she told him firmly.

"I don't want to come back. Just let me in. I promise I'll behave myself," Trevor teased.

"I'm not even dressed yet, Trevor."

"I don't mind," he said with a chuckle. "Seriously, Michelle, I won't look. Just let me in. It's lonely out here."

Michelle groaned. "OK, just a second." She closed the door, threw on her robe, and finger combed her hair.

"Welcome to my humble abode," she teased as she opened the door.

"My little butterfly, all dressed in yellow," Trevor crooned gesturing to her yellow terry cloth robe.

Michelle picked up a pillow off the bed and nailed him with it. In a moment the room was a flurry of pillows as they exchanged fire. Trevor finally tackled her, landing both of them on the bed. The whole escapade reminded her so much of the pillow fights she and Steve had, that she just naturally responded as if it were her husband. She yielded freely to his embrace and a moment later was kissing Trevor.

"*STOP, MICHELLE!*" a voice in her head exploded. She pulled away a tiny bit, but her body was crying for more. She let herself go for another moment. Then simultaneously she and Trevor pulled away from each other.

"I'm sorry, Michelle. I don't know what got into me."

"No, it was my fault. I shouldn't have let you in my room in the first place," she replied.

They sat side by side on the edge of the bed. "What's happening here?" she finally asked.

"I don't know, Michelle. But from the moment I met you at class, I've felt this connection to you. I can't explain it, but some power is drawing us together."

"I know what you mean," she said. "I've felt it, too. But, Trevor, I'm married. I can't do this."

"Tell you what. Let's not worry about it for now. Let's just enjoy the rest of the conference, and let whatever this is go away on its own," he suggested, seeming to ignore her comment about being married.

"Okay," she agreed reluctantly.

He patted her hand and stood up. "I'll go downstairs to the lobby and get us some coffee while you get dressed."

After he walked out the door, a barrage of emotions hit Michelle. Guilt was first to attack, followed by fear that Steve might find out about her encounter with Trevor. But those were not the only feelings she was experiencing.

Much as she loved Steve, she could not deny her growing attraction for Trevor. He was so good for her in so many ways. Already she had learned so much more about herself and her nightmares. He was the only one who seemed to really understand her from the inside out.

Just then the hotel phone rang. As she picked it up, she noticed the blinking message light.

"Hello?" she said.

"Hi, babe!" Steve replied affectionately.

Michelle was thankful that he could not see her cheeks turn crimson. "Hi back!" she said in a voice as light as she could muster.

"How's everything?" he asked innocently.

"Fine," she said. "How are things at home? Is Max okay?"

"Everything's fine here, Michelle, but I'm really worried about your parents. Did your mom get a hold of you yet?"

"No, why? What's up?" Michelle asked, feeling her body tense. She dug through her purse on the nightstand and pulled out her cell phone. Flipping it open, she saw that she had a voicemail. Then she remembered she'd silenced the ringer for one of the sessions and had forgotten to turn it back up.

Steve's voice interrupted her thoughts, "I think you'd better call her, honey. Your dad just took off. Left some kind of note for her saying that he had to get away from everything and think. Your mom is really upset and worried."

"Oh no," Michelle started twisting her hair. "Is she at home?"

"As far as I know. Oh, and Michelle, you got a letter from your dad in the mail yesterday. Do you have any idea what that's about?"

"A letter? That's strange. Dad never sends me letters. What does it say, Steve?"

"I don't know. I haven't opened it. Do you want me to read it to you?" he asked.

"Yeah, I think you'd better."

She could hear him rustling papers, and then he began to read it to her. She listened silently, a strand of her hair wrapped so firmly around her finger that it almost cut off the circulation.

"Are you still there?" he asked when he finished and she was still silently searching her mind for an explanation.

"Yeah. I'm thinking. Something is really wrong, Steve. This is not like my father."

"I know. That's just what your mom said about his leaving."

"I'll call her right now. Thanks for calling me. Let me know if you hear any more."

"I will. Try not to worry too much, Michelle. Your dad's got a good head on his shoulders."

"I know. Thanks. I'll call from the airport before our plane takes off," she said, remembering her earlier promise to let him know when she left.

"Good. I'm eager to see you and hear all about your conference," Steve said lovingly. "Miss you, babe."

"Me, too," she replied, realizing with gratitude that she really meant it. Whatever this thing was with Trevor, she really did love Steve.

"How did she sound?" Ben asked.

"Worried," Steve replied.

Ben nodded and bowed his head in another silent prayer. He rested his hand on his shaking leg, a nervous habit he'd started in childhood. He wished he had the right words for Steve. Sometimes he felt so inept. Maybe he wasn't really cut out to be a pastor after all. Sure he had a lot of knowledge about the Bible. But wasn't a pastor supposed to know what to do or say in a situation like this?

Steve stirred his coffee absentmindedly as he stared into space. "John's always been such a pillar of strength. I'd hate to see him crack over something like this."

"Where does your father-in-law stand with God?" Ben asked.

"Where do any of us stand with God?" Steve shrugged his shoulders as he looked up from his coffee.

Ben prayed silently, *Help me know how to answer that one, Lord.* He paused for a moment and replied, "Well, that's a loaded question. If you've invited Jesus to be the Lord of your life, then you can know for certain you are a member of His family." Ben could see the concern on Steve's face.

"If that's what you're talking about, then I'd say that John is standing outside of what you call the family of God. He's always referred to religion as a crutch for weak people. He raised Michelle and Tim to believe in themselves and to believe that they could do anything they set their minds to." Steve paused. "But if you're talking about being a decent human being and trying to live by the Golden Rule, I'd say John Ackerman is a good role model for the rest of us."

"Too bad you can't earn your way into heaven," Ben said somberly as he shook his head. *Was that too harsh? Please help me, God.*

"What do you mean?" Steve asked.

"Let me see if I can explain it," Ben replied. He stretched his legs and stood up. "Mind if I grab a refill for my coffee first?"

"Help yourself," Steve stood up, grabbing his coffee cup and following Ben over to the kitchen counter.

After they had gotten more coffee, they walked into the family room. Ben spent the next hour explaining to Steve about the gospel. He showed him scriptures that explained the imperfection of man and the sacrifice Jesus made on the cross to reconcile humanity to God. He talked a lot about grace and God's love.

"I see what you're saying, Ben. It's not like I don't believe in God or anything like that. It's just that I'm not sure about this 'born again' stuff," Steve explained.

"I know what you mean. That was hard for me, too. But check this out, Steve." Ben showed him the passage in the book of John where Jesus said, "I tell you the truth, no one can see the kingdom of God unless he is born again."

"So are you basically saying that you really believe that Jesus and Christianity are the only way to God? That seems so narrow-minded to me."

"*I'm* not saying that, Steve. *Jesus* himself is the one who said that. Listen to this passage in chapter fourteen verse six: *'I am the way, the truth, and the life. No one comes to the Father except through Me.'* That was Jesus, Steve. *He* said it." Ben paused for a minute and studied Steve's face. "Maybe this is the time for you to decide if you believe it." Ben sat back in the couch and watched for his reaction.

Steve turned and looked earnestly at him. "I want to make sure I understand all of this, Ben. I can see that you really believe in what you're saying. Keep going. Tell me more."

Ben smiled with relief and anticipation. "Instead of reading you more scriptures, let me tell you about what God has done for me in my life."

Steve nodded. "Sounds good to me."

"You remember how I was in high school. I thought I was God's gift to planet Earth, and I treated the girls like they were my toys." He cringed and shook his head as he looked away.

"I remember. They didn't seem to mind at the time," Steve added.

"Hmmm. Well, the part you didn't see was the beer bottle I kept hidden in the glove box of my car. I'd start sipping from that bottle before first period even began."

Now it was Steve's turn to shake his head. "So that's where you got your confidence?"

"That's where I got my courage. The courage to face another day. Yeah, I was the big man on the outside, but a coward on the inside."

"So what happened? How did you get into the Bible?"

"About a year after I graduated, I realized I had a serious drinking problem. I'd shake like a leaf if I wasn't drinking. But I was still convinced that I had the power to do anything. So I made up my mind to quit."

"Just like that? Cold turkey?"

"Well, yeah, except I gave myself one last fling. I decided to go out and party with some friends I'd met at the beach." He paused and winced as the memories flooded back.

"So what happened?"

"When I came to in the morning, I was in bed with some girl. I didn't even know her name. She was crying. When I asked her what was wrong, she just kept shaking her head and hugging herself, kind of rocking back and forth."

He stood up and started to pace the floor. "I kept asking, 'Did I hurt you?' but she just ignored me. Finally, I got up and left. I still don't know what happened that night. I can't remember anything after my buddies and I were drinking on the pier."

Ben turned and looked at Steve. "God used that night to get my attention. I looked in the mirror and saw what a jerk I had become. As much as I'd like to have blamed it on the booze, I knew it was more than just my drinking. I'd lost all sight of right and wrong. All I cared about was having a good time."

Steve listened intently. He seemed surprised that Ben was being so candid about such painful memories.

"That afternoon my cousin called. He asked me if I wanted to go to a concert with him at his church. I don't know why, but I said yes. The music was great—awesome bands. But it was weird because they were all Christians. Their music sounded a lot like the music I listened to on the radio, but their message was totally different.

"It got my attention, and afterward I went up and talked to a couple of them. Before I knew it, I was telling them what a mess my life was.

"Those guys took the time to spend hours with me that night. We went to a coffee shop. They told me a lot of the stuff I've been telling you tonight. It was my time, Steve. Know what I mean?"

Steve nodded. "So you became a Christian that night?"

"Yep. And I haven't regretted it for a minute since. As soon as I laid down my old life and turned my new life over to God, I felt a huge weight lift off of me. I knew I had a fresh start. And get this, Steve. I haven't had one drink since then. Don't even want the stuff."

"That's great! You know, I could tell when I first saw you up here that you had changed."

Ben smiled at his comment.

"I mean it. You're not the same guy you were in high school. Maybe it's God, like you say."

"It is, Steve. So what do you think? I know you're not coming from the same place I was, but we all could use a helping hand and the knowledge that God is on our side."

"Yeah, I guess you're right. So what do I have to do?" Steve rubbed his hands together as if he felt nervous.

"Well, let's pray and seal the deal." Ben clapped Steve on the back.

"Okay. I'm game."

Ben placed his hand on Steve's shoulder and both men bowed their heads as Ben led Steve in a prayer asking Jesus to become the Lord of his life.

As Ben stretched out in bed that night, he thanked God for bringing him to Sandy Cove. Flashing back to his youth and the cocky arrogance that dominated his life at that time, he was amazed the Lord could use him to impact one of his old classmate's lives so profoundly in such a short time.

Everything Ben was doing in this venture to Oregon relied on his faith in God. He didn't know where the money would come from to start a new church, but he knew God had called him to go. As he drifted off to sleep, he thought about his bride back home, who believed in him and encouraged him to step out in faith. And he thought about his God, who had already blessed him with the time he had spent with Steve. Maybe he really *was* supposed to become a pastor!

Sheila's hand was resting on the phone receiver, her mind lost in a fog of concern. John was not answering his cell phone even after she left repeated messages. And why wasn't Michelle calling her back?

Who else could she call? Someone must know something about where John might have gone. Groping for ideas, she gazed across the dimly lit study and sighed. It seemed a bit eerie to be sitting at her husband's huge desk, surrounded by his books and papers. No one used this room but John. It was his private sanctuary and she felt almost as if she were trespassing. She could picture him sitting at this desk, his pipe cradled in his hand as he hunched over his work. Even Sheila did not dare to interrupt him at times like that.

A moment later a ring of the phone jolted her back to the present. Hoping that John would be on the other end, Sheila quickly picked up the receiver.

"Hello?" she said tentatively.

CHAPTER SIXTEEN

"Mom? Is that you?" Michelle asked.

"Yes, Mimi. It's me." Sheila's voice caught in her throat as tears welled up in her eyes. "Thank God. I need to talk to you."

"I know about Dad. Steve told me," her daughter began. "Have you heard anything at all from him?"

"No. I was hoping this might be him calling," she replied. "Where do you think he could be, Michelle?"

"I don't know, Mom. This just isn't like him. Have you called anyone from work?"

"No. He doesn't want me to do that. You know. Because of the lawsuit. He told me to tell them he's out of town on urgent family business if they call here," she said, beginning to sob softly.

"Oh, Mom," Michelle said. "Do you want me to come home?" Sheila could hear the concern in her voice.

"I don't know what I want yet, Mimi. Your grandfather suggested I go to their house for a few days."

"That sounds like a good idea. I think it would be good for you to be with them. Grandma and Grandpa always seem to know what to do."

"You're right, dear. Your grandparents are very wise," she agreed, sniffling softly as she thought about her parents. "But what if your father tries to reach me? Maybe I should just stay here."

"Do this, Mom. Leave a message on your answering machine that says you are visiting your parents. Then if he does call home, he'll know to call you there."

"Yeah, I guess I could do that," she replied. "Do you think he'll be okay?"

"He'll be okay," Michelle said, but her voice didn't sound convincing. "Dad is strong. He can take care of himself. I'm sure he'll be calling you pretty soon."

Her well-meaning words of reassurance sounded hollow to Sheila. "I hope you're right. I've never seen him like this—so distraught and frantic."

"Maybe Tim could go out and look for him," Michelle suggested.

"He's already begun driving around town asking people we know whether they've seen him."

"That's good. I'm sure he can't be too far away. Dad's not just going to disappear off the face of the earth. He's too responsible for that."

"So you think I should go to your grandparents' house?"

"I think you should go, Mom. Tim can reach you at any hour of the day or night, and Dad will call your cell phone if he calls home and gets your answering machine."

"Okay, Mimi. Are you home now?"

"No, but I'll be back soon."

"Call my cell phone when you get back."

"I will, Mom. And try not to worry, okay? We'll find Dad somehow, and get this mess straightened out."

After she hung up the phone, Michelle sunk back against the bed pillows. She tried to imagine her brother driving around town asking about their dad. What would people think? And would Tim have any luck tracking him down? This just wasn't like the big, strong, self-sufficient dad who raised them. In spite of her attempts to reassure her mom, Michelle was deeply troubled in her mind and spirit.

The flight home was quiet. Sitting next to Trevor, Michelle thought about her mom and dad.

"You okay?" Trevor asked, noticing her pensive expression.

"Yeah, just a little worried about my parents."

"Anything I can help with?" he asked.

"No. It's kind of complicated," she answered, looking away so he wouldn't notice the tears in her eyes. This was one problem that Steve would definitely understand better. She was eager to get home and discuss it with him. He always had great ideas for resolving a crisis or solving a mystery. He'd know what to do.

Trevor, himself, was also running intermittently through her mind. How could she have let things get this close? Admittedly, she felt much more comfortable with him now.

There was such ease to their friendship while they were together at the conference. A level of intimacy had broken through the nervous energy that once permeated their contacts. But getting off the plane and greeting Steve, with Trevor on her heels, was something that she was not looking forward to experiencing.

Trevor didn't push the conversation about Michelle's parents. He was deep in thoughts of his own. He could see her out of the corner of his eye. Her beauty was so striking, even when she was wrestling with worries.

He thought back to their encounter over the pillow fight. There was definitely something positive developing between the two of them. He hadn't experienced these feelings since the early years of his relationship with Trisha. The magnetism was undeniable. Even Michelle had to admit there was something special between them.

Clearly their relationship could evolve from here. It was in the stars for both of them. He could feel it, but he knew this was no time to push her. She had too much on her mind already. His own inner wisdom told him to leave her alone with her thoughts for the time being.

As the plane was about to land, he reached over, took her hand and said, "When we get off the plane, you go first by yourself. I'll hang back here. It might be awkward greeting Steve with me there."

She squeezed his hand. "Thanks, Trevor. That would be much easier." Leaning her head back against, she let out a deep sigh.

"How can I explain all that I've learned to Michelle?" Steve asked Ben as he dropped him off at his hotel. "I really want her to know and understand this stuff."

"That's only natural, Steve," Ben assured him. "But you've got to remember that Michelle is in a different place than you are, spiritually speaking. She's intrigued by the New Age approach to spirituality. You can't just jump in and spin her around to Christianity. What you need to do is to hold on tight to what you've got. Sink your roots deep into the Word of God. We'll keep studying together. And pray for Michelle. Ask God to show you any open doors to share with her, but don't try to bombard her immediately and start setting out to convert her. Only God can do that. The Holy Spirit must draw her to Him. Do you understand what I mean?"

"Yeah, I guess I do. I remember several times when people tried to push me in the past. It didn't work," Steve agreed.

They both prayed for Michelle and that God would woo her into an intimate relationship with Him. Then Ben gave Steve a handshake and a hug and waved good-bye as he walked into the lobby of the hotel.

Steve drove to a florist, picked up a dozen red roses for Michelle, and then went to meet her at the airport.

Michelle realized how tired she was as she walked through the airport. The carry-on bag she was pulling behind her felt heavier than ever, and a bag of conference material was slung over her shoulder. Scanning the area, she saw Steve walking toward her holding a bouquet of roses. He hurried in her direction with a smile.

"Welcome home," he said, extending the roses.

"Thanks!" She grinned, and they embraced. From the corner of her eye she caught sight of Trevor. He smiled and nodded his head, then walked off without saying a word.

"It's so good to have you back, babe," Steve said.

"It's good to be back," she replied. She looked up at her husband. His familiar smile and the warmth of his body against hers gave her a feeling of safety. Everything would be okay. Her dad would come home soon, and she'd explain to Trevor the limits on their relationship.

They spent most of the ride home talking about Michelle's parents. Steve seemed really concerned, too. He asked her if she thought he should hire one of the private detectives Roger sometimes used on their cases to help find her father. But she was reluctant to do anything that drastic. She wanted to give her dad some time alone to think. Hopefully he would contact them soon.

Steve glanced over at Michelle as they approached Sandy Cove. He wanted to tell her all about his weekend and about his new commitment to God. But he knew he needed to wait.

Michelle talked vaguely about the classes and seminars she had attended. Even though she didn't say much, it was obvious from the enthusiasm in her voice that she was as thrilled about her new spiritual discoveries as he was about his. Steve listened patiently, trying to understand this world of mysticism and occult that was so fascinating to his bride.

They decided to pick up Chinese food for dinner. When they arrived home, Steve proudly showed her how he had already straightened up the house and set the coffee table in the family room for their dinner. While she went upstairs to change, he started a fire in the fireplace.

As soon as she came back down, she told him she wanted to give her mom a quick call before they ate. Sitting on the couch, she picked up the phone and dialed. She seemed relieved to hear her mom's voice. Steve heard her say, "You sound a lot better, Mom."

Then there was a pause.

"Yeah. I've noticed that with Steve sometimes," Michelle said.

Steve wondered what she was talking about.

"I'm sure you're right. Well, tell Grandma and Grandpa I said hi."

Another pause.

"Love you, too, Mom. Bye."

Steve glanced over at her. She looked more relaxed. "So, what did your mom say?"

"She's doing better now that she's at my grandparents' house."

"What was the bit about noticing something with me?"

Michelle looked confused for a moment and then replied, "Oh. Mom was saying that Grandpa told her men sometimes need to get away from everything and think things out by themselves. I just said that I'd noticed the same thing about you."

"Yeah, I guess I do that sometimes. So does your grandfather think your dad will be okay?"

"He seems to. You know how Grandpa is. Always trusting that God will take care of everything."

"You don't sound so sure about that yourself," Steve said. He could feel his heart speeding up at the mention of God, and he wondered how far he should take the topic.

"Well, it really doesn't matter what I think right now. I'm just glad Mom is feeling better." She got up and walked into the kitchen to serve up the takeout food.

Steve cleared off the coffee table and lit the pillar candle. Then he started some soft music.

Walking back into the family room, Michelle was impressed and touched to see Steve's efforts at atmosphere. She remembered how attractive that aspect of his personality was when they were dating. When he wanted to, he knew how to romance a woman.

Pushing all remnants of Trevor out of her mind, she settled on the couch beside him. She noticed him silently pause for a moment with his head down as if in thought, and then he looked up, kissed her softly, and said, "Let's eat!"

After dinner, they snuggled in each other's arms and reminisced about their dating days. She laughed as he reminded her of their second date. They had eaten dinner at an elegant restaurant overlooking the ocean in Malibu, and when Steve had reached for his wallet to pay the bill, he'd realized he'd forgotten it. He had to call his dad to bring it.

"You looked like you'd seen a ghost!" she said. "I couldn't figure out where you were going in such a hurry."

"Well, how was I supposed to tell you that I had to go call my dad to bring money to pay for our dinner?" he asked with a chuckle.

"We've had a lot of good times, haven't we Steve?" Michelle said.

"We sure have. And they're not over yet." He smiled as he draped his arm over her shoulder.

She looked into his eyes, reaching out and touching his check with her hand. He leaned toward her and his lips met hers tenderly. His kiss felt like home.

Trevor was alone in his apartment. He sat with a glass of wine, staring into the dancing flames in the fireplace, and thinking about Michelle. There was something special about her—innocence somehow mixed with grace and sophistication. She seemed so fragile in his arms, and yet there was a passion inside that he had sensed in their kiss.

She loved the things he loved—the mysteries of the cosmos, the lure of the occult, and the drive to evolve. He smiled as he thought about her childlike awe of his knowledge and understanding of mystical matters. He wanted to take her to higher and higher levels—to teach her things that had taken him years to learn.

Trevor took another sip of wine and sighed. "I will know that woman in every way," he promised himself. "Eventually Michelle will realize that we are meant to be together."

CHAPTER SEVENTEEN

Michelle could feel herself moving in perfect harmony with her partner. They danced to a melody that only the two of them could hear. Perched on a cliff in a clearing surrounded by beautiful wildflowers, they were alone together with nothing but the sound of the crashing surf far below and the music in their minds.

An incredible feeling of peace and joy caressed her soul. She moved with grace and perfect rhythm. Clearly, they were made for each other. Everything felt so right. She looked up into Trevor's seductive eyes, and she felt herself stir as his hand on her lower back drew her closer to him. The smell of the salt air mingled with the aroma of his scent.

They began twirling and swaying with more passion and fervor, moving closer and closer to the edge of the cliff. Michelle knew there was danger, but she refused to let the moment slip from her hands. As they reached the drop-off point, Trevor gently pressed his lips to hers. She leaned into his kiss, and they started to fall through space.

The ringing of the phone awakened her with a start. She sat up feeling lost and confused. Where was she? Her mind groped for its bearings. Was she at home with her parents? Or in a hotel with Trevor? Reaching for the phone, she saw a framed photo of Steve and Max. Reality rushed at her.

"Hello?" she said in an uneasy voice.

"Good morning!" a familiar, masculine tone replied.

"Trevor?" she asked, sitting up and rubbing her eyes.

"One and the same!" he said cheerfully. "Are you awake?"

"Well I am now," she murmured, rubbing her eyes and brushing her hair off of her face.

"Oh, sorry. I didn't mean to wake you."

"It's okay. I need to get up anyway," she admitted as she struggled to push her dream aside and focus on reality.

"Okay, then I won't feel too bad. Hey, I bought you a present," he announced.

"What are you talking about?"

"A present. As in a gift. You've heard of them before, I'm sure," he teased.

Michelle was a little taken aback. "Why would you get me a present?"

"Let's just say it's my way of thanking you for the great companionship at the conference."

"I don't know about you giving me presents, Trevor," she said guardedly.

"Since when does the receiver of the gift make that decision?" he quipped in reply.

"You're making me crazy, Trevor." *What is it about this guy?*

"Good. Then we can be crazy together," he laughed. "I'll meet you at the Coffee Stop at ten. Bye!"

Before she could reply, the phone connection was cut off. She shook her head and crawled out of bed, almost stepping on Max in the process. "Sorry, pal! I'm not quite with it yet!"

Michelle was becoming accustomed to Steve leaving for work before she woke up in the morning, but she usually had some awareness that he was gone. This morning she was totally oblivious to everything.

It took her a moment to realize she was not a young lady living at home with her parents and being courted by another man. Her mind was reeling with such a conglomeration of thoughts and feelings. Part of her was aware of the danger of this friendship with Trevor, but another part was flattered by all the attention and intrigued by his charm.

"I'm totally in control of myself," she said aloud as she got dressed. "I won't do anything stupid."

Trevor stared absentmindedly at the phone while he pictured Michelle in her yellow bathrobe. In his imagination, he could feel her silky, black hair and see her bright, sparkling eyes. The olive complexion of her neck, with its flawless finish, would have the fragrance of jasmine. Undressing her with his thoughts, he pictured the naked curves of a goddess. He smiled, pleased with himself for thinking of the little symbolic gift he had purchased. It would bring them closer than ever.

Pressing the phone to his ear, John listened as to it rang at the other end. He just wanted to hear Sheila's voice for a minute and wasn't even sure if he would say anything back or not. After four rings, the answering machine clicked on. Sheila's recording told him that she had gone to her parents' house. No matter. He hung up the phone and stared off into space. There was no way he would call her there. He didn't need Phil or Joan questioning him.

His head was throbbing. He hadn't eaten in forty-eight hours. A tight knot kept twisting in his gut, robbing him of any appetite. Standing, he walked across the room, picked up a manila envelope, and left the hotel.

Steve sat at his desk looking at the brochure about the cabin at the lake. Although he'd enjoyed his weekend of Bible study with Ben, he was yearning for some time alone with Michelle. She seemed so preoccupied with her father's situation and all of her New Age studies. He knew there was nothing either of them could do at this point to bring John home any sooner, and Sheila seemed to be okay at her parents' house for a while.

Two days of enjoying nature and each other's company would be the perfect opportunity to catch up on their relationship and possibly open the door to some important issues such as his new faith. He was eager to share *something* about it with Michelle. Although he wasn't sure what to say, he needed to somehow begin to tell her about this wonderful new facet of his life.

"You look like a man deep in thought," his partner, Roger, said with a smile.

"Just thinking about my wife," he replied.

"Now there's something worth thinking about. I'll bet you missed her last weekend."

"That would be a smart bet. Are you a gambler?"

"No. But if I were, I'd be gambling on you asking for the day off on Friday to get a head start on your little getaway."

"Right again!" Steve feigned astonishment.

"Go ahead and take it, pal. You've been working too hard this past month, and with that new land merger case starting up next week, you might be burning the midnight oil around here again soon."

Steve thanked Roger for understanding and promised he'd be ready to tackle the new case bright and early Monday morning.

He started to call Michelle but then changed his mind. "I'll tell her tonight," he thought with a smile.

"It's not really a big deal," Trevor said as he handed the gift box to her.

Michelle looked into his eyes and could see a confidence that was very attractive. Why did he always seem so self-assured? She carefully unwrapped the box, which she could see was obviously wrapped by male hands, and lifted the cotton inside to reveal a key chain with a copper enameled butterfly on it. Patterns of sapphire blue, sun-kissed yellow, and glittering crimson were delicately detailed on the outstretched wings.

"It's beautiful!" Michelle said.

"Just like you, Miss Butterfly!" Trevor smiled.

In an instant, her mind recalled the moment of freedom and release when he had guided her out of the cocoon of her past. She surprised herself when a tear slipped down her cheek.

"Now what is that for?" he asked as he wiped the tear away with his thumb.

"I don't know, Trevor. It's just that I . . . well. . . I really appreciate all that you've done for me."

"Michelle, believe me, I've wanted to do all of it. Watching you grow like this has inspired and encouraged me as much as it's helped you. And I thought this little butterfly would be a good reminder to you to always keep stretching and learning and never let the past hold you back."

"Thanks, Trevor. You've been good for me," she acknowledged.

"We're good for each other. Your enthusiasm and freshness about all that you're learning, encourages me to keep growing too," he said reassuringly. He reached over and flipped her hair away from her face. "Besides, I like you."

"I like you too, Mr. Wind!" Michelle said with a smile, while she fought the voice inside that warned her to back away.

Steve pushed his paperwork aside and left the office to go pick up some lunch. Before returning to work, he decided to swing by the house and pick up his Bible.

Michelle's car was parked in the garage, and he could hear the washing machine running in the adjacent laundry room. When he got to the door, he saw that her keys were still in the lock, and an unusual butterfly decoration was hanging from the key ring beside the familiar wooden carving of her name.

"Michelle! You left your keys in the door!" Steve called to her as he came into the kitchen.

"Hi, Steve! What are you doing home?" she asked with a surprised expression on her face.

"I just came by to pick up something. Where did you go this morning?

She looked a bit flustered and said, "I was just out for coffee at the Coffee Stop."

"What's this butterfly thing? Is that new?" he asked as he handed her the keys that he had retrieved from the lock.

Michelle blushed. "It's just a little something my teacher gave me," she stammered, beginning to twist her hair.

"What teacher?" He could tell she was really nervous.

"You know, the teacher of the class I take at the bookstore."

"Since when do teachers give gifts to students? I thought it was supposed to be the other way around," he said, feeling confused.

"I don't know, Steve. I guess it just reminded him of something about me," she replied defensively. "It's not a big deal."

"Okay, if you say so. But I don't really like another guy giving my wife gifts," he said.

Michelle just looked at him, picked up the laundry basket, and headed up the stairs.

He shrugged his shoulders, grabbed his Bible off the end table in the living room and a banana from the fruit bowl for his lunch, and then headed back to work without saying good-bye. This was obviously not the time to talk to Michelle about their weekend getaway.

It was late in the day. Sheila walked out to the front porch of her parents' home. The aging wood beneath her feet creaked with a familiar sound. Something about this place comforted her. Maybe it was the view of wide-open spaces so foreign to her life in Southern California.

She leaned against the railing and looked out over the expansive front lawn, breathing in the sweet fragrances of gardenias planted at the base of the steps leading from the concrete walkway to the porch. The deep blue tones of the sky were beginning to fade as dusk approached.

She could remember her childhood years and how she loved this porch. Flashbacks of sitting on the steps telling secrets with her best friend, swinging on the porch swing with her dog, Muffin, and those special times of cuddling on her father's lap in the big wicker rocker, all spoke peace and safety into her soul.

How she wished she could retreat to those simpler times. But at least she had a chance to relax here for a few days while she decided what to do about John.

Phil strolled up the walkway from the mailbox. Seeing his daughter on the porch touched his heart. She looked so drawn and fragile. He wanted to somehow take the burden of worry off of her shoulders, but he knew deep inside that only God could do that.

"How about some tea, honey?" he asked with a gentle smile. "We can sit here and sip while we watch the sun go down."

"That sounds good, Dad. I'll go fix it," Sheila replied.

"You just sit down here on the swing and let your old pop pamper you for a change," Phil insisted.

"Okay, if you insist," she said, sinking down into the soft cushion on the swing.

As she rocked, Sheila could hear her father puttering around in the kitchen. He was making the tea by himself since Joan was at the library serving her volunteer time reading to the local children.

She was glad for this little window of time alone with her father. He had always been such a beacon of wisdom for her, and she really needed his input now. But that was not the only reason. There was something about their relationship that eased her anxieties. He had a calmness, an inner peace that spilled over onto her.

A few minutes later, he nudged the screen door open with his foot and carefully carried the tray with tea and cookies on the little wicker table beside her. Then he handed Sheila her cup. "Two sugars, right?" he said with a wink.

"Two sugars," she replied, smiling in return.

Later that night, John walked the streets of another town, his shoulders sagging as if burdened by a heavy weight. Cradled in his dangling left hand was the large legal size envelope containing paperwork on his lawsuit. Why was he carrying this thing around? Logic and purpose evaded him. He had no particular destination and no awareness of how long or how far he had wandered. His mind was dead tired, and he felt numb all over.

As if observing himself from afar, he continued to move mechanically through town without any sense of connection to his environment or his own body. Looking down at the sidewalk when anyone passed, he avoided even the most trivial encounter with another human being. One word kept repeating itself in his mind. *Escape.* Somehow he must escape.

CHAPTER EIGHTEEN

Eventually the darkening skies and the cool dampness of evening began to settle on John's shoulders. A fragrant aroma of Italian cuisine and the warm sounds of conversation and laughter drew him into a corner restaurant. The red carpet, dark wood tables with barrel chairs, and round candlelit tables gave the place a traditional Mediterranean look.

Noticing that all the tables were occupied, John wandered over to the bar. He absentmindedly placed his envelope on the counter and slid onto a bar stool.

"What can I do for you?" the bartender asked with a friendly voice.

"Sort this mess out," John muttered under his breath as he pushed the envelope off to the side.

"Pardon me?"

"Never mind. Just get me a vodka tonic," he replied with a sigh.

"Coming right up."

Glancing around the dining area, John noticed a woman who appeared to be in her late thirties looking his way. She smiled, and he made a feeble attempt to smile back then turned away.

A moment later she was beside him at the bar asking the bartender for a glass of Perrier. "The food's great here, but the waiters can be a little slow," she said after making eye contact with John. "You look like you're carrying the world on those shoulders," she observed. "My name's Sylvia."

John looked her over more carefully. Curly auburn hair and sparkling green eyes complemented her cameo complexion. "John," he replied and extended his hand. Her handshake was firm and confident.

"What's got you so down, John?" she asked, settling herself on the bar stool next to him and sipping on her Perrier.

"It's a long story."

"Well, I've got all evening," she replied. "Maybe just talking about it will help."

He glanced over at her and saw what appeared to be genuine concern and compassion in her eyes. Part of him wanted to collapse and be comforted while the other part wanted to run.

She reached over and touched the envelope. "This have something to do with your worries?" she asked intuitively.

"You might say that," he replied.

"Mind if I take a look?"

"Go ahead." John could not believe his own words.

She carefully slipped the stack of papers out of the envelope. Her eyebrows rose when she saw they were legal documents. "Looks like you've got yourself in quite a pickle here," she said as she perused the paperwork.

"You familiar with court documents?" he asked tentatively.

"You might say that. I'm a paralegal. My brother's an attorney. He got me interested in law, and now he works me to the bone at his office."

"I wonder what your brother would have to say about this mess," John said, almost as if he was talking to himself.

"It's hard to say. Maybe I could set you up with an appointment," she suggested, blushing as her stomach growled. "Sorry about that. I haven't eaten anything all day. Are you going to have dinner?"

"I hadn't really thought about it, but now that you mention it, I am feeling a bit hungry."

"Tell you what. Let's order some food. I'll look through this more while we eat. Maybe I can get you in to talk to Jeff tomorrow."

John looked her in the eye. Was this some kind of pass? She looked back with a sisterly smile, and as if reading his mind said, "Look, John Whoever-You-Are, all I'm talking about here is a friendly dinner. I can see that wedding ring."

He looked down at his left hand and twisted the gold band. Glancing over to hers, he noticed that she did not wear any rings.

"Widowed," she said, and then added, "So what do you say? The manicotti here is out of this world."

"You know, I think I'll take you up on that. I haven't eaten for two days. Maybe a good meal will help me think more clearly," he agreed.

She patted his arm, slipped off the bar stool, and gestured for him to follow her back to her table.

Phil studied his daughter's face as she stared out toward the horizon. The sunset bathed the sky in hues of purple and pink. Sheila looked mesmerized and deep in thought.

"Penny for your thoughts," he said softly.

She turned and looked him in the eye. "Oh, Dad. Remember when it used to be that simple? I had a jelly jar full of pennies from you asking me that after school every day!"

He smiled and nodded. "I always looked forward to those moments in the rocker."

"Me, too. No matter how bad my day might have gone, I could always look forward to a penny and a stick of gum!"

"I wish I could make everything okay for you now, honey. I know you're worried about John. Your mother and I have been praying for him continuously."

"I know you have. Thanks, Dad, but it's going to take more than prayer to fix this mess."

His heart broke as he looked at his daughter. She didn't understand God's power and she was unable to find his peace. If only there was some way to guarantee a transfer of faith from parent to child, but God had not encoded faith into DNA, and all he could do was pray and wait for her heart and mind to reopen. He knew from past conversations that it was no use trying to talk her into returning to her childhood faith.

A few minutes later, Joan's car pulled into the gravel driveway, and Sheila stood up. "Mom's home. I'd better take this tray back to the kitchen and help her get dinner started. Thanks for caring, Dad. Keep praying. Who knows? Maybe it will help."

Sylvia's smile was contagious. A great conversationalist and a down-home friendly countenance made her a pleasure to be with. In a very short time, she was able to put John at ease, which was a rare feat in his current mindset.

In spite of his legal dilemma, he found himself relaxing and smiling as he listened to her tales about the people in this small town. For the first time in over a month, he was actually hungry. It was as if the dark cloud hovering over him had evaporated.

Maybe this gal and her brother are the answer I've been looking for. There must be some reason why he was feeling so much better.

"Hey, Sylvia, I really appreciate you taking the time to do this," he offered as she studied his paperwork over her salad.

"No problem. I'm glad to help if I can," she replied. "Besides, I hate to eat dinner by myself. I never could get used to it after my husband passed away."

John's eyebrows rose. "I'm sorry," he said awkwardly.

"Don't be sorry. He's in a better place. Cancer consumed most of him long before he actually died. It was a relief to know he wouldn't have to suffer any more," she added. "God's taken good care of me since then." She gazed off into space for a few moments then looked back at him. "So tell me about yourself," she asked.

"Not too much to tell. I've got a wonderful wife named Sheila and two grown children—Michelle, who's married and lives in Oregon, and Tim, my free-spirit son," he said, looking away and shaking his head.

"You live around here?"

"No. We live in Seal Beach, down in Orange County."

"By Long Beach. I've been there. It's a quaint little town. My husband and I stopped there overnight on a trip to San Diego." She looked away and seemed lost in thought for a brief moment but rapidly rallied her attention back to John. "So what brings you up to this neck of the woods?"

"I needed to get away. Be by myself and sort through this mess."

"Well, let's hope that my brother can give you some helpful suggestions, and you can get back to your wife and son. They must be worried."

"Yeah."

The waiter showed up with their main course, and they both began to eat. The dinner was delicious and the company charming. As the conversation steered to less weighty topics, John began to recoup a feeling of normalcy.

Clearly he had needed a break from thinking about or discussing his case, and Sylvia effectively entertained him with other topics, including an annual town festival that she was helping to coordinate the following month. Both of them were surprised to realize that two hours had passed while they ate and chatted.

Busboys were putting the clean tablecloths onto the tables around them for the next day, and the bartender was drying and reshelving the last few glasses, as their server approached the table one last time.

"Anything else you two need tonight?" she asked with a practiced smile.

"No thanks. We're just about to leave," John replied.

As they stood up, Sylvia asked him for his phone number so she could contact him in the morning about meeting with her brother. John explained that he was temporarily staying at the Redwood Lodge. He gave her his cell phone number and thanked her for the enjoyable evening. She smiled, shook his hand, and promised to call him.

After she left, John dropped a couple of twenties on top of the bill, picked up his envelope, and headed back to his motel. The cool night air made him feel refreshed and alive again. He pulled his cell phone out of his pocket and turned the ringer on. *Wouldn't want to miss her call.*

A full stomach and a diversion from his problems had been great medicine. John slept soundly that night and did not awaken until the phone rang at nine-fifteen the next morning.

CHAPTER NINETEEN

"Hello?" John said after flipping his phone open. He struggled to prop himself up in bed and rubbed his eyes with his thumb and index finger.

"John?"

"Hello?"

"This is Sylvia. Are you awake?" she asked.

"I am now," John replied and, glancing at the clock beside the bed, hastily added, "I can't believe I slept this long!"

"Sorry to wake you up, but I wanted to see if you could drop by in about an hour. Jeff has a half hour break between two meetings, and he's agreed to look over your case."

"An hour? Yeah, that would be great. I'll just get cleaned up and catch a cab. What's the address?"

He grabbed a small pad of paper and pen and jotted down the address and suite number. "What's your brother's name again?" he asked.

"Jeff. Jeff Morgan. You'll see his shingle hanging beside the entrance to the office. Suite 105. You can't miss it. See you around ten-fifteen."

"Okay. And Sylvia?"

"Yes?"

"Thanks. I mean it. This might be the break I've been looking for."

"No problem," she said lightly.

John got out of bed and glanced around the room. His clothes were thrown rather carelessly over the back of the chair. He shook them out, hung them on hangers, and hung the hangers on the towel rack in the bathroom, hoping the steam from his shower would help diminish the wrinkles.

Never imagining that he would need more than one dress shirt and slacks, he had only brought along a duffel bag with his shaving kit and some jeans and sweats. But this appointment was important, and he wanted to look his best.

Michelle was deeply engrossed in her latest book, *Evolving to New Heights,* when Steve got home that night. Startled by the sound of the garage door, she realized that time had escaped her and she hadn't begun to prepare dinner. Even Max seemed oblivious to the hour and was still sleeping soundly in the overstuffed easy chair.

"Michelle, you home?" came Steve's voice from the kitchen.

"In here," she called back.

"Hi, babe," Steve said with a kiss as he placed his Bible on the coffee table. "What's for dinner?"

"Well, actually, I just spaced out reading this new book and lost track of time. How about soup and sandwiches? I could whip that up pretty quickly," she replied hopefully.

"I've got a better idea. Let's go out. I've been craving Chinese food all day," Steve suggested.

"You and your Chinese food!" Michelle replied, putting her book on the end table. "I'll feed Max, while you change clothes."

Steve went upstairs. When he came back down he was wearing jeans and a sweatshirt.

"Ready?" Michelle asked.

"Let's go," he replied, grabbing his keys from the coffee table.

Fifteen minutes later they were at the Panda Palace seated in a comfortable corner booth surrounded by bamboo wallpaper, reading their menus by the light of the round, paper lamp that hung overhead.

After ordering their dinners, Steve asked about Michelle's mom's plans. "Do you think she'll stay out at your grandparents' house until she hears from your dad?"

"I don't know. Maybe. Hopefully it won't be too long. Tim's still looking, and Mom's started calling some of the hotels in the area."

Steve nodded. Their conversation lagged as Michelle stared off into space. Steve assumed she was thinking about her parents. Meanwhile, his mind pondered all the new and exciting revelations he had been studying in his Bible. He yearned to talk to Michelle about them.

"I've been reading some great stuff this week," he began tentatively.

"Really? Me, too. You should read this book I'm in the middle of. It explains how people move from one plain of evolutionary thinking to another through a succession of experiences and lives. I never really understood the theory of reincarnation until now. It makes a lot of sense when you study it."

Steve didn't know what to say. He was so new to his faith and to his study of the Bible that he really didn't have an argument to give his wife, but deep inside his spirit was telling him that she was way out in left field.

"That's interesting, honey," was all he could think to say. His mind reeled as he realized how deeply Michelle was plunging into this New Age stuff.

"I wish you'd take the time to study all this," Michelle said earnestly. "Maybe you could take an afternoon off and come to my class with me."

"That's impossible, Michelle. You know I can't just take off early like that with the caseload we've got right now. Besides, maybe your teacher wouldn't like having your husband there," he added and then wished that he hadn't.

"What's that supposed to mean?"

"Nothing. Forget I said it."

A tension filled the air as they sat quietly reading their menus. Steve could feel the rift that was developing in their relationship, and he wondered if Michelle sensed it, too. She seemed convinced she was on the path to ultimate truth, but Steve was certain he had discovered the one and only way.

The remainder of their dinner conversation was strained and focused on small talk. By the time they left to go home, an uncomfortable chasm of silence separated them. Michelle took her book upstairs and crawled into bed. Meanwhile, Steve picked up his Bible and poured his heart out to the Lord in prayer.

"Please, God. Help me know what to say when Michelle brings up all this stuff. We are drifting apart. Show me what to do."

Michelle was packing her bags for the weekend. A getaway with Steve sounded so attractive three weeks ago. Now, with the tension that permeated their relationship, she almost dreaded spending two days alone with him.

Her original plans of a romantic retreat dissolved, and rather than packing her honeymoon nighties, she threw old tee shirts and sweats into her suitcase.

Last, but not least, she carefully tucked her new book into the top pouch of the bag. Hopefully she'd be able to finish it while Steve was fishing. She usually sat pole-in-hand beside him, but this time she planned to sit nearby and read.

At their last session, Trevor urged the class to try to complete the book before their next meeting, when he hoped to teach them about past life regressions. Everyone in the group liked to tease her about being the star pupil, but Trevor always rose to her defense indicating that she was just more growth-oriented than some of the others.

As she latched the suitcase shut, the doorbell rang. Glancing at the clock, she smiled. Monica was always so prompt.

She was out of breath as she reached the door. "Hey, there!" she said with a gasp.

"Did I catch you at a bad time?" her friend asked.

"No, I was upstairs finishing packing when you rang the bell. I almost tripped over Max on the way down the stairs," she explained, catching her breath. "Come on in."

Monica followed her into the kitchen while Michelle gave her some directions about taking care of the cat while they were gone. As if sensing he was the topic of conversation, Max trotted up to them and began rubbing against Michelle's leg.

"Hey, goofy. Monica's here to learn about babysitting you while we're gone," she said, as if speaking to a child.

Max mewed in response and sat at Monica's feet licking his paw and then rubbing his head with it.

"We're going to have a blast, Max," Monica added, playing along.

Michelle handed her a piece of paper listing Max's needs. She started reciting them to Monica and then stopped herself. "I guess you could read this without my help." She smiled.

"Just show me where the food is, and we'll be fine!" Monica replied reassuringly. "I'll be here tonight around seven o'clock and come back in the morning by eight. Anything I should know about tucking him into bed?" she teased.

"Don't worry. Max will tell you everything you need to know," Michelle replied with a grin. "Steve won't be here for about two more hours. Do you want to stay for a cup of coffee?"

"That sounds great, but are you sure you're all packed and ready? I don't want to put a damper on your little getaway!"

"You don't have to worry about that," Michelle said. "But yes, I'm sure that everything is packed and ready."

She poured the coffee, and handed Monica a cup as they sat down at the kitchen table.

"Is everything okay?" Monica asked, seeming to pick up on her mood.

"I guess. Steve and I are just having some difficulties right now. It's nothing serious. He just doesn't understand about our class and the stuff I'm learning."

Monica listened patiently. "It's probably good you're going away this weekend. Maybe everything will go back to normal once you get up to the cabin and have some time together."

"I hope so. It just seems like we're both going in different directions. Steve has got this Bible thing going, and I'm finding myself more and more interested in the more mystical side of spirituality."

"I know what you're saying, Michelle, but maybe Steve will eventually grow to see the bigger picture. Give

181

him some time to explore. Maybe the Bible is part of his own evolution," she said thoughtfully. "Wow, I'm starting to sound like Trevor!" she added with a giggle.

"You are," Michelle agreed with a smile.

John looked into the mirror and began adjusting his tie. Although his face was creased from weeks of worry, the bags under his eyes had receded somewhat after last night's rest. His stomach growled, and he smiled, relieved that his appetite had returned. He'd grab a muffin from the vending machine out in front before he caught the cab.

In his haste to get to the appointment with Jeff Morgan, he almost walked out without his envelope. Fortunately, it caught his eye as he stepped into his shoes. "Don't want to leave without that," he mumbled under his breath, retrieving the package and heading out the door.

He'd instructed the cabby to meet him by the lobby, and he had just enough time to buy his muffin and a cup of coffee before climbing into the backseat. Handing the driver the slip of paper with the address, they headed to the law office of Jeff Morgan.

In ten minutes they pulled up in front of a brick and glass building at the corner of First and Larkin. John paid the cabby and, grasping the envelope tightly in his hand, walked up the open-air stairway leading to a row of offices. Number plaques with arrows pointed him to Suite 105. The shingle beside the door read, "Jefferson T. Morgan, Attorney". John sighed, smiled hopefully, and pushed open the door.

Sylvia was sitting at the front desk in a tweed suit. She looked up and welcomed him.

"Feeling better after a good night's sleep?" she asked.

"Much. Thanks. And thanks again for setting up this appointment with your brother."

"My pleasure. He's almost finished with his nine-thirty appointment," Sylvia said as she glanced at the clock. "Why don't you just have a seat and make yourself comfortable for a few minutes."

He sat in the leather chair beside the couch and picked up a *Newsweek* magazine from the glass end table.

"Would you like something to drink? Coffee maybe or some tea?" Sylvia asked.

"No, thanks. I'm fine. I had a cup of coffee on the way over in the cab," he replied.

Flipping through the pages of the magazine, he was not able to concentrate on reading anything. As he set it down, the door from Mr. Morgan's office to the reception area opened, and two men stepped out shaking hands and saying good-bye.

John rose to his feet. One of the men, a tall thin guy with wavy dark hair and a friendly smile looked toward him and said, "You must be John Ackerman." He extended his hand to John, and they exchanged a firm handshake. "Jeff Morgan. My sister told me that you needed some advice."

"I really appreciate you fitting me into your schedule like this. Your sister must be as persuasive as she is encouraging," John replied with a smile.

The two men walked back into Jeff's office. His large oak desk revealed a hodgepodge of file folders, with one small clearing in front of his chair. He gestured to the caramel-colored leather chair facing the desk, and John took a seat.

"So tell me a little about your case. Sylvia mentioned something about an embezzlement situation at your company. Mathers, Inc. I believe she said."

"Yes. I've been with Mathers for over twenty years now. Competition at the management level has been getting pretty cutthroat lately with the parent company restructuring and forcing many upper level workers into early retirement." John hesitated, groping for words. "I love my job, Mr. Morgan..."

"Call me Jeff."

"Okay, Jeff. Anyway as I was saying, I love what I do. It challenges me and gives purpose to my life. I'm doing all I can to resist this early retirement push."

"And?"

"And now I'm in this mess. Someone at Mathers has used my signature to authorize large cash withdrawals from the general fund. I really thought it would be no big deal to clear this all up, but now I'm in over my head."

"Let's see what you brought," Jeff said, indicating the envelope on John's lap.

His hand shaking, John handed him the envelope.

Jeff carefully slid the paperwork out and began flipping through it. He was silent as he read. John studied his face, looking for some glimmer of hope. After what seemed like an eternity, he looked up.

"Is this your signature?" he asked pointing.

"Yes and no. It looks like my signature, but I did not sign that document."

"How about this one?"

"The same."

"Did you ever sign for a cash withdrawal of this nature?" Jeff asked earnestly.

John Ackerman hesitated, looking down at the floor.

"Look, Mr. Ackerman,"

"John."

"John. If you want my advice, you've got to level with me. Did you ever sign one of these authorizations?"

John sighed; his shoulders dropping as he looked down at his own clasped hands. "I did sign one awhile ago. My daughter was getting married, and I needed a temporary loan to cover some of the expenses, so I took an advance on my pay for the following month."

"I see," Jeff said sitting back in his chair.

"But I didn't draw any pay the next month. The company had a huge cushion in the account anyway. It was no loss to them, and it got me through a tight spot. Certainly I'm entitled to a little help like that from a company I've given so much of my time and life to."

"We're not talking about what you are entitled to, John. We're talking about the law. What you did was illegal. Granted the company was not hurt in the process, but this is a form of embezzlement." He paused to let his words sink in.

"But I didn't sign any of the authorizations for withdrawals that you are looking at, and they are trying to nail me on all of them."

"The problem we have here, John, is that even if you could prove these were not your signatures, any prosecutor worth his salt will find the one transaction you did sign and then your goose is cooked."

"So what should I do?" John asked, desperation evident in his voice.

"Get yourself a good attorney and start praying. I'd also get my affairs in order, just in case."

"In case?"

"It's possible you could serve a prison term for this, John. The courts are becoming more and more aggressive with white-collar crimes. They may let you serve your time on weekends or in community service, but even if they do, it's likely Mathers will cut the cord, so you'll need to find another job. It's not easy finding work when you are a felon."

Jeff paused and looked at John. "Listen, I'm not trying to scare you. It's possible they'll find the real culprit here. But I wouldn't be doing you any favors to soft pedal this. It's better to be prepared for the worst and be relieved if it doesn't happen."

John dropped his head into his hands, rubbing his scalp, and trying to process what he was hearing. "Can you help me? I mean, will you take on my case? I really didn't think I'd need an attorney because I knew I didn't sign those papers, and I was sure the whole thing would be cleared up. But now I see that I'm going to need some really shrewd counsel if I have any hope of getting myself out of this mess."

"I wish I could help you, but I'm overloaded right now, and this case is out of my jurisdiction anyway. But I could recommend some good attorneys in your area," Jeff replied, reaching for his iPad.

He searched his contacts and jotted down two names and phone numbers. "Try these guys. They are both experts in corporate law; it just depends on who is available. Good attorneys are often backlogged with cases. Hopefully one will be able to fit you in."

Jeff gathered the papers together and slid them back into the envelope. "I've seen people get out of bigger messes than this. Just be prepared. Worst case scenario you'll serve a couple of years and pay a stiff fine."

John nodded numbly and stood to his feet. Jeff walked around to the front of the desk and handed him the envelope, stretching his hand out to John. They shook hands, and John took the envelope and walked toward the door.

"Let me know how it turns out," Jeff said.

"Yeah, okay. Hey, thanks for your time," John said sincerely. He forced a smile and then left the office.

Sylvia was not at the front desk. As he was leaving, she came back in from outside carrying the mail in one hand and some court dockets in another.

"How'd it go?" she asked softly.

"Not good," was all he could say in reply.

"I'm sorry, John. I'll be praying for you."

"Yeah, thanks," he said in a defeated tone as he left.

CHAPTER TWENTY

Steve had meticulously packed the car, and they were ready to go. Michelle handed him a small cooler to take out to the car, filled with tasty treats like their favorite chicken salad sandwiches, apples, and miniature candy bars to munch on during the drive to the lake. Then she cuddled Max one last time, fed him a liver-flavored kitty treat, and placed him on his favorite chair.

"We'll be back before you know it, little guy," she told him reassuringly.

Max seemed oblivious to the trauma of the moment and curled up to snooze.

Michelle noticed the mail delivery truck driving off as she walked out of the kitchen door toward the car. She made a quick trip to the box and retrieved the mail, then climbed in beside Steve. He looked happy and almost a little nervous.

"What's that grin about?" Michelle asked.

"Nothing, babe. I'm just glad we're getting away. I hope this will be a great weekend for both of us."

"Me, too," she agreed. She reached across and squeezed his hand. "Let's go."

"Okay, Lakeside Bed and Breakfast here we come." He started the car and backed out of the driveway, pressing the remote to close the garage behind them. The sun was shining, and he looked more relaxed than Michelle had seen him in a while. They rode out of Sandy Cove and onto the open highway.

"Pretty day," Michelle commented, grasping for conversation.

"Yep," he replied with a smile.

She flipped through the mail on her lap and was pleasantly surprised to find a letter from Kristin. Although email was great, it was fun to get a real letter in the mail. She opened the envelope and pulled out the familiar sunflower stationery she'd given Kristin before she moved away. "You'd better write lots of letters to me on this paper!" she had teased at the time.

Steve popped in his favorite CD and was tapping on the steering wheel and humming along as she read the contents.

The letter was more of a note. It started with the usual greetings and questions, but quickly moved on to the point. Kristin had met someone special, very special, and she wanted to bring him up to Sandy Cove for Michelle and Steve to meet.

"Listen to this, Steve," Michelle said, reaching over and turning the music down before she began to read the brief letter.

He kept his eyes on the road while she read.

"This must be pretty serious," Michelle commented after finishing. "Kristin would never bring some guy up for us to meet unless she thought he was *the one*."

"You're right. We've been trying to get her to visit us for a while now. Maybe that's why we haven't heard from her lately. She's been busy with this guy. What did you say his name is?"

"Mark. That's all she said. No last name."

"You should call her when we get back and set something up. Maybe they could come up over Memorial Day weekend."

"That's a great idea. I'm still hoping Mom and Dad will come then, too," she said, and then added with concern, "Steve, do you really think my dad is going to be okay?"

"He'll be fine, honey. Once he gets this mess cleared up, he'll be back to his old self," he said reassuringly, reaching over and patting her on the knee.

"But how will he ever get cleared of those charges? You yourself even admitted that it's a challenging case."

"I'm just getting started in this field, Michelle. There are many attorneys who deal with cases much tougher than your dad's, and they manage to clear their clients—some of whom are actually guilty, I might add. Your dad's an innocent man. The truth will prevail."

"Well, I hope he gets the right counsel. At this point, I'm not sure how clearly he's thinking. Mom is worried sick. I hope she's getting some rest out at Grandpa's."

"I'm sure they're are taking good care of her." He reached over and took her hand in his, giving it a little squeeze of reassurance. She thought about how she'd held Trevor's hand at the conference and winced, hoping Steve didn't notice.

"Want to listen to the music again?" he asked.

"Okay." She let go of his hand and turned the volume back up.

The melody of a soft love song caressed them from the CD player. They rode without talking for a while. The day was breathtakingly beautiful, with sapphire blue skies, a few pristine, billowy clouds, and the rare commodity of full sun. A breeze was blowing gently through the leaves on the trees lining the highway, and traffic was virtually nonexistent.

Michelle pushed away the worries about her dad and tried to imagine what Mark must be like. She pictured Kristin as a bride and thought about how exciting it would be to help plan her wedding.

190

After a while, her stomach started growling. "Are you getting hungry yet?" she asked Steve.

"Hmmm?"

"Hungry. Are you getting hungry?" she asked. "Why don't we stop somewhere and have a picnic?"

"Okay, that's a great idea. Isn't there a campground a few more miles down off the highway?"

"Yeah, I think there is. Remember we noticed the sign last time on our way home?" She thought back to their last visit to the lake—a summer camping outing shortly after they got settled into Sandy Cove.

Steve nodded. "I think it's just past the interstate turnoff."

They were able to locate Camp Meadowlark about ten minutes later. Pulling off the highway, Steve followed the signs down the winding side road until they entered a parking area with a rustic playground comprised of two tire swings and a shallow slide beside some redwood picnic tables. It was peacefully vacant and the sun provided a relatively warm spot to enjoy the lush surroundings and their lunches. The fragrance of pine trees filled the air and the scampering of chipmunks and squirrels were the only sounds breaking the silence.

Michelle took an old quilt from the trunk of the car. She draped it across the picnic table as a tablecloth and spread out their lunches. Using napkins as plates, they sat down to their picnic feast.

"This place is gorgeous," she replied with delight as she looked around.

Steve's head had been bowed, but he looked up and smiled saying, "There's nothing like God's creation."

Michelle wondered if he had been praying. All of this "God" stuff was so foreign coming from him. It made her feel almost awkward with her own husband. She really hoped he'd come to see things from a more open-minded perspective. How would she ever adjust to

191

living with some conservative Bible thumper after all that she was learning and experiencing in her classes? Her mind strayed to Trevor and his engaging smile. He was really helping her to expand her horizons.

Thinking about him gave her an inspiration. *Trevor would love this place!* She jumped up with a start and quickly walked over to the car to get the camera.

"What are you doing?" Steve asked.

"I'm going to take a picture of this place! It's the perfect image to gaze at during my newest meditation. In our class we're learning about our inherent oneness with Mother Earth, and this place really helps me feel that spiritual connection."

Steve just said, "Oh." He didn't look impressed.

She surveyed the area and chose the angle she liked best, and then began snapping pictures. After taking half a dozen, Michelle sat back down and started to eat.

"Give me that camera," Steve said.

"Why?"

"I want to take a picture of you so I can have something to gaze at, too."

"Are you mocking me, Steve?"

"No. I just want to take your picture."

"Okay," she replied, handing over the camera and giving him her best smile.

It was quiet in his motel room that afternoon as John sat slumped over in the chair. Jeff Morgan's words, "Get your affairs in order," kept echoing in his mind.

Finally, he rallied his energies to sit up at the small table and write a letter. In the letter he explained his one-time involvement in borrowing funds from the company's account. Then he described the confusion and anguish he was now experiencing in this fabricated set of charges that were being leveled against him. Admitting that the signatures on the documents matched his own with flawless precision, he adamantly denied any involvement in the actual embezzlement itself.

At one point the letter took a turn as he asked a series of questions he knew would never be answered. Why was this happening to him? Who wanted to see him destroyed? What would this do to his family? How would the real guilty party ever be brought to justice?

He concluded with a message of love to his family and a reiteration of his loyalty and steadfast devotion to Mathers, Inc. Without even bothering to look the letter over, John pushed it aside and walked away. He eased his body onto the bed, picked up his cell phone and punched in the number for Phil and Joan's house, hoping that Sheila would answer.

A moment later his heart skipped a beat, hearing his wife's voice on the other end. He hesitated for just a moment and then said, "Hi hon. It's me."

"John! It's so good to hear your voice. Are you okay? Where are you?"

"I'm calling from a motel up north. I miss you, sweetheart."

"I miss you, too," she said. "Where exactly are you, John? Give me the name of the motel, honey."

"I'd rather not, Sheila. I'll be home soon anyway."

"When, John? I've been worried sick."

His heart was wrenched from his chest. "I don't know yet, honey. I just wanted to make sure you know how much I love you, and that none of this stuff has to do with you."

"Oh, John. Please come home. I love you, too, and I want to help you," she urged.

"I know you do, but I just can't drag you through this mess. It's better this way. Believe me."

"How much longer will you be gone?" she persisted in a concerned voice.

"Not much. I've figured out what I need to do, so please don't worry. How are your mom and dad?" he asked, changing the subject.

"They're fine," she replied. "What are you going to do?"

"I'll explain it to you as soon as I can. How are Tim and Michelle?"

"Tim's been looking for you, honey. He's really been worried."

"Call him, Sheila. Tell him I'm fine and to stop looking, okay?"

There was a long pause on the other end.

"I mean it, honey. Call him up and tell him not to worry. I'll be home sooner than you think," he persisted.

"When?"

"Within a week at the longest."

"Promise?"

"Promise. Now tell Tim what I said, okay?"

"All right, I'll tell him."

"And Michelle, how's she doing?" he asked, thinking about his beautiful daughter, who had grown into such a lovely young lady.

"She's good. Steve took today off, and they're headed out to the lake for a weekend away. I think it will be good for them. He's been working so hard. They need the time together."

"I'm glad they're making time for each other," John replied with a sigh. "Life is too short."

"What?" Sheila asked.

"Nothing. I was just thinking out loud. Well, I guess I'd better finish up my business here. Just remember that I love you, Sheila. You're a wonderful wife. Everything will work out for the best," he said.

"Okay, honey. I love you too."

"Bye, sweetheart."

"Bye, John."

Sheila was slowly lowering the receiver to the phone when her dad walked into the room.

"Are you okay?" he asked.

Turning to him, she confessed, "I'm scared, Dad. That was John on the phone. He tried to reassure me, but I know that he's upset. His voice wasn't normal, and he was trying too hard to make it sound like everything is okay." She looked up at him with tears filling her eyes.

"Oh, baby," he said softly. She collapsed against him and began to sob.

CHAPTER TWENTY-ONE

Tim Ackerman's baby face belied his age. At twenty-six, he could easily pass for eighteen. His sandy hair and gray-green eyes were captivating, and his matching dimples drew attention to his broad smile. A football star in high school and junior college, Tim's frame was sturdy and muscular. Narrow hips and long legs complemented his broad shoulders.

Girls were easily attracted to Tim, but he was in no hurry to settle down. The bachelor life with its freedom and mobility appealed to his restless nature. Consequently, he steered clear of commitments, including any particular career path, preferring a string of temporary positions earning just enough to meet his weekly expenses.

Tim was an avid surfer. Since he worked until four o'clock, he usually spent late afternoons at the beach. It wasn't just the sport that drew him. Sometimes he'd sit on his board and watch the waves go by. It gave him a place to think, and today he had a lot on his mind as he wondered about his father and where he could have gone.

He was getting ready to head down to the water when his cell phone beeped. It was his mother. She sounded horrible. He could tell this would take some time. Switching to his Bluetooth, he wandered through his small apartment looking for the keys to his truck while he listened to her talk.

She told him about her conversation with his father and explained how bad he sounded. She asked him where he had looked so far on his search to track his father down. He named a few neighboring towns and some of the acquaintances he had called. Every attempt had led to a dead end.

"Listen, Tim," she said gravely. "I don't think this can wait another day. I have a terrible feeling. Something is going to happen to your father if we don't find him right away."

He sunk down into the sofa and put his bare feet on the coffee table. "You really think it is that serious?"

"I do. I'm coming home tonight, and I want you to be there to help me. Your dad mentioned something about being up north in a motel. We've got to figure out where he is and try to find him."

"Okay, Mom. I'll call the guys and tell them to go without me. What time do you think you'll be here?"

"Probably by seven. Maybe we can have dinner together and figure out what to do."

"Alright. I'll meet you at the house."

"Thanks, honey. I really appreciate this."

"No problem. See you at seven. And Mom, don't worry. We'll find him," he added, hoping his voice sounded more convincing than he felt. He also had a bad feeling about all of this.

"I just hope we can do it before it's too late," his mother said softly before saying good-bye.

"We will," Tim replied.

By mid-afternoon Steve was pulling up a narrow, winding driveway to the Lakeside Bed and Breakfast. Tall trees lining the driveway towered above them, and the air was thick with the fragrance of pine. At the summit, the trees parted and revealed a sprawling lawn and an A-frame redwood mansion.

Steve drove up to the curb in front of a flight of wooden stairs leading to a huge, wraparound porch and the massive wood and glass entry door. As they got out of the car, Michelle spotted the lake off to the side behind the inn. She watched Steve breathe in the fresh mountain air and nodded with a smile as he pointed toward the water. At the door, they were greeted by a middle-aged woman in jeans and a plaid flannel shirt.

"You must be the Barons," she said, extending her hand to them. "My name is Hannah. My husband, Tom, and I are the innkeepers. Welcome to the Lakeside Bed and Breakfast."

"You have a beautiful place here," Michelle said as she gazed around the lobby and living room. Exquisite Persian rugs in rich colors adorned the polished, hardwood floors, and elegant antiques furnished the rooms. Steve signed in at the register and gave Hannah their credit card.

"I hope you'll find everything to your liking," she said after swiping the card and handing it back to him. "Make yourself at home. We have a game room downstairs with a TV and VCR, as well as a pool table and a variety of board games. The spa is right out this door," she pointed toward a little alcove with a small door leading out to the back of the porch.

"Breakfast is served family style at eight. If you need to eat earlier, just check in with the cook before she goes home at nine tonight. She'll be happy to whip you up something delicious."

Steve thanked her and took the key. Then Hannah escorted them to their room at the top of the winding oak staircase. "If you need anything, just let me know," she said, leaving them alone to explore the room.

It was decorated in a homey country style. The queen-size, four-poster oak bed was covered with an intricate hand sewn quilt of blues, browns, and cream colors. A nubby textured teddy bear sat propped up against the multitude of pillows at the headboard. In his lap was a small package of Hershey's kisses.

On the wall directly across from the bed was a large bay window overlooking the lake. A sitting ledge with a blue cushion and coordinating quilted pillows made the window into a lovely place to read or just gaze out over the lake and relax.

Against another wall was a beautiful carved oak bureau holding plush, white terry cloth robes inviting use. Beside the bureau was a matching dresser and a tea cart already set with a steaming pot of tea and several shortcake biscuits, fresh from the oven. Michelle looked at Steve and smiled. It was her favorite flavor—cinnamon spice.

"Did you have something to do with this?" she asked as she wagged her finger at him suspiciously. He just grinned and shrugged.

She walked over and peeked into the attached bathroom. It had oak cabinets with brass fixtures and an old-fashioned claw-foot bathtub. Cinnamon potpourri spiced the air with a sweet fragrance, and the towels and washcloths were specially folded to look like flowers.

She looked around, soaking in all the quaint and appealing details, then looked over at her husband and smiled. "This place is perfect. I love it."

"For the amount I'm paying per night, it'd better be perfect," Steve said half kidding.

She walked over and gave him a peck on the cheek, and insisted on serving them both some tea. So Steve made himself comfortable on the bed, while she waited on him. He seemed a little disappointed when, after serving him, she settled with her tea and biscuit in the window seat across from him.

"Look at the view, Steve. I could spend the whole weekend in this little nook looking out over that sparkling lake," she said, thinking about her book and how relaxing it would be to lounge there and read.

"Don't even let that thought enter your pretty little head," Steve chided. "We're setting the alarm for six A.M. and heading out to fish."

"Let's talk about it later. Right now I just want to relax and enjoy our tea," she replied.

After they were finished, Steve decided to go down to the lobby and ask the innkeeper about dinner options. A flier had indicated several nearby restaurants, and he wanted to get some recommendations. While he was gone, Michelle decided to try to read a chapter or two in her book. She was just getting immersed in her second chapter when he returned.

"We've got reservations for seven-thirty at the Steak and Stein," he reported.

"Okay, that sounds great," she replied without looking up from her reading.

"Want to go for a walk down by the water?" he asked.

"Maybe in a little while. I'm right in the middle of this section, and I'd like to finish it first if you don't mind."

"Okay. Guess I'll get some reading in too," he said as he took his Bible out of the suitcase.

He didn't appear to notice her look of disdain as she glanced over at his reading material. There must be a way she could get him to realize the Bible was only one small tool in the quest for spirituality. But how?

Back at his apartment in the outskirts of Seal Beach, Tim was getting ready to go over to his parents' house. He threw a few clothes into a duffel bag, turned off the stereo, and headed out to his red pickup truck parked in the carport under his apartment. While he drove across town, he thought about his dad and wondered how he would find him.

Tim loved his father, but their relationship had always been a bit strained. His dad was a hard-driven man who saw success in business as the true measure of a person's worth. He pushed him to strive for perfection in all areas, and Tim did his best to win his father's approval, always striving for good grades and trying to be the star athlete his dad hoped he would become.

All of that ended after high school. Tim burned out on trying to win the love he felt he was missing, and his goals began to change.

He wanted to have fun, and his dad's serious and seemingly joyless existence did not appeal to him. Rather than argue, he just tuned his dad out. Trying to clamp down harder only led to further resistance, until finally Tim opted to move out a year after graduating.

Since that time, their relationship was distant and their interactions confined to surface conversations only. It wasn't until he disappeared, in such a radical departure from his character, that Tim's heart was again stirred toward his father.

His mother had sounded so worried, and her concern became Tim's as well. Lost in thought, he almost drove past the deli without stopping to pick up dinner. Veering quickly across two lanes, he just missed clipping a small sports car. The driver honked and made an obscene gesture.

"Whatever!" Tim murmured to himself as he navigated the truck into a parking place. He bolted into the store, purchased some fried chicken and potato salad, and took off for his parents' house.

Pulling into their driveway, he thought about all the basketball games he and his dad played on that same driveway when he was a boy. Then he thought about the day he moved out, and how his mother stood by herself waving good-bye, while his dad was stewing in the living room over their angry parting words.

Tim hoped finding his father would somehow patch up the broken pieces. Though they did not see eye to eye on many life issues, he yearned for a close bond with him. For the first time, he could see his dad's vulnerability, something he had never seen growing up. If there was any way he could help him now, he wanted to do it.

A pile of newspapers near the front door indicated that his mother had not thought to cancel the paper while she was off visiting her parents. He decided to check the mailbox and found it was also loaded. He took the mail and the papers inside through the front door, reminded by the soft beeping sound to shut off the security system as he entered.

The living room was dark and the house seemed stuffy. He parted the shutters to open the front windows. A soft breeze wafted in, sweetening the stale air with the fragrance of ocean breezes.

"That's better," he said to himself, as he walked into the kitchen.

Everything looked neat and tidy as usual. Peering into the refrigerator, he suddenly remembered the chicken and potato salad sitting on the front seat of his truck. He went out, retrieved them, and then turned the oven on low, removing the plastic wrap on the chicken and replacing it with foil, before putting it inside. He popped the potato salad into the fridge and grabbed a can of beer to drink while he waited for his mom. It was only six-thirty, so he knew it might be awhile.

Wandering through the house, he strolled into his father's study. He never felt comfortable in this room. The imposing desk and burgundy leather executive chair were the focal points. The walls were lined in matching bookshelves, each housing volume after volume of manuals, biographies, and investment literature. The subtle aromas of leather and pipe tobacco mingled in the air. It was his father's sanctuary, a place of retreat and concentration. No one was allowed in without his permission, and Tim felt a little uneasy walking around in there sipping his beer.

His cell phone startled him, and he pulled it out of his pocket and flipped it open. His mom was on the other end, wanting him to know that she was running a little late and might not make it there until seven-thirty.

He reassured her he would wait and told her that he had picked up dinner. After hanging up, he slowly sat down at his father's desk. The big leather chair smelled masculine, and he felt out of place as he sat there looking at the paperwork stacked in piles in front of him.

"I wonder if I'll have a study like this someday," he thought to himself. He shook his head suddenly as if to perish the thought and was just rising to leave the room when something on the desk caught his eye. It was the corner of a yellow piece of paper poking out from under the edge of the desk blotter. Tim lifted the blotter to find a small sticky note with a phone number scrawled across it. Nothing else. Just a phone number. But the area code was out of the Southern California area, and it struck him as odd that there was nothing else written on the paper. He picked it up, sat back for a moment and thought, then leaned forward and punched in the number.

After two rings, a pleasant voice answered, "Redwood Lodge, may I help you?"

Redwood Lodge. That was the place where they sometimes stopped overnight on their way camping in the Sierras. It was a modest motel that was clean and had almost a cabin-like feel to it.

"Hello?" the voice asked. "May I help you?"

"Uh… yeah," Tim mumbled, turning his focus back to the phone. "I'm trying to locate someone who may be staying at your motel. Do you have anyone named Ackerman registered there?"

"One moment please," she responded and put him on hold. The sound of country music softly replaced her voice. He leaned back in the leather chair and waited, his heart pounding in his chest, and his mouth suddenly dry. He cleared his throat and took a swig of beer so he'd be able to speak when she came back on the line.

The voice returned. "Thank you for holding. Yes, there is a John Ackerman registered. Would you like me to try ringing his room?"

"Um… yeah, sure. That would be great." Tim sat upright, grasping in his mind for words to say should his father answer the call. His breathing was tight and his knuckles were white from tightly gripping the receiver.

The phone rang several times. No one answered. After the fifth ring, the same woman's voice came back on the line.

"He doesn't appear to be answering. Would you like to leave a message?" she asked.

"No. That's okay. Thanks anyway," he replied and hung up the phone.

He looked at his watch. It said 6:30. If he left right away, he could make it to the lodge before midnight. Something inside was urging him to go quickly. He stood up, paced back and forth in front of the desk, flipped open his phone, and dialed his mom's cell phone.

"Hello?" her voice responded after only one ring.

"It's me, Mom. I found out where Dad is," he said.

"What? Where is he? How did you find him?"

"I found a phone number on a piece of paper under his desk blotter. It's for the Redwood Lodge."

"The Redwood Lodge?"

"Yeah, remember that place we used to stay on the way up to Running Falls?"

"Of course I remember. Your dad is at the Redwood Lodge?" she asked again. "I thought I looked through all the paperwork on his desk before I left."

"It was under the blotter, Mom. It caught my eye somehow. Anyway, I just talked to the front desk at the lodge. They tried to ring his room, but there was no answer. I think I should go up there, Mom. Do you want me to leave now or wait till you get here?"

"Oh, Tim. Let me think a minute." She paused, and then said, "It's about a five hour drive, isn't it?"

"At least."

"I hate for you to drive that by yourself. Besides, maybe it would be better if I were with you when you talk to him. Who knows what kind of state of mind you'll find him in."

"It's up to you, Mom. The drive is not a problem. I've driven further than that by myself many times. But if you think Dad might need you up there, I can wait here. How much longer do you think till you get home?"

"I'm just getting off the interstate now. I could probably be there in about twenty minutes. You just wait there. I'll hurry."

"Okay, but be careful, Mom," he said, imagining the worried look on his mother's face.

"I will, dear. See you in a bit," she said and then hung up.

Tim continued to pace. He could not settle himself. A sense of urgency pressed on him, and he could feel his adrenaline pumping. Trashing the empty beer can under the kitchen sink, he remembered about the chicken, turned off the oven, and pulled the carton out, setting it on the counter. There would be no time to eat once his mom got there. He decided to gnaw on a leg while he waited and paced. He would pack some chicken and salad into containers for his mom to eat during the long drive.

Although he wasn't sure what he would say, he tried calling his father's cell phone several times, and even tried texting a short message. No response except the same voicemail message stating that John Ackerman was unavailable to take the call.

Every few minutes a car would drive down the street, and Tim would peer out through the open windows. Time was dragging, and he was eager to get on the road. Relief at having located his father was mixed with a horrible feeling of dread that something was terribly wrong. Something he might not be able to fix.

CHAPTER TWENTY-TWO

John ignored the buzzing of his cell phone. The pistol rested in his right hand as he held the letter to his family in his left. Surely this was the only way out. He was not willing to drag his family through a messy trial, no matter how innocent he knew he was in his own heart and mind.

His thoughts haunted him. *They don't deserve this humiliation. You'll probably end up losing them once you are locked up.*

For several moments, he thought about his wife and children. Remembering the good times, he whispered softly, "I'll always love you." Sweat trickled down his neck and back, and he was trembling. Rallying all of his courage, he lifted the barrel to his temple and pulled the trigger.

Jessica Jones was working the front desk of the Redwood Lodge. She heard a sound like an explosion and ran to the window. There was no sign of any trouble in the parking lot or on the street out front. Something urged her to investigate, but she was not supposed to leave the desk unattended. She decided to call the police.

"Bridgeport 911. What is the nature of your emergency?" a voice asked briskly.

"I just heard an explosion," the woman replied. "It sounded like it was very close."

"What is your location?"

"I'm at the Redwood Lodge, on the corner of Madison and Main."

"Any sign of a fire?" the officer asked.

"No. Everything looks fine, but it was a really loud boom."

"We'll send a unit right over." The officer continued to question her while the patrol car was heading for the motel. As soon as the officers arrived, she hung up the phone and explained to them the loud explosion she had heard.

"Did it sound like a gunshot?" one of the officers asked.

"I don't know. Maybe. It was pretty loud. I thought maybe someone set off a firecracker in the parking lot or something, but when I looked outside, everything looked normal."

"We'll have a look around," the other officer said. They walked out of the motel lobby and proceeded along the building that housed the rooms for rent.

A few minutes later they returned to the motel office. "Nothing looks out of the ordinary. Which of your rooms are occupied?" the first officer asked.

She pulled out the register and made a list of the occupied rooms, including the names of the occupants. The officers asked her if she knew which tenants were currently on the premises, but she admitted she had no way of knowing. They asked her for a master key to the rooms, and she produced one without hesitation.

"All we can do right now is to go by and check each room. If no one answers the door, we'll use the master key."

Within five minutes, the officers had discovered the source of the explosion. Sprawled on his bed, blood splattered over the bedspread, was the body of a man. He appeared lifeless until one of the officers placed his finger on the carotid artery to check for a pulse. Then a soft moan came from a place deep inside.

"This guy's still alive. Get the paramedics!"

Immediately the other officer began speaking rapidly into his radio. Within a couple of minutes a siren could be heard approaching.

Jessica stood at the doorway of the office looking down the row of rooms and watching the ambulance pull up to an open door about halfway down the corridor. She hurried back to the register and saw the name of the occupant of room 45—John Ackerman. Someone had just called about him earlier that evening. Had someone shot him? She decided she'd better call the motel owner. He would want to know about this.

Sheila and her son rode in silence most of the long journey. Both of them were lost in their own thoughts and concerns, and she was exhausted from her trip home and the immediate departure on another five-hour drive. They only stopped once at a fast-food restaurant to grab some coffee, and they were back on the road within ten minutes.

It was nearly midnight when they drove into the parking lot of the Redwood Lodge. Sheila's heart froze in her chest when she saw the ambulance pulling away. Two police officers were walking toward the front office, and they arrived at the door simultaneously, the older one holding it open for Sheila and Tim as they entered.

Jessica and her boss were sitting behind the desk and arose immediately. The motel owner looked over at Sheila and asked, "Can I help you?"

"I'm looking for my husband, John Ackerman," she explained.

The officers exchanged glances and the one who had held the door for them said, "Mrs. Ackerman, we need to talk. Come over here and have a seat."

Sheila felt faint. Tim put his arm around her shoulder and gently escorted her to the chair. She sank down without ever taking her eyes off the officer's face. "What happened? Is my husband alright?" she asked, tears filling her eyes.

"Your husband is on the way to the hospital, Ma'am. He has been seriously injured. A gunshot wound. It appears to have been self-inflicted."

"Oh, no. Oh, Tim. We're too late." Tears spilled down her face, and she began to rock back and forth, moaning.

Tim held onto her and kept repeating, "Oh, my God. Oh, my God." All he could think of was how he had somehow let his father down again. Why hadn't he searched the house earlier? If he had found the phone number yesterday instead of today, this never would have happened. But no, all he had been thinking about was getting away for the weekend with his buddies. Now his dad might die, and it would be his fault for not finding him sooner.

Sheila reached out and took her son's hand in hers as she searched the officer's face for some sign of hope. Tears were pooling in her eyes as she thought about John and how desperate he must have felt to do something so drastic.

"I know that this is very difficult for you, Mrs. Ackerman. Can we give you and your son a ride to the hospital?" the first officer asked gently.

"Yes, please. We need to be with him."

"Of course." The man touched Tim on the shoulder and nodded toward the door. He helped his mother up, and the four of them walked out to the patrol car.

As they got into the backseat, Sheila's head was spinning. Part of her wanted to know the extent of John's injuries, and part of her wanted to run and hide. She felt so helpless and afraid. Then a thought came to her. She reached into her purse and pulled out her cell phone.

"Call Grandpa," she said to Tim. "Tell him to pray."

As they pulled out of the parking lot, Tim punched in his grandparents' phone number.

Phil awoke with a start and reached for the phone. The reception was marginal, but he could hear enough to understand that it was Tim calling on Sheila's cell phone.

"We found Dad, Grandpa. He was... and we are on our way ... hospital," Tim's voice came and went as the connection cut on and off.

"What, Tim? Is your dad okay?"

"He's in the hospital, Grandpa. Mom wants you to pray. I'll .... later." The phone went dead. Phil tried calling back, but a recording said the user was out of range or had the phone turned off.

"What's happening, Phil?" Joan asked as she sat up in bed. "Where was Tim calling from?"

"I don't know, honey. The phone kept cutting out. But something is definitely wrong. John is in the hospital."

"Why? What happened?" She reached out and put her hand on his shoulder.

"Tim was trying to tell me, but the connection was horrible. He said Sheila wants us to pray. I think he said he'd call us back later."

"I wish we knew where they were," Joan said, wringing her hands. "Sheila needs us, Phil. I want to be there with her."

"I know. All we can do right now is wait to hear back. In the meantime, let's pray."

She scooted herself next to him on the edge of the bed. They held each other as Phil poured out a prayer, pleading with God to reach down and touch John and to be with Sheila and Tim.

John could hear beeping sounds. He felt very cold and could tell that his body was shaking. People were talking around him, but he could not open his eyes to see them. He realized that he was unable to speak.

"Blood pressure is 70 over 40. Pulse is 65."

"The CT scan should be back. That will give us a better idea of the extent of the damage."

"Are there any family members here?"

"Yes, his wife and son just arrived with the two officers."

"Tell them I'll be ready to meet with them in about ten minutes. Have them wait in my office."

John wanted to call out to them, but his mouth only chattered with the shivers that wracked his body. Someone was putting blankets on him, but the cold was so deep in his bones that he felt like he was buried in a mountain of snow.

"This guy's a goner. If we don't get his temperature and blood pressure up, we'll lose him."

"Could be damage to the brain stem. Let's try the heat lamps."

"He probably won't make it through the night. Dr. Jeffries usually recommends a 'no code' in these cases."

"I'll stay here with him. You go talk to the family and get them to Dr. Jeffries' office."

Michelle stirred softly in her sleep. She rolled over and glanced at the clock. It was one-thirty. Feeling restless, she gently slipped out of bed, hoping not to wake Steve.

The light of a full moon was streaming in through the window and bathing the room in a soft glow. She walked over to the window seat and sat down. Looking over the lake, she could see the water glistening peacefully.

As she gazed out, she was transported back in time and space to a cabin in the mountains of Southern California, where her family spent many weekends when she and Tim were little. She remembered one special Saturday evening when her grandfather took her for a moonlit walk by the water's edge.

That night, as they both soaked in the beauty of the lake reflecting the giant yellow moon, her grandfather said, "Look at the wondrous painting God created for us tonight." She'd stood in awe, imagining God up in heaven with a giant paintbrush, creating the beautiful scene before them.

I miss you, Grandpa, she whispered in her mind. Suddenly she felt very far away from her family. Thoughts of her mother and father began to stir inside. She hadn't talked to her mother in several days, and she wondered if there was any news about her dad.

"Please, God, watch over my father," she said softly. Then she smiled and shook her head, halfheartedly chastening herself for falling back on her childish ways of talking to God, as if he were some benevolent Father figure sitting on a throne in the heavens waiting to hear her requests.

Trevor had taught her that she had her own God-consciousness and she merely needed to look within for all the power of the universe. Still, he did admit that it was possible to tap into the "universal consciousness" of God in everyone and everything, so perhaps that was what she was doing with her prayer.

A few moments later, she felt someone's eyes on her. She turned to see Steve propped up on his elbow, gazing at her thoughtfully.

"Are you okay, babe?" he asked quietly.

"Yeah, I'm fine. I just felt restless and decided to sit here and drink in the view of the lake. It's really beautiful with the full moon shining on it."

He got out of bed and walked over to where she was sitting. Resting his hands on her shoulders, he looked out over the water. "You seem a little distant this weekend. Is everything okay?" he asked as he gently massaged her shoulders.

"I guess. It just seems like everything is changing in my life so fast. I love all that I'm learning and doing, but I miss my family and the ways things used to be."

Steve didn't know quite what to say. He loved Michelle so much that his heart ached. Had he been wrong to move her so far away from everything and everyone she knew? He thought about her grandparents. Their godly example always impressed him.

Maybe if they were back in California, Michelle would be sharing the same faith that he had come to embrace, rather than going off on these metaphysical tangents. Yet, if they had stayed in California, would he have found the truth? It seemed a divine appointment that he and Ben had ended up back together in the same distant town after all these years. Steve shook his head and sighed.

"What, Steve? What's wrong?"

"It's nothing, Michelle. I was just thinking about how much I love you, and wishing that you could still be close to your family and friends."

"I'm fine, honey. Really. I've made new friends, and I can always catch a plane and be with my family in a couple hours time. Besides, I'm really growing and stretching. That's important, too."

"I guess."

They embraced for a moment and then Michelle surprised Steve by announcing, "I'm hungry! Are you up for a snack at that twenty-four-hour coffee shop we saw on the highway?"

"You're crazy! At two in the morning, you want to go out for a snack?"

"Please," Michelle begged.

"Okay, okay!" Steve replied, holding his hands up in a gesture of surrender.

CHAPTER TWENTY-THREE

The nurse escorted Tim and Sheila to Dr. Jeffries' office. They sat down in two chairs facing a large rosewood desk. Neither of them said much as they waited for information about John's condition. Sheila seemed subdued. Her eyes were red-rimmed and her shoulders sagged under the tremendous weight. To fill the silence, Tim commented on the vast array of credentials with Dr. Jeffries' name on them displayed on the wall behind the desk.

"This guy's been everywhere," he started, gesturing to the framed accolades. "Look, Mom. U.S.C. Dad would be happy about that."

Sheila nodded numbly. She managed to give him a weak smile and then reached over and patted his hand. "Did you get a hold of Michelle?" she asked.

"No. Still just voicemail. They're probably out of range."

A moment later, Dr. Jeffries entered the room carrying a folder and some films. He introduced himself and then sat down across from them.

"We've run some tests on your husband, Mrs. Ackerman. According to the CT scan, the bullet seems to have fragmented into several small pieces. The brain is a complex organ and, quite frankly, it is difficult to assess the extent of the damages in a case like this.

"From what we can see, it appears that the brain stem was not compromised, although there is some trauma to the other parts of the brain. This means that the basic life functions of respiration and circulation will probably stabilize over the next day or so, providing there is no further intracranial hemorrhaging.

"Because of the fragmentation of the bullet, we are dealing with an inoperable situation here. All we can do is to wait and observe your husband's progress, and hope for the best."

"What are his chances?" Sheila asked, focusing all of her attention directly on his large brown eyes.

"As I said, it's difficult to tell. I've seen cases like this with some degree of recovery, and I've seen others where the patients never regain consciousness. Although researchers have mapped out the brain fairly well, and we can take educated guesses about the damage from the location of these fragments, the brain is different from any other organ in the human body. It has back-up mechanisms we are far from understanding.

"Perhaps you have heard of cases where someone has lost a portion of his brain function due to injury or stroke and then has been fully rehabilitated, through therapy, to resume all normal functioning. It is possible to train parts of the brain to compensate and take over for other damaged or destroyed parts. Let's take a look at your husband's films."

Following his lead, they walked over to a light bar on the side wall of the office. Dr. Jeffries attached a series of images along the light.

"Do you see this small white shape here?" he asked, indicating a spot on one of the pictures. "This fragment is lodged in what we call the speech center. This portion of the brain allows thoughts to be translated into speech.

"Now, look at this next segment. Here we can see a smaller fragment has entered the cerebellum, which controls balance and muscle coordination. And then

217

here," he added pointing to a third image, "is a third sliver that is pressing against the hypothalamus, which regulates body temperature and appetite.

"This could help explain why your husband's temperature is not stable, as evidenced by his shivering. However, shock alone will also produce those symptoms, so we have to wait and see if he will stabilize in that area."

He waited a moment as if to let the information soak in. Then he asked, "Do you have any questions?"

"What are you doing for him right now?" Sheila asked.

"We are keeping him as comfortable as possible and trying to alleviate the swelling. He is in a coma. He could go either way at this point."

The doctor escorted them back to their seats. Then he pulled up a side chair and sat facing them. "This is one of the most difficult part of my job, Mrs. Ackerman. But we need to make some important decisions here, and it is up to you and your family to make those decisions for your husband since he can't speak for himself."

She nodded and looked at Tim. He reached over and took her hand.

"Suicide is a terrible tragedy for any family to endure. It appears that your husband made the decision to take his life. Perhaps you know what brought him to that point. As an outsider, it is not my business to determine whether or not your husband had legitimate reasons to think his life should be terminated. The bottom line is that it appears to have been his wish."

Tim squeezed his mom's hand and gave her a tissue from the doctor's desk.

"What are you saying, doctor?" she asked with a pleading look in her eyes.

"I'm saying that if your husband survives this trauma, he will have even more problems to deal with than he had going into it. The road to recovery from this type of injury is long and difficult. He may never fully recover his speech or the use of his limbs. It is possible he could remain in a nonresponsive state, semi-comatose, for years. I've seen families go through that. I don't advise it."

"What *are* you advising?" Tim asked.

"I'm advising we put your husband on what we call 'no code'."

"What does that mean?" Sheila asked, tears filling her eyes again.

"It means that we will let nature take its course. If your husband goes into cardiac or respiratory arrest, we would not resuscitate."

Sheila and Tim grasped hands again. "What do you think?" she asked him.

"I don't know, Mom."

Sheila pulled her hand away and stood. She walked over and looked at the films from the scan. Turning toward the doctor, she asked, "Do you believe in God, Dr. Jeffries?"

He paused. "Let me answer that this way. I'm a man of science, but I've seen recoveries that no amount of science or medicine can explain. You might call them miracles. However, let's consider this. If there is a God, and He really does perform miracles, He certainly doesn't need our medical intervention to do that."

Sheila's brow was furrowed, and she seemed to be wrestling with what the doctor said. "I'd like some time to think about all of this," she finally answered. "I need to talk to someone."

"Would you like me to get the hospital chaplain?" the doctor asked.

"No. Thanks anyway. I want to talk to my father. He's a retired pastor," she answered.

Dr. Jeffries nodded.

"Can we see my dad?" Tim asked.

"By all means," the doctor said, standing to his feet and gesturing toward the door. "I'll take you to his room in the ICU."

They proceeded down several long corridors that eventually opened into a hub of activity. The ICU had a wheel-like shape, with a round nursing station at the center and a myriad of rooms that rayed outward like spokes.

Each room had glass windows facing the station, and a multitude of machines beeped steadily, monitoring patients in various cubicles. The doctor took them to the nurses' desk first and introduced them to the head nurse, Vivian Moore.

Vivian had a kind face, framed by a wreath of soft curls. Her compassionate spirit radiated from her large green eyes. Before taking them in to see John, she explained what they could expect.

"He is on several monitors right now, so there will be wires attached to his chest and his scalp. He has an IV with antibiotics and medication to reduce the swelling in his brain. Since he is unconscious and his eyes are closed, he'll look like he's asleep."

She led them into his cubicle. Tim could see tears immediately began to roll down his mother's face as she looked at her husband. He looked so cold and vulnerable there with all the wires, monitors, and IV lines. Where was the strong, intelligent man they both knew?

Vivian walked over to the side of his bed and put her face near his ear. In a rather peculiarly loud voice she said, "John, your wife and son are here to see you."

A moan came from somewhere inside of him.

"That is the only response we've been able to get from him," she said softly. "It's important to keep talking to him. Hearing is often retained in comatose patients. Perhaps your voices will stimulate more responses."

Vivian adjusted the sheets and blanket and then touched Sheila gently on the shoulder. She pointed to a young nurse, who was sitting in the corner of the cubicle by the foot of John's bed. "This is Sherrene. She will be here throughout the night. I'll be at the nurses' station if you need me." Then Vivian made eye contact with Sheila and added, "I'm praying for your husband."

Sheila sighed and embraced her. "Thank you so much. I needed to hear that."

After Vivian left the room, Sheila turned to Tim. "Go call Grandpa again. Tell him everything, and ask him to come. I need him here. And try Michelle again. Maybe a text will get through."

"Okay. I'll be back in a few minutes. Do you want me to bring you some coffee or something?"

"Coffee would be good. I'm not hungry, but I need something warm."

As soon as Tim was gone, Sheila walked over and pulled a chair up next to her husband. She sat down and took his hand in hers.

"I love you, John," was all she could manage before the tears started flowing again. There was no response on his face, but his thumb gently moved back and forth, caressing her hand.

"He's moving his thumb," she said to Sherrene.

"That could be a reflex, or he might be trying to tell you that he hears you," she replied.

Sheila was trying to remain composed, but she couldn't seem to hold back the flood of tears. Sherrene handed her a box of tissue. "Is there anything else I can get you?" she asked.

"No thanks. I just can't believe this is happening," she said between sniffles.

"I'm so sorry," the nurse said softly, and then added, "Your son seems like a great guy."

"Yes, he is. I don't know what I'd do without him," Sheila said, thinking about all they'd been through in the past few hours.

Tim walked in a few minutes later, carrying two cups of hot coffee. "I talked to Grandpa. He and Grandma are on their way. They said it would probably be the middle of the morning before they arrive. They've called the prayer chain at their church, and Grandpa says to tell you Jeremiah 29:11, whatever that means. He said you would know."

She smiled through her tears. "Yes, I know. He taught me that verse when I was in high school. It's a long story. Maybe I'll tell you someday."

"Okay. Well at least it made you smile," he said. "I texted Michelle. When do you think she and Steve will be back home?"

His question interrupted her flashback. "What?" she asked.

"When do you think Michelle and Steve will be home?"

"I don't know. Hopefully by the middle of the afternoon tomorrow. I wish we knew the name of that place they're staying in," she added. "I'm not even certain of the town, or we could call all the B & B's in that area."

"Maybe I should call the airlines and book her a late flight for tomorrow night," Tim suggested.

"That's a great idea, honey. Reserve two seats in case Steve is able to come with her."

"Alright. I'll go take care of that and then come back with something for you to eat. You've got to eat something, Mom, even if you're not hungry."

"He's right, Mrs. Ackerman. You'll need your strength," Sherrene added.

"Okay. I don't have the energy to fight both of you. Just bring something light, like a sandwich or something. Maybe you'd better take a cab back to the motel and get my car."

"There's a decent hotel across the street," Sherrene said. "Maybe you two should see if you can get a room there."

Sheila looked at Tim.

"I'll handle it, Mom. After I get the car, I'll get a room and pick up something for you to eat."

He took off, and Sheila was left gazing at her husband and feeling very lost and afraid.

Sylvia could not get John Ackerman off of her mind. All night long she kept recalling his downcast countenance when he left the law office. She felt compelled to pray for him each time she tossed or turned over in bed.

By morning she was convinced that she needed to go talk to him again. Perhaps there would be an open door to share the Lord with him, though she did not consider herself much of an evangelist.

Rather than calling on the phone, she decided to drive by the Redwood Lodge on her way to work. Maybe she would be able to talk him into having a donut and some coffee with her.

Since she wasn't sure which room was John's, she went to the office first. A middle-aged woman was sitting behind the counter talking on the phone. She told whomever she was talking to that she would have to call back later.

"Can I help you?" she asked in a very businesslike way.

"I'm looking for a man by the name of John Ackerman. He's staying here."

ROSEMARY HINES

"Well, actually, he's not here anymore," the woman replied evasively.

"When did he check out?"

"I guess you might say that he 'checked out' in the middle of the night."

"What do you mean, you guess?"

"Well, he didn't exactly walk in here and check out. He left in an ambulance. Gunshot wound," she added under her breath.

"Oh, no." Sylvia took a deep breath as she used the counter to help balance herself. "Was he alive?"

"Yes. They took him to St. John's Methodist."

"Okay. Thanks," Sylvia mumbled, pushing away from the counter and returning to her car. She pulled her cell phone out of the glove box and called her brother.

"Jeff, it's me. You know that guy, John Ackerman, who you talked to yesterday?"

"Yeah."

"Well, he's in the hospital with a gunshot wound. Either those people who were trying to frame him were pretty desperate, or he lost hope himself and decided to end it all. I'm heading over to St. John's Methodist to find out if he made it through the night. I don't know when I'll be in. Can you manage for a few hours?"

"Oh, man. Sorry to hear that. Yeah. I have that big meeting with Stanley Brothers, which will probably last until eleven. I'll have the switchboard downstairs pick up my calls until you get back. Leave me a message about Ackerman, and maybe I'll try to come by the hospital," Jeff said.

"Okay. I'll call as soon as I know anything," she promised.

224

Phil and Joan pulled into a roadside coffee shop for breakfast. They had been driving since two-thirty that morning and needed something to eat. The florescent lights of the restaurant were harsh and the yellow, orange, and brown patterned carpet was reminiscent of the '70s.

"Let's just grab a quick muffin and some coffee and get out of here," Joan suggested.

"Good idea," her husband agreed.

They ordered bran muffins and coffee to go and were back on the road in fifteen minutes. Bridgeport was only seventy miles away, so they would be there by nine-thirty. As they drove, Joan silently prayed for John, pleading with God to reach out to her son-in-law with the gift of salvation.

She thought about the fifty-three people who had been praying through the night, as the urgent prayer request for John had pressed through the church prayer chain. *Thank you, Lord, for prayer warriors who are willing to be awakened at all hours to stand in the gap for our loved ones,* she spoke silently to God.

His wife sat on a large boulder beside the lake, a fishing pole in one hand, her book in the other. Steve had refused to take no as an answer to his fishing quest, so she was trying to accommodate him while getting her reading done at the same time.

"This isn't exactly what I had in mind," he observed from his perch on a tree stump. "You're buried up to your ears in that book." *Why can't she just forget all that stuff for a while.*

"Sorry," she replied, then added teasingly, "Maybe the fish will keep you company."

Ouch. After a few minutes, he said, "Okay. Guess we'll call it a day. Nothing's biting anyway. Let's go back to our room and clean up for breakfast."

She smiled in agreement. They packed up the fishing gear and hiked back up the short, winding path to the bed and breakfast. As they approached the property, wonderful aromas of cinnamon and bacon wafted through the morning air.

"Smells like heaven to me," he commented with a smile, hoping to reconnect with her.

"Race you to the room!" she countered, taking off running. He looked down at the gear in his hands and shook his head as she disappeared into the inn.

Fifteen minutes later they were sitting at the dining room table feasting their eyes on the spread before them. One large platter was piled high with giant homemade cinnamon buns. Two quiches flanked the treats. One was a vegetarian recipe, and the other was filled with ham and three kinds of cheese. Plates with bacon and sausage were placed strategically around the table and each place setting had a small bowl of fresh fruit and a roll that looked like squaw bread.

The cook explained the various dishes and beckoned the guests to help themselves. Twelve people of various ages were seated around the table, and they began introducing themselves to each other as they passed the various dishes around. One of the other younger couples was from Southern California, so Michelle launched into a conversation with them.

As it turned out, the wife knew Kristin, Michelle's best friend, from a woman's Bible study at her church. Michelle seemed surprised to hear Kristin would be attending a Bible study, but she looked happy to meet an acquaintance of her friend. By the time breakfast was over, they'd exchanged addresses and phone numbers.

Out of a Dream

Afterward, she told Steve she wanted to go for a walk along the lake by herself. He felt a little concerned, but she said, "It's no big deal, Steve. I just want to be alone for a little while and soak up the scenery."

"Are you sure you'll be okay by yourself?" he asked. Michelle had never acted like this before. When it came to hiking or taking walks, she always wanted someone to go along with her.

She was really changing—becoming more independent and more distant. He didn't know what to think. Although he didn't want to become a jealous or suffocating husband, he didn't like the way she seemed to be pulling away from him and from their relationship.

"Don't be silly, Steve. I'll be fine. I'm a big girl," she laughed and winked as she strolled out the door.

"I see," Steve replied to the air after she was gone. He decided he would stay in the room and pray for her while she was gone. Maybe God would touch her with the beauty of creation during her little walk and use that as another seed to draw her back toward the faith she once possessed.

As Michelle walked along the path at the water's edge, she thought about many things: her marriage, her relationship with Trevor, and her father. *The men in my life,* she thought to herself, realizing they were the focal point of her mind on this walk, rather than the natural beauty she had sought to embrace.

She sat under a tree and tried meditating, but as she sat there all she could think about was the unsettling feeling she had about her father. It had stirred her to awaken in the middle of the night, and now it was coming back to haunt her. Something must be wrong.

She decided to try to tap into the power of universal consciousness that Trevor had told her about.

Maybe she could send vibrations of encouragement and hope to her father.

Twenty minutes later she felt as concerned and disconnected as ever. Try as she might, she couldn't seem to reach into this dimension. She wished Trevor was there to help her or to channel these powers to her father himself.

Meanwhile her husband was fervently interceding on her behalf, pleading with God to reopen her eyes to the truth.

CHAPTER TWENTY-FOUR

Sylvia arrived at St. John's Methodist and worked her way through the maze of corridors to the ICU. The front desk had informed her that she would be able to locate John Ackerman there.

Feeling awkward and like an outsider, she approached the nurses' station and spoke to a woman who seemed to be in charge.

"I've come to inquire about a friend, John Ackerman," she started.

"His wife and son are with him right now," the nurse replied. "Why don't you have a seat right over there, and I'll tell them you're here. What was your name again?"

"My name is Sylvia, but I don't know his wife or son. I just recently met John when he consulted with my brother, who is an attorney," she explained haltingly. "I know this sounds crazy, but when I heard he was in the hospital, I felt like I should come over and pray for him."

At that comment, the nurse smiled. "Sometimes God prompts us to do things we don't fully understand. John Ackerman can use all the prayers he can get."

Sylvia relaxed a little, realizing that she was in the company of another believer. "I've been really concerned about Mr. Ackerman since he left my brother's office. He seemed to have lost all hope in a matter that has been consuming his life."

"Sometimes those impossible circumstances are the only things that can bring us to our knees," the nurse said thoughtfully. "Would you like me to introduce you to his family, or would you prefer to just sit out here and pray?"

"I think I'll pray for a while. If his wife comes out, you can introduce us. But I don't want to interrupt her time with him. Besides, my brother is hoping to get by later, and maybe he can talk to her about his meeting with John. I'm just his secretary, so I'm not privy to all they discussed," she said.

"Make yourself comfortable, dear," the nurse replied with a warm smile. "It's always great to have a fellow prayer warrior in this ward."

Sylvia returned her smile and settled down on a soft crescent-shaped couch that rested against one of the curved walls. Bowing her head in silence, she fervently interceded for John Ackerman, praying that God would reach him and make Himself real to this man who so desperately needed His touch.

Phil and Joan paused momentarily before getting out of their car in the hospital parking lot. Grasping hands, they pleaded with God to set John free—free from his own bondage to independence, self-sufficiency, and pride.

They asked for wisdom to comfort their daughter and grandchildren, and boldness to speak the truth in love. They prayed for John's salvation first and foremost and for his complete physical healing as well.

Then they looked into each other's eyes, and went to face their greatest challenge—bringing light to someone trapped in darkness.

The receptionist at the information desk gave them a map of the hospital and showed them the path to the ICU. Walking hand-in-hand, they found their way to the large circular center.

It was relatively quiet that morning in intensive care. A nurse was doing some paperwork at the central desk, and a woman was sitting alone on the couch in what appeared to be a posture of grief or prayer.

Because of the glass walls facing toward the desk, it was clear that five beds were occupied. Before the nurse could address them, they spotted Tim heading out of the public restroom off to the side of the cubicles.

"Tim!" Joan cried.

They came together and embraced, Tim's eyes filling with tears. "It's okay, Son," Phil said, noticing Tim's embarrassment at his show of emotions. "You don't have to be strong for us."

"Take us to him," Joan said softly, using her thumb to wipe a tear that had escaped the corner of Tim's eye.

He led them into cubicle 4, and Sheila looked up with an expression of relief as she saw them enter.

"Mom, Dad," was all she could say before collapsing into their open arms. The three huddled together in a prolonged embrace as Sheila began to cry again softly.

"You'd think I'd be out of tears by now," she said.

"The Lord sees each tear, honey. He knows what you are going through," Phil replied with earnest genuineness, his own heart breaking as he held her.

"I know, Dad. He's been with me here."

Joan nodded and hugged her daughter tightly again. "He'll get you through this, baby."

"I just hope He can get John through it, too," she replied.

"We need to pray together for that, Sheila. Your husband needs God's touch on his spirit as well as his body," Phil explained.

"Please pray for him, Dad. I'm really worried," their daughter admitted, looking at him with the pleading look of a frightened and confused child.

Joan held her close while Phil walked over to the side of John's hospital bed. He looked down at the broken man who lay there helpless. His heart swelled with compassion, and he began to pray.

"Lord, I want to lift John to your throne of grace. Please reach down and touch him. In the midst of this darkness, send the light of your love into his heart and spirit. Remove the blinders of self-sufficiency and pride, and give him a new and clear view of you. Bring to his remembrance every word he has ever heard spoken about your Son. Take him to the foot of the cross and show him the way of salvation. Set him free to choose the path of life, and touch and heal the wounds in his body, mind, and spirit."

Phil was so focused on the urgency of his pleas that he did not see a tear that escaped from John's eye. Sheila saw it though and drew in her breath, looking over at her mother, who nodded, acknowledging that she, too, had seen it.

A sense of peace flooded Sylvia, and she looked up at Nurse Vivian. Their eyes met and communicated an unspoken, shared experience. Though neither of them could see John or the tear that signaled his response, it seemed they both knew in their spirits that God was at work in that cubicle, and that John would never be the

232

same again. In the spiritual battle for John's soul, a significant victory had been won. His heart and spirit were opening to God.

Without saying a word, Sylvia rose and walked out of the ICU. Her divine appointment was over.

Michelle and Steve packed their bags and took one last look around the beautiful room they had shared for the weekend. "Let's remember this place for our anniversary," he said.

"Good idea," she replied, resting one knee on the window seat and gazing out over the lake. "Let's request this room, too. I love this window seat."

"Yeah, I noticed," Steve said with a smile.

Michelle realized he was referring to all the time she'd spent sitting there reading. She gave him a mock evil eye and then threw one of the pillows from the window ledge, hitting him squarely in the face. For a brief moment she flashed back to her pillow fight with Trevor in the hotel room and their kiss afterwards. But Steve's voice brought her back to the present.

"Very funny!" he retorted. "I'll get you back when you're not expecting it!"

He walked over and hugged her, but she seemed a little stiff. "I'm just kidding!" he said with a smile.

Michelle's returned his smile, hoping he hadn't noticed her blush. "Yeah. Right."

"Are you okay?" he asked.

"I'm fine. Let's get this stuff packed and out of here before we have to pay for another night."

"Good plan," Steve replied.

After everything was packed, they headed out to the car. Steve did his usual routine of carefully placing each piece in the trunk in a specific and perfect fit.

"Let's see if they have any cookies left in the sitting room to take with us on the road," Michelle suggested.

"Okay. You get the cookies, I'll sign us out," Steve replied.

They found a plateful of freshly baked oatmeal cookies on the sideboard and the cook gave Michelle a bag to fill for the ride home. Steve paid the bill with cash, thanked the innkeepers, and told them how he and Michelle had really enjoyed staying there.

The drive home was quiet and peaceful, both Steve and Michelle lost in their own private thoughts. Sunshine tickled the leaves of the trees along the highway, and Michelle soaked in the cheerful scene. If only Oregon was sunny more often. It was so beautiful when the sun finally did come out. There was always a freshness in the air that she didn't remember from Southern California.

In what seemed like a short time, they were pulling into their driveway. Michelle had drifted off to sleep, but awakened as the car slowed to a stop. *I love this house,* she thought to herself, enjoying its homey and inviting appearance in the final spray of afternoon sun. She looked over at Steve and smiled.

He took her hand and squeezed it. "Here we are."

They got out of the car, and Steve began unloading the trunk. Michelle grabbed one of the bags, and he grabbed another. Walking into the kitchen, they were immediately assaulted by Max, who seemed indignant about their absence. He rubbed up against their legs and nearly tripped them with his weavings as he loudly chided them for being so neglectful.

"Get over it, Max," Steve said with a smile. "It looks like you've survived to tell the story."

The cat ignored his remark and gently bit Michelle on the ankle.

"Ouch! You little stinker!" she said, picking him up and kissing the top of his head.

"Oh, that will teach him," Steve observed teasingly.

"He's just a baby, Steve. He doesn't know any better," she said in Max's defense.

"I see. Well, I'll get the rest of the stuff from the car, and you check the answering machine. If Max will let you, that is."

"Funny," she replied. Walking into the family room, she pressed the play button on the recorder.

A familiar male voice came from the machine. "Steve, it's Roger. Call me at home. Nothing big, I just wanted to run by some information you'll need for the meeting Monday."

Next came, "Hi, Michelle, it's Monica. There was this great medium at the bookstore on Saturday. You would have loved her. She has amazing abilities to contact spirits. I bought her book. I'll tell you all about it when you get back. Give me a call."

And finally, "Michelle, it's Tim," Michelle's heart skipped a beat. Tim didn't usually call her on the house phone. "Something's happened to Dad. Call St. John's Methodist Hospital in Bridgeport." He rattled off the hospital phone number then continued. "We'll be in the ICU. Mom's here with me. We got you two tickets for a flight out of Portland on Northwest #312 leaving at eleven Sunday night. I'll meet you at the airport here at one-fifteen."

Michelle's mind was racing. "Steve! Get in here, quick!" she called.

He was just coming into the house with the last of their things. He dropped everything and went straight to her. "What is it?" he asked, visibly shaken by Michelle's expression.

"It's my dad, Steve," Michelle said, starting to cry. "Listen to this."

She pushed the repeat button on the answering machine, and Tim's message replayed. Steve stood there with his hand on Michelle's shoulder as he listened. "I'm glad they got two tickets. I'll call Roger and let him know I won't be in tomorrow."

She turned and clung to him, feeling like she might pass out. He guided her over to the couch. "Listen, Michelle. We don't really know anything yet. Let's call the hospital and talk to your mom."

Michelle just nodded, trying to stop the tears. As she retrieved her cell phone and turned it back on, she saw the text from Tim and the numerous missed calls.

CHAPTER TWENTY-FIVE

The doorbell rang, and Steve swung open the front door, hoping it wouldn't be a salesman. Monica was standing there. Her brown hair was somewhat disheveled, but her eyes were sparkling.

"I thought I'd better come by and check on Max, in case you guys weren't home yet. We wouldn't want him to miss his dinner!" she added with a dimpled smile.

"Come on in, Monica," he said, failing to smile in return as he gestured for her to enter.

"What's the matter, Steve?" Monica asked, concern creeping into her voice as she noticed his grim expression.

"Something's happened to Michelle's dad. She's on the phone with the hospital right now trying to get more information." They could hear Michelle's muffled voice in the other room.

Monica didn't seem to know what to say. Finally she just offered, "Is there anything I can do?"

"As a matter of fact, yes. We'll need you to look after Max and the house for a few more days. Michelle and I will be leaving out of Portland Airport on the red eye tonight. I'm not sure how long we'll be gone," he added.

"Hey, no problem. Max and I have become fast friends." Monica glanced at the cat, who was watching her from across the room.

"Thanks, Monica. I'll leave the hospital phone number on the refrigerator, and you've got Michelle's cell number in case you need to reach us. We'll call you from Bridgeport tomorrow. Here's some money, in case you need any more cat food or litter while we're gone," Steve said, handing her some cash.

Monica nodded. Then she asked, "Bridgeport? Isn't that in Northern California? I thought Michelle's parents lived in Orange County."

"They do. It's kind of a long story, but her dad is in a hospital up in Bridgeport right now." Since he didn't know much about it himself, he was relieved when she didn't press for more information.

"Okay, well I'd better let you get back to Michelle. Don't worry about Max or the house. I'll take care of everything," Monica said reassuringly.

"Could you bring in the mail and the paper, too?" Steve wracked his brain, making sure he covered all the details in case they ended up being gone for a week or more.

"Will do."

"Thanks. We'll let you know when we'll be back."

"Tell Michelle I'll be thinking about her," Monica offered as she turned to leave.

Steve was escorting her to the door when he heard Michelle's distressed voice calling him from the family room. Monica nodded for him to go to Michelle, and she let herself out.

He hurried to the family room. Michelle was rocking back and forth on the couch and crying. For a moment, Steve thought that John must be dead. He gently reached down and touched his wife's shoulder. She looked up at him, tears streaming down her face.

"Tell me what Tim said," Steve asked, trying not to panic.

"He shot himself, Steve," was all she could manage before her body was wracked with sobs.

"Oh, Michelle. No." He sat down beside her and cradled her in his arms. They both rocked together as he tried to comfort her. She buried her face in his chest and let the torrent of tears run dry.

As he held her tightly, confusion and sorrow for his wife gripped his heart like a vise. What could he say or do to help? Was this all partly his fault for not taking John's case more seriously and intervening? His head shook back and forth involuntarily as if trying to deny what he'd heard. Meanwhile Michelle continued to cry, murmuring "Why?" over and over as the tears flowed freely down her cheeks.

When her sobs finally receded into a black silence, Steve loosened his grip and looked into her eyes, searching for information.

"He's not dead, Steve. But they don't expect him to last long. We've got to go to Bridgeport right away. We've got to get to the airport."

Steve was relieved to hear that John was still alive, but distressed to learn the seriousness of his condition. "Let's throw a few more things in the suitcases in case we are there for a while. I'm glad Tim was able to book the flight." He pulled her back into an embrace and immediately started to silently pray. *Please God,* he pleaded in his heart, *let him live long enough for Michelle to get to the hospital and see him.*

A moment later Michelle pulled away from him again. "Who was at the door?" she asked.

"It was Monica. She came by to check on Max. She'll take care of him while we're gone."

"Okay, good," she said, looking relieved and overwhelmed at the same time.

"It's all worked out," he assured her. "We'll just repack our bags and I'll heat up some soup for dinner. I'll see if Roger can drive us to the airport, so we don't have to leave the car there." He wondered how Roger would manage the workload without him, but Steve knew he had to be with his wife.

"Okay," she said numbly as she stood to walk upstairs.

Steve carried their bags from the kitchen to the bedroom, and they worked together to sort clothes and repack for the trip. When they got finished, it was almost six o'clock.

"Ready to eat a little something?" Steve asked.

"I'm not really hungry. You can eat, though," Michelle answered, exhaustion and concern etching lines in her face.

"I'll heat the soup. Maybe you'll change your mind. In the meantime, why don't you just stretch out on the sofa under a blanket," he suggested, noticing the darkening skies outside.

He led Michelle downstairs and helped her get settled. Max jumped up on the couch beside her and inspected her closely. It seemed as if he could sense that something was wrong. She stroked his head. "You can keep me company, Max," she said softly. Tears oozed out of her lower lids. She closed her eyes tightly as if to shut out reality.

Steve shook his head. Looking at Michelle's puffy red eyelids and seeing the tears begin to escape out of the thick, closed lashes wrenched him. His heart ached. He handed her a tissue and kissed the top of her head. "Be right back," he told her.

While Steve was heating the soup, her phone rang. Michelle could feel her heart pound as she flipped it open, wondering if it was more news about her father.

"Hello?"

"Michelle? It's Trevor."

"Trevor?"

"Yeah. I just ran into Monica at the gas station and she said that something happened to your father,"

"It's really serious, Trevor. He tried to kill himself," she said, surprised to hear herself repeating this to someone outside the family.

"Wow. I'm sorry to hear that." Trevor seemed to be at a loss for words.

"Remember my dream about the river?" she asked him.

"Yeah. I was just thinking about it. Don't jump to any conclusions, Michelle. Let's think positive thoughts," he suggested. "Remember, the river might just symbolize some kind of big change or challenge. Your dad will need all the encouragement and good thoughts he can get. Maybe this crisis will bring positive changes into his life."

"Maybe." Michelle was not convinced.

"How bad is he?"

"All I know is that he's in intensive care. Steve and I will be flying down there tonight," she continued.

"I'll keep sending positive thoughts for you and your dad," Trevor added.

It sounded so hollow to Michelle. "Thanks, Trevor," was all she could say in return.

Just then, Steve came into the family room carrying a cup of hot tea for her. She turned to him and smiled weakly, then spoke into the phone, "I've got to go now. I'll talk to you when I get back."

"Okay. Take care, Michelle," Trevor said before hanging up.

"Who was that?" Steve asked curiously.

"Trevor," Michelle replied. "He saw Monica at the gas station, and she told him about my dad."

"Oh," Steve said. He gave her the tea then headed back toward the kitchen. "I'll be back with some soup in a minute. Just try to eat a little."

Their meal was a quiet one. Michelle sipped her soup and nibbled on the crackers, but she wasn't able to finish the small serving that he'd brought for her. He didn't push her to eat more, and she was glad. Her stomach was in knots.

After they were both finished, Steve collected the bowls, silverware, and glasses and told her to try to take a nap before they left. She could hear him rinsing the dishes and putting them in the dishwasher as she snuggled down under the afghan and closed her eyes.

In what seemed like a few minutes, he was gently rubbing her shoulder and saying, "It's time to go, honey. Roger is here to take us to the airport."

She sat up, rubbing her eyes, and noticed Steve's partner standing just inside the front door. She tried to smile. "Hi, Roger."

He gave her a compassionate look and returned her greeting. Then Steve helped her up and walked her to the stairs. "You go on upstairs and freshen up. Roger and I will get the bags in his car."

She nodded and walked up to their room. Her mouth felt cottony and her head ached. Walking into the bathroom, she caught sight of herself in the mirror. Her eyes were red and puffy with dark circles under them. There were streaks of mascara on her cheeks and her hair was a mess.

After brushing through the tangles, she pulled her hair back into a ponytail and proceeded to wash her face with cool water. It helped revive her, and she felt a little better when she looked back into the mirror and could begin to recognize herself. She brushed her teeth, threw on some makeup, and started back downstairs.

Roger and Steve were waiting for her. She glanced at the grandfather clock. They would have to hurry to get to the airport in plenty of time to get their tickets and seat assignments. Giving Max a quick kiss, she darted into the kitchen and grabbed a water bottle out of the refrigerator, then headed out the front door.

CHAPTER TWENTY-SIX

Roger dropped them off outside of the terminal. It had begun to sprinkle lightly, and they hurried inside. The airport was relatively quiet, as would be expected on a Sunday night. They had no problem checking their luggage, and getting their tickets and seat assignments before boarding.

Once settled on the plane, Steve sunk back into his seat and sighed.

"You must be exhausted," Michelle said as she noticed his drawn expression.

"I'm fine, honey." He reached over and squeezed her hand.

"Why don't you try to sleep during the flight?" she suggested.

"I might close my eyes for a few minutes. Will you be okay?" he asked.

"Yeah. I'm feeling a little better after that nap. I'll probably just look at one of these magazines," Michelle answered, reaching for one of the periodicals in the seat pocket in front of her.

As she absentmindedly paged through the glossy pages, she thought about her mom and what she must be going through. The daughter in her wanted to hurry up and get to the hospital, while another part wanted to run in the opposite direction. Could she bear to see her dad in this condition? Would she be able to keep it together for her mom or would she fall apart?

Realizing that she was unable to concentrate on reading the magazine, she put it back into the pocket and glanced over at Steve. His eyes were shut, and he was breathing in a slow, rhythmic manner. She reclined her seat and closed her eyes.

A picture of her father appeared on the screen of her mind. It was a memory from her wedding when he had presented her with a special wedding gift—a heart-shaped locket made of white gold. "In my heart, you will always be my little girl," he'd said with a tear in his eye. "Don't forget that, princess."

Thinking about that intimate moment brought fresh tears to her eyes. She could feel one escape under her closed lids and slip down her cheek. Hoping that no one had noticed, she brushed it away with the back of her hand. *Hang on, Daddy,* her heart pleaded as she willed the plane to hurry.

Back at St. John's Methodist Hospital, Sheila and her parents were keeping a bedside vigil. While still very grave, John's condition seemed to have stabilized somewhat. Vivian, the head nurse, smiled kindly as she spoke to them. "He seems to be holding his own. His vital signs are improving." Then she turned her attention to John. "Can you hear me, John?" she asked firmly, leaning over his bed.

There was no response. "Squeeze my finger," she persisted, placing her finger in his open palm. John's fingers made small jerking movements. "That's great, John. Good job," she said, adjusting his bed to elevate his head slightly. She removed the bandage on the right side of his scalp and replaced it with a clean gauze pad. There did not appear to be any fresh bleeding from the wound, and it looked relatively small and insignificant.

"Keep praying," Vivian smiled. "He's in there somewhere."

Sheila thanked her for the encouragement and for her tender care. "We couldn't have asked for better nurses," she added glancing at Sherrene as well.

"Just doing our jobs," Vivian replied, directing a smile to the other nurse, who nodded in agreement.

Michelle was standing on the top of a hill looking down over a vast valley. The soft afternoon breeze was blowing gently through her hair and the warm sun felt wonderful. She could see some sheep grazing on the lower parts of the hillside. As she soaked in the peaceful scene, a dark shadow caught her eye. Something was stalking the sheep. It was low to the ground and moved stealthily through the low brush. None of the sheep seemed aware of the imminent danger.

Michelle wanted to call out to warn them, but she had no voice. She waved her arms, trying to get their attention, but they continued to graze, innocently ignoring her gestures. Her heart started to pound as she saw the rapidly approaching threat to these gentle creatures. Her chest was rising and falling with each anxious breath as she sat fixated on the scene. Unable to help them herself, she pleaded in her mind, "Please save them."

Almost immediately a man stepped out from behind a large outcropping of rock. He threw a rock in the direction of the shadow. It froze momentarily then jetted away in the opposite direction, disappearing completely from sight. The sheep looked up at him and then calmly resumed their grazing.

The shepherd turned to Michelle and smiled. The good shepherd. All is well. Michelle was about to return his smile when she felt something touch her shoulder.

"Please return your seat to the upright position," a woman's voice said.

Michelle looked around, startled. "What? Oh. Okay." She leaned forward and pushed the button to bring the seat back up.

"You must have been dreaming. You were breathing pretty hard there for a minute," Steve commented after she got resettled.

"It was a weird dream, Steve. Peaceful, then scary, then the shepherd came and everything was fine," Michelle said rather incoherently as she tried to piece her dream together. "I think it's a good sign, though. The sheep were threatened, but the shepherd came and protected them. It kind of reminds me of the Bible stories Grandpa Phil used to tell me when I was little," she continued, and then paused before adding, "Maybe it means that God's power is with my dad."

"You might be right. Lots of people are praying for him," he replied. He explained that he had called Ben while she was napping after dinner and had asked him to put John onto their church prayer chain.

Michelle smiled. "Thanks, babe. You think of everything."

The plane began its descent into the airport. Steve took her hand in his while they waited for the wheels to make contact with the runway. The landing was smooth, and they were disembarking within minutes. He carried her carry-on and rolled his behind him, leaving her unencumbered except for her small purse. The aisles were not crowded on this late flight, so they exited quickly.

As they headed for baggage claim, Michelle spotted Tim standing with his hands in his jacket pockets. His usually shiny light hair was dirty and pushed back haphazardly from his face, and his eyes looked red and heavy. He pulled his right hand out of his jacket pocket and lifted it only to shoulder height as he waved to them, attempting a smile that rapidly faded back into an expression of exhaustion. Soon the three were embracing. Michelle felt worse than ever after seeing Tim's face. She wished she had the words to encourage him, to somehow lighten the burden he appeared to be carrying.

"How's he doing?" was all she could manage.

"About the same. He's not responsive."

"How's Mom?"

"She's holding up the best she can. Grandma and Grandpa are here. They arrived this morning."

"Oh, that's good. I'm glad they're with Mom," she added.

The airport was practically empty, giving her an eerie feeling as they walked silently through the large, open corridors. By the time they got to the baggage carousels, the suitcases were already waiting for them. Tim grabbed one and Steve got the other.

Her brother looked bone tired, his eyelids drooping as if from fighting sleep and his shoulders slumped forward. But he seemed to rally and do his best to fill them in on the events of the past twenty-eight hours. He described his discovery of the phone number, the call to the lodge that confirmed their father's location, and the nightmare they'd encountered when they finally arrived at Bridgeport.

As he spoke, Michelle thought about her mother. What must it be like for her to see her husband in this condition? She was thankful Tim had been with her throughout that long night and day. Knowing that their grandparents were at the hospital also comforted Michelle.

They loaded the luggage into the trunk of the car, and Michelle gestured for Steve to drive, but Tim insisted that he could make it and it would be easier for him to drive since he knew the way to the hospital. She climbed into the backseat, and Steve got in the front passenger side.

The highway and streets were empty at this hour. Steve and Tim made small talk for most of the drive to St. John's Methodist.

"How's work?" Tim asked.

"Fine. Busy as usual," Steve replied. "How about you? Still working at the same place?"

"Yeah. It pays the bills."

"I hear you."

Silence replaced their shallow conversation. They rode for at least ten minutes without a word being spoken. Michelle's stomach was twisting with anxiety. Her emotions vacillated between a sense of urgency to be with her father and a strange surreal sensation of being an outsider in someone else's drama. How could something of such magnitude seem so unreal? It was almost like she had become two people. One reacting, the other observing from a distance.

She noticed that her husband kept an eye on Tim, who appeared to be coming close to drifting off several times. All Steve had to do was clear his throat or cough slightly, and Tim's head nodded back to attention. After what was beginning to seem like an endless ribbon of highway, they finally arrived at the hospital.

Tim knew exactly where to park the car, and they walked in through the E.R. entrance, the only door open at three in the morning. The woman at the front desk looked up and smiled compassionately at them. Tim nodded in acknowledgement and then skillfully led them through the various hospital wings to the ICU.

Michelle was relieved to see her mother and grandparents still in the cubicle keeping vigil. Sheila sat in a chair beside the head of the bed, Grandma Joan in a chair next to her, and Grandpa Phil standing behind them both with his hand resting on Sheila's shoulder. An air of quiet solemnity pervaded the small glass room.

Michelle's heart swelled with love and concern when she saw how vulnerable her father looked, lying so still on his back with wires and IV lines connected to him in various places. Machines surrounded the head of his bed monitoring his vital signs. His skin looked pale and his face sagged, his chin and jaws darkened by unshaved stubble. Deep furrows etched his forehead and framed his mouth. His eyes were closed and appeared somewhat sunken in their sockets.

As they walked in, Sheila rose from her seat and embraced Michelle, guiding her to the head of the bed. "Why don't you sit here for a little while? You can hold his hand if you'd like." Michelle just nodded and sat down. Before she could ask how he was doing, her mother added, "There haven't been any changes. He seems to be resting comfortably."

The tiny cubicle was now crowded with people. Michelle and her grandmother were seated, but Sheila, Phil, Tim, and Steve were all standing along the wall beside the bed. "Let's give Michelle some time alone with her father," Phil suggested. "I think Sheila could use a little break. We can walk down to the cafeteria and come back in a little while."

Joan put her hand on her granddaughter. "Do you want me to stay here with you?"

"No. I'll be okay. You go with Grandpa and Mom."

"Okay, baby. We won't be gone long," her grandmother promised, rising to her feet and giving her a kiss on the cheek.

As soon as they were gone, Nurse Sherrene spoke from her chair in the far corner by the foot of the bed.

"Hi, Michelle," she began softly. Michelle turned to see her for the first time. "Your mom has been eager for you to get here. I'm going to get a refill for the IV solution. If you need anything, Vivian will be right there," she indicated, pointing to the woman at the nurses' desk. "It's okay to talk to your father," she added. "He might respond to your voice."

Michelle tried to smile and nodded. When Sherrene was gone, she reached over and took her father's hand. "Daddy?" she said softly. John's hand moved slightly, but his head did not turn. "Can you hear me?" Michelle asked, squeezing her father's hand gently.

Again, his hand moved in hers, but there was no other response. Not knowing what to say or do, Michelle sat quietly for a few minutes. Then she said, "I love you, Dad. I know we can get through this somehow. Fight. We need you."

At that point John's chest rose in a noticeable intake of air, followed by a deep sigh. Then he was still again.

A gamut of memories flooded Michelle's mind. Looking down at her father's face, she thought about the many times he had conveyed such strength and love to his family. Now what she saw was brokenness. Maybe it would help to talk about her happy memories. Maybe that would inspire him to press on and fight for his very life.

Beginning with her earliest memories from childhood, Michelle talked to her father about their life as a family. She reminded him of the day he rescued her from the scary dog in the park, the tea parties they used to have with her doll and teddy bear, the times he used to sit her on his lap and let her "drive" the car, the props he helped construct for the sixth grade play, the occasional camping trips as a family, and then the later years of interviewing her dates and finally walking her down the aisle when she married Steve.

John lay still throughout her recollections, with the exception of occasional movements of his thumb, which seemed to be rubbing her hand, especially after she would say something funny or particularly poignant. Despite his closed eyes and expressionless face, Michelle sensed that he heard every word. This prompted her to urge him on even more.

"I know you have been really upset, Dad. But you can't give up. There has to be an answer. We'll find the right attorney and get this mess straightened out. But you've got to hold on. You have to fight to live. Please, Daddy. We need you."

John Ackerman could hear his daughter pleading with him, but he couldn't answer her pleas. It was as if he were locked in a suit of metal armor that kept him perfectly still. Only his hand obeyed his commands to move. He hoped that she could feel his love coming through his touch. Never before had he felt so powerless, so out of control. A sense of desperation engulfed him. *Please help me*, his spirit cried out, not even knowing to whom he was calling.

Suddenly he felt himself being drawn into a tunnel. He experienced a sensation of acceleration and then a strange phenomenon of weightlessness and freedom.

The steady beeping sound of the heart monitor became erratic and then switched to one continuous tone. Within seconds, Vivian was in the cubicle pressing buttons and calling out "Code blue, ICU 4" over a speaker. She quickly told Michelle to wait outside and began working on John. As Michelle fled out the door, two male nurses appeared from nowhere pushing a loaded cart and racing into the cubicle.

Michelle could not see what was happening, but she knew her father was dying. "Please, God. Save him!" she cried earnestly, tears flooding her eyes as she paced back and forth. "Don't die, Daddy. I need you!" she repeated, over and over, under her breath. What seemed like an eternity later, Vivian came out and intercepted her pacing.

"It's okay. We've got him stabilized again. You can go back in," she added, looking compassionately into Michelle's eyes.

Without thinking, Michelle collapsed into her arms sobbing. Vivian soothed her, stroking her hair and saying, "It's okay. Let it all out." Michelle cried for several minutes, unable to stop herself. She was wiping her nose on the back of her hand when Vivian offered her a tissue.

As Michelle blew her nose and wiped her eyes, she saw the rest of the family return to the ICU. Michelle's mom looked at her with a panicky expression. "He's okay, Mom," Michelle said, her voice still shaky.

Steve started to go to his wife, but Phil put out his hand and stopped him. "Let me talk to her," he said to his grandson-in-law.

While the rest of the family moved in the direction of cubicle 4, Phil walked over and took Michelle's hand. "Let's go for a little walk, pumpkin," he said affectionately. "Your brother needs some time with your dad."

Michelle sniffed and tried to dry her eyes with what was left of the tissue. Phil pulled a handkerchief out of his pocket and handed it to her. "These things still come in handy," he said with a wink, and a nervous giggle escaped from Michelle. After she'd wiped her eyes and blown her nose, Grandpa Phil put his arm around her shoulder and led her out of the ICU.

She leaned against him while they walked, feeling his steadfastly solid strength of character, compassion, and faith. Though she loved her father deeply, Grandpa Phil held a piece of her heart that no other man could claim. His sense of humor, generous and loving nature, and constant faith evoked a tenderness and respect in Michelle that grew deeper and deeper over the years. It had been a long time since she'd been alone with him, and she was deeply grateful for this opportunity to be in his calming presence.

The crisis with her father magnified her sense of confusion about the meaning and purpose of life. She wanted to talk to her grandfather and give him the opportunity to help her sort through her thoughts and experiences over the past year. But another part of her hesitated. She knew that he could never fully understand some of the things she had been exploring and learning.

For the time being, she just wanted to lean on him and let him take her away from the horror of her father's condition. She walked along beside him without saying a word, as they headed down a long, shiny corridor toward the hospital chapel.

Tim sat back in the chair beside his father's bed, his elbows resting on the metal arms. He felt awkward as he glanced around the room. It was his first time to really be alone with his dad, and he wasn't even sure he should be there. But Grandma had convinced Mom and Steve to go for a short walk with her so he could have this time.

The steady beeping of the heart monitor momentarily skipped a beat, and Tim sat upright, clutching the arms of the chair. Within a couple of seconds, his father's heart resumed its normal rhythm again. Tim glanced through the doorway but did not see any added concern on Sherrene's face. Apparently the momentary change in the heart rate did not alarm her.

Relaxing back in the chair again, Tim thought about how strong his dad had always seemed to him throughout his childhood. He remembered his father's stern voice and sometimes overbearing presence. But he also remembered the feeling of safety in his father's arms when he used to climb up onto his lap and watch a football game or listen to a story.

How on earth did this happen? he thought to himself as he stared at his dad.

Tim closed his eyes and leaned his head back against the wall. Scenes from his childhood came rushing back to him. A game of miniature golf on a Sunday afternoon. A hike through a section of Yosemite Valley on one of their few family vacations. A weekend fishing trip with his father and the Boy Scouts. Like magic moments frozen in time, Tim collected his special memories with his father.

Where did we lose touch with each other? he wondered as he opened his eyes and gazed at the still body of his father once again.

Tim stood up and moved closer to the bed. "Dad?" He placed his hand on his father's shoulder. No response.

He was just about to turn and sit back down when he saw his father's hand lift slightly off the bed.

A wave of emotion washed over Tim. He placed his hand on his father's hand. "You've got to make it through this, Dad."

His father took a deep breath. It jolted Tim. "Dad? Can you hear me?"

The air rushed back out of his father's lungs. Silence. Then he resumed his steady, shallow breathing.

Anxiety and regret battled for Tim's attention. Every little change in his father's heart rate or breathing could signal the end. Would Tim ever get a chance to make things right with his dad?

I need you, Dad. Don't leave us. The words seemed trapped in his throat, but he knew this might be his last chance to talk to his father.

"Uh…Dad… I've got some stuff to tell you." He paused as he looked down into his lap, searching for the right words. "I know I haven't always been the best son." He sighed and then continued. "I guess I've been kind of stubborn. Anyway, what I'm trying to say," Tim looked up at his father's face, "is that I'm sorry." He paused again and then added, "I love you, Dad."

John took another deep breath. At that very moment, Tim resolved to work through his issues with his dad and rebuild their relationship, if he ever got the chance.

CHAPTER TWENTY-SEVEN

The chapel was a small, quiet room with several beautiful watercolor scenes on the walls depicting the countryside of Israel. There were a multitude of lush plants on the altar. A simple, but large cross hung from the ceiling in the front. Across it was engraved the verse, "Peace I give unto you."

Michelle and her grandfather sat down in the front pew. They were both silent for a time, as Michelle thought about her father and all that had happened. Thankfully, there was no one else in the room.

Michelle's grandfather took her hand in his. "Do you remember the stories I used to tell you about the shepherd and the sheep?"

Her heart leapt, remembering not only the stories, but also her dream on the airplane. "Yes, Grandpa. I remember," she replied. "I had a dream about sheep on the airplane on our way here. It was kinda scary. They were grazing on a hillside when a dark shadow of something began creeping toward them. I tried to call out and warn the sheep, but I didn't have a voice. Then, when I was convinced they would be killed, a man stepped out from behind some rocks and drove the darkness away."

Grandpa Phil nodded. "You know, Michelle, the Lord never takes His eyes off of us. Just like the shepherd diligently guards his flock, God is always watching over us. Even now." He squeezed her hand as if to emphasize that last thought.

"Then what happened to Dad? Why didn't God stop him from doing this?" she asked, looking squarely into her grandfather's eyes. "Things like this make me doubt that God is the good shepherd you talk about."

"Listen to me, Michelle. God was there when your father shot himself. But your dad has been running from the Lord all his life. He has prided himself in his own success and self-sufficiency." She nodded, and he continued, "Sometimes it's hard for an intellectual like your father to realize his own weaknesses and needs. Maybe the only way God could break through to him was to let this happen."

"You think so, Grandpa?"

"It's possible, honey. You know, God loves us enough to give us the free will to make our own choices. But ultimately, He yearns for us to choose Him—to choose the eternal life He designed for us. Do you understand what I'm saying?"

She looked into her grandfather's eyes. They were filled with compassion, not judgment. She nodded her head again and looked back down to the floor. She knew he spoke with heartfelt sincerity, but she also knew that many of the things she had been learning in her BlendTherapy class seemed valid, too. From what she'd seen and heard, Trevor was as convinced about his beliefs as Grandpa was about his own. While a part of her yearned for the simple faith of her childhood, she was confused and uncertain about what to believe.

"Grandpa?" she began as she twisted her hair nervously.

"Yes, darlin'?"

"Have you ever wondered if there might be more to life than knowing and serving the God of the Bible?" she asked tentatively, looking down at her lap instead of making eye contact.

"What do you mean?" he asked.

"I mean, like maybe it's more complicated than that. Maybe God isn't really like a person, but more like a force in the universe, some kind of power that everyone can tap into," she said, trying to explain. The more she struggled to put it into the words, the more she realized how vague it must sound to him.

"It's hard to explain, Grandpa. It's just that I wonder if maybe there is something to the New Age ideas that I've been learning about in Oregon," she concluded.

"Well, kiddo, I don't profess to know everything about New Age ideas, but I can tell you that there really isn't anything 'new' about them. Where do you think ideas like reincarnation and karma come from?" Phil asked.

"I guess most of them come from Eastern religions."

"Right. Those religions have been around for centuries, Michelle. Now let me ask you an important question," he added, lifting her face and looking into her eyes. "Who do you think Jesus is?"

"Well, I used to think He was… like… a part of God. But now I wonder if He was really just another great teacher, like Buddha and Mohammed." Her voice quivered, and she glanced downward again.

"Maybe you should know what Jesus said about Himself," her grandfather replied.

"What did He say?" she asked looking up again.

"He said that He was the Son of God and that He was the only way to the Father. That's pretty serious stuff, honey. The Jewish religious leaders tried to stone Him for claiming to be deity. Once you've studied Jesus' teachings and what He said about Himself, you realize either He really is God or He was a con artist or a deluded lunatic."

Grandpa Phil squeezed her hand again. "Unless you completely ignore what Jesus said, you can't label

Him as just a good teacher and put Him on the same level as Buddha or Mohammed."

Michelle nodded.

"Don't accept the teaching of your friends without really thinking about that and reading Jesus' own words yourself." He lifted her chin again and looked into her eyes. "None of the New Age ideas you have been learning can offer you the hope that you will find in the pages of this book," he said, gesturing to the worn leather Bible on the bench beside him. He took a deep breath and continued. "You've probably never thought of it this way, Michelle, but when you get right down to it, New Age thought is based on the idea of creating your own god."

"What do you mean?"

"I mean that most people who follow the New Age perspective are really just creating a religion of their own—making a god that fits their own views. What do your teachers tell you about the world religions?"

She thought for a moment before replying. "I guess they say that there is good in every religion; that we should choose the good parts of each and reject the parts that don't fit for us."

"That's what I mean. Can you see how this is like making your own god? It's a god fashioned after your own opinions and desires. It's a god who lets you live any way you want without consequences. While that may be fine when life is going along smoothly, how can you run to that kind of god for wisdom in a situation like you're in now with your dad? Those gods don't know any more than you do."

He paused as if to let his words sink in. Michelle sat still, staring toward the cross.

Her grandfather placed his arm over her shoulder and continued. "Honey, man has been trying to understand God since the beginning of time. All kinds of ideas and practices have evolved throughout the world from those attempts."

She nodded. "So how do we know which ideas are right, or that there is only one path to God?"

"That's why God came to earth, putting on humanity in the form of His Son, Jesus. He became flesh so that we could really know Him. And through His death on the cross, He opened the gates of heaven so all who believe could spend eternity with Him."

Michelle listened silently, staring down at the floor.

Her grandfather continued, "I know that New Age philosophy says all paths lead to God. But what did Jesus say about it, Michelle? He said, 'I am the way, the truth, and the life. No one comes to the Father except by Me.'"

"It just sounds so narrow, Grandpa," she countered.

"Yep. It does sound that way, because it is. Remember that verse from Matthew where Jesus said, 'the way is narrow that leads to life'? Even though it may seem unfair, it's important to remember that *everyone* is invited to take that path. It doesn't matter if you're rich or poor, what your ancestral lineage is, or whether you've lived an exemplary life or one filled with mistakes—all are welcome to come to God through Jesus. Anyone can have open access to God, just by recognizing and believing that Jesus' death paid the penalty for sin."

"But don't you think that it's possible Christianity is just a step along the way to personal enlightenment?" she asked earnestly.

He paused and then replied. "No, Michelle. It is not a step along the way. It is *the way*. Besides, what is personal enlightenment, anyway? If God is the most enlightened being in the universe, do your teachers believe that you can become as enlightened as Him? If so, they are teaching the same lie as the serpent in the Garden of Eden—that you, too, can be as God, knowing all things."

She didn't say anything.

He gently turned her face toward hers. "Why don't you tell me more about what you've been learning?"

"Well, I've learned about the importance of personal evolution—always growing to new levels of understanding and awareness. I've learned some things about psychic energy and power through yoga, meditation, and certain tools like the tarot cards. And I've been studying dream interpretations, to help me uncover the hidden messages of my dreams."

While she spoke, she felt that the words sounded somehow childlike or naïve, yet she knew the experiences and lessons she was trying to explain had impacted her life over the past year. Why did they sound almost silly when she tried to explain them to her grandfather?

Groping for words, she continued. "Weird things have been happening to me, Grandpa."

"Like what?"

"Like I have these vivid dreams and they seem to have messages in them, almost like they are trying to teach me something."

Phil nodded, looking at her closely.

"And my yoga teacher reads tarot cards. When she read them for me, I asked her about what would happen with Dad's lawsuit. She spread out the cards and the one in the center was the death card. It was a skeleton holding a scythe. Later I dreamed that Dad was drowning in a river, and I couldn't get to him. Now all this happens. It's almost like I can see into the future." She was twisting her hair as tears clouded her vision.

He wrapped his arm around her. "Oh, sweetheart," he said softly. "Dreams can be peculiar creatures. My guess is that your worries about your father triggered that one."

Michelle just nodded as she tried to inconspicuously brush away her tears.

"Sometimes dreams *do* hold special messages. Maybe you remember some of the dreams in the Bible stories we used to read together. God can use dreams to teach us more about ourselves or about the events we have encountered or are about to experience. But most of the time, dreams are just our mind's way of trying to help us sort out our thoughts and fears."

"What about the tarot cards, Grandpa? Why do you think they were so accurate?" She looked up and listened intently.

"I think there are spiritual forces that give power to the tarot cards, Michelle, but I don't think they are godly forces, honey."

Even though Michelle was reluctant to admit it, she knew what her grandfather was saying could be true.

"What you've been studying and exploring is intriguing, but it's not the answer you're looking for. While I don't discount your experiences, I believe they are, at best, a weak substitute for the truth." He paused and leaned toward her. He looked into her eyes with an expression of great tenderness and added, "I love you, kiddo. There's no way I can sit here and nod at what you're saying without giving you my perspective."

"I know, Grandpa. And as much as I'd like to say that I'm right there with you on what you believe, I guess I still have more sorting out to do first," she replied, hoping he'd understand.

"Think it all through carefully, Michelle. There is no other path to the peace that God can offer. Real peace will come when you let the *real* God of the universe be the God of your life—when you take Him at His word and lean on Him for your strength and for your guidance."

He looked her in the eye and continued. "Remember, none of us is guaranteed a tomorrow. Today may be your day to decide whether or not to follow Jesus. If you are sincere about wanting to know the truth, God will show it to you. I have no doubt about that." He smiled and gently embraced his granddaughter.

"I hope you're right," she said, returning his smile. Then she asked, "What do you think will happen to Dad?"

"I don't know, sweetheart. I'm praying for a miracle. But more important than that, I'm praying your father will come to his own understanding of the truth. If he survives this, he'll really need the Lord. And if it's his time to go, I want him on the right path." He paused and then added, "Your mom says that the doctor wants to put him on what they call 'no code'."

"What does that mean?" she asked.

"It means they won't resuscitate him if his breathing or heart stops. Dr. Jeffries doesn't think it's in your dad's best interests to keep him alive like that," Grandpa Phil tried to explain. "He wants to have a meeting with us tomorrow afternoon. Actually, I guess it's *this* afternoon," he added, glancing down at his watch.

"What do *you* think, Grandpa?"

"I believe that your father should be given every opportunity to recover. We'll discuss it together as a family, along with the doctor. In the meantime, you're looking awfully tired, honey. Why don't you just rest your head on my shoulder and relax for a few minutes?"

"Don't you think we should get back to the ICU?" she asked hesitantly.

"You know, Michelle, your brother has not had any real time alone with your father since he got here. Tim's been so busy looking after the details of taking care of insurance forms, finding food and coffee for your mother, and getting you here from Oregon, that he's had no opportunity to sit there alone with your dad. I think we should give him more time." He wrapped his arm around her and gently pulled her head to rest on his shoulder.

She understood what he was saying and knew that he was right. Closing her eyes, she leaned against him, listening to his steady breathing and feeling herself melt into his embrace. Gentle memories of childhood snuggles and stories of the Good Shepherd enveloped her and gave her a peace she'd almost forgotten.

Trevor could not get Michelle out of his mind. He thought about their weekend together at the conference and her incredible, positive energy. Though she was growing rapidly in her grasp of personal evolution, there was so much potential she had not tapped into yet. At a time like this, with her father in critical condition, there were many tools he could give her that might be helpful, not only to Michelle, but to her father as well.

He picked up the phone and dialed Monica's number.

"Hello?" came a male voice from the other end, surprising Trevor who expected Monica's husband to be gone to work by eight-thirty in the morning.

"Hello," Trevor began. "Is Monica there?"

"Who's this?" asked the man.

"This is Trevor Wind. I'm trying to get a hold of a mutual friend of ours named Michelle," he added to counter the suspicious tone of voice he heard on the other end.

"Just a minute," came the reply.

A few moments later Monica was on the line. "Hi, Trevor. What's up?"

"I've got some things I want to send to Michelle. They might help her right now. Her cell phone is going straight to voicemail whenever I call."

"I don't think she's taking any calls, Trevor. I can tell you the name of the hospital if that's any help, but I don't have the phone number here. It's on their refrigerator in case I need to reach them about their cat I'm babysitting," she added.

"Oh, okay. Give me the name of the hospital. I can get the phone number from the Internet," replied Trevor. He grabbed a paper and pen.

"Okay, it's St. John's Methodist Hospital. It's in the Bridgeport area of California."

"St. John's Methodist. Got it. Thanks, Monica," he added.

"You're welcome. Oh, and Trevor, if you get a hold of her, tell her that I decided to bring Max here for a few days so he won't be so lonely."

"Max?"

"Yeah. He's their cat."

"Okay. I'll tell her. Thanks again, Monica. See you Thursday."

"Okay, bye."

Trevor set the phone down, logged onto the computer, and looked up the hospital's phone number. He walked over to an oak filing cabinet and pulled open the top drawer. While he called the hospital, he glanced over the tops of the file folders, looking for specific articles.

"Here's a good one," he said aloud, pulling out a file that read, "Healing Through Guided Imagery".

In it were several articles about the supernatural powers of healing that can be released by visualizing the tissues in the body repairing themselves. Also in the folder was a meditation he had been given during his studies at the Wellness Institute in Spokane. "These might help her," he muttered under his breath.

After several rings, a young woman's voice answered, "St. John's. How may I direct your call?"

"I'm not sure," he began. "I'm looking for the daughter of John Ackerman. He is a patient there."

"One moment, please." There was a pause, and then she continued, "Ackerman. He's in the ICU. There are no phones in those rooms, but I can transfer you to the nurses' station."

"Thank you," Trevor replied. He tried to imagine Michelle in the clinical setting of a hospital intensive care ward. She was so sensitive and fragile. He ached to be there with her.

His mind was brought back to attention when a nurse in the ICU answered the phone a moment later.

"ICU. Vivian speaking."

"Ummm, I'm looking for the daughter of a patient there," he started to explain.

"Name of the patient please?"

"John Ackerman."

"You must be looking for Michelle," she replied.

"Yes. I want to send some information to her. Do you have a fax number I could use?"

"Yes, we do." She proceeded to give him the number. "Would you like to speak with Michelle?"

"I really don't want to bother her, but I thought she might appreciate these files. They might be able to help with her father."

"Are you family?"

"No, just a friend. You can tell her Trevor called. Tell her I'm faxing some things to her."

"Are you sure you don't want to talk to her? She's just coming back in from the cafeteria," she said.

"Okay, if you don't think I'd be bothering her."

"Here she is."

"Hello?" Michelle's voice sounded weak.

"Hi, Michelle. It's me, Trevor."

"Trevor? How did you know where to find me?"

"Monica gave me the name of the hospital. Oh, and she told me to tell you that she took your cat over to her house so he wouldn't be so lonely."

"Oh, she didn't have to do that," Michelle replied, but her voice gave away her appreciation for Monica's thoughtfulness.

Trevor continued, "Well anyway, Michelle, I'm calling because I have some articles that I thought might help you and your dad, and I want to fax them to you."

"Okay. Did the nurse give you a fax number?"

"Yeah. I'll send them as soon as we get off the phone."

"Alright. I'll be waiting for them. Thanks for thinking of me, Trevor."

"I think about you all the time, " he admitted. He heard her take a deep breath and let it out. "Are you holding up okay?" he asked, wishing he could be there with her.

"I'm fine. It's my dad I'm worried about. He's in a coma, Trevor. The doctor thinks we should put him on 'no code'." Her voice was quivering.

"Before you do anything, read through this material," he urged. "Maybe it will help."

"Okay. Thanks."

He could hear a man's voice in the background talking to Michelle. *Must be Steve.*

Her voice spoke again. "I've got to go."

After hanging up the phone, Trevor arranged the articles in a stack and fed them into his fax machine. He punched in the hospital fax number and sent them off. Then he grabbed his helmet and headed out the door to take a ride along the coast. He needed to escape his apartment and clear his head. Maybe he'd also drop by the bookstore later and talk to Starla for a while. She could always help him regain his center.

Michelle had some kind of pull on him that was consuming his mind and energies. He needed to get a grip and refocus.

CHAPTER TWENTY-EIGHT

Michelle was sitting by her father's bedside. The rest of the familyhad gone tothe cafeteria for a quick lunch, and they were bringing back a sandwich for her.

While she listened to the steady beeping of the monitors, she looked through the papers Trevor had faxed to her. Although she was exhausted from lack of sleep and little to eat, she didn't want to miss out on anything that might help her father.

Vivian had left early that morning and was replaced by a drill sergeant of a nurse named Stephanie. She was very businesslike and efficient, but lacked the warmth and compassion that had helped sustain all of them throughout the long night.

Sherrene had also gone home, and a nurse from cardiac care was substituting for her usual day replacement. Brittany was in her thirties, a young mother of three, who connected well with Michelle. She was also interested in mysticism and New Age philosophies and was helping Michelle sift through the various articles and information from Trevor.

"You know, I've heard a lot about healing through imagery," Brittany said with enthusiasm as she read the top page from the stack. "There is a center in Arizona that teaches this. Oh yeah—here's the information about that place."

"So what does it say to do?" Michelle asked with a hopeful expression.

"Well, basically, you just imagine the various cells that have been attacked by disease or damaged by injury, and you begin to see them repairing themselves."

"You just do it all in your mind?"

"Yeah. It sounds crazy, but there are terminal cancer patients who have been completely cured through this type of therapy."

"But weren't those people doing the imaging themselves?" Michelle asked.

"I think you're right. But here's an idea. You could talk to your dad about all of this, and even though he can't answer us right now, maybe he'll try to follow your directions in his mind. It couldn't hurt to try. We don't know how our own thoughts can impact physical matter. Think about those guys who can actually move heavy furniture from across a room just by thinking thoughts to move it."

"Yeah. I've heard about that. Well, I guess it's worth a try," she agreed.

Michelle leaned over her father's bed. She began speaking positive thoughts into her father's mind, hoping that he would hear and think the healing images she was describing. There was no response from John. He remained totally still, not even moving his fingers. It was as if he was sinking deeper and deeper into his coma.

After several minutes, Michelle sat back and sighed. As if Brittany could see the discouragement written all over her face, she touched Michelle's arm and said, "Give him time. He'll come around. Just keep thinking positive thoughts."

Michelle nodded and turned her face away, not wanting the nurse to see her eyes filling with tears again. Positive thoughts escaped her like a vapor. She was almost totally lost in fear and despair.

Help me, she cried out in her mind.

"I will," replied a still small voice from somewhere in her spirit.

Instantly a picture of the shepherd from her dream flashed across the screen of her mind. Michelle could see a depth of compassion in His eyes that penetrated to the darkest part of her soul.

It was three in the afternoon and the sun filtered in through the metal mini-blinds in the hospital conference room. Sheila, Phil, Joan, Michelle, Steve, and Tim were all seated around the massive oblong table with Dr. Jeffries at the head position. A cold draft from the air conditioning caused Michelle to shiver and Steve reached over, placing his arm around her and drawing her up against his side.

Dr. Jeffries had spread out John's various test results in the center of the table for everyone to see. "I've consulted with several other neurosurgeons on staff here including the chief of neurosurgery, and they have all conferred with my evaluation of John's condition," he began. "We all came to the same conclusion," he continued solemnly. "We believe that the most appropriate response is to place him on a 'no code' status."

He paused as various members of the family shifted in their chairs and searched each other's faces for reactions. No one said a word, but volumes were spoken by their expressions alone. Dr. Jeffries continued, "From what the nurses and his chart tell me, John suffered respiratory arrest during the early morning hours. He was resuscitated and returned to his prior level of unconsciousness. There has been no significant improvement in his condition; in fact he seems to be slipping deeper into the coma."

Sheila began to weep quietly, and Phil handed her a handkerchief, rubbing her shoulders gently in an attempt to reassure her.

"I know that this is a tremendously difficult decision for you to make," he said looking at Sheila. "But have you had a chance to discuss it as a family?"

"Not really. Is there some reason why it is critical for us to make this decision right away?" she asked.

"It's been my experience that the longer you keep a loved one on full code, the harder it is to decide to change their status. Watching someone hang onto life can give a false sense of hope for recovery."

"Are you saying that it's not possible for John to recover from his injuries?" Phil asked.

"Nothing is impossible," Dr. Jeffries said, turning to Sheila's father. "But the complete recovery of someone in John Ackerman's condition is very unlikely."

"I think you're underestimating my dad," Tim said sitting forward in his chair and looking Dr. Jeffries squarely in the eye.

"That may be, but think about this. Compounding the multiple injuries to your father's brain is the likelihood that his will to live is marginal, considering the circumstances leading to his injury."

Tim just shook his head as if to shake off what he had just heard. He ran his fingers through his dirty, disheveled hair, and slumped back into his chair.

Looking around the table at each family member, Dr. Jeffries added, "Let me ask all of you this question. What kind of man would you describe John to be?"

It was silent in the room for a few moments, and then Sheila spoke. "My husband has always been a pillar of strength. He is hard-working and independent. A self-made man. And he is a loving husband and father, who

273

always put his family first." Her voice began to waver, as Michelle reached out and took her hand.

"Mom's right," agreed Tim. "Dad has always been a determined guy with a strong sense of responsibility."

Michelle nodded, looking at the doctor and twisting a piece of her hair until it was a tightly woven strand.

"All right," began Dr. Jeffries. "Let's think about what you are saying in relation to his current condition. We're dealing with someone who is used to being strong and independent, right?"

Several heads nodded in agreement.

"How do you think he would feel about a life of weakness and dependency?" he continued, pausing to let the question sink in.

Michelle started to cry again softly, and Steve pulled his chair closer so he could comfort her. It was clear where Dr. Jeffries was going with his question. No one in the room could say that John Ackerman would gracefully accept the life of an invalid, should it come to that.

"Here's another question for you. You say that he is very loving and would always want what's best for his family. You, his family, would like to hold on to him, which is perfectly normal. But would he think it was best for you to have to care for him for the rest of his life, should he live a normal life span in a crippled body?"

He tried to make eye contact with each person at the table, but many of them were avoiding his glances as much as they were trying to avoid his questions.

"Dr. Jeffries," Phil spoke up, "we are all trying to understand your perspective on John's condition, but you need to understand ours. Yes, we are trying to hold on to him, but it is not just for ourselves. As you know, human life is complex and there are many layers to consider. I, for one, am concerned for John's spiritual condition as well as his physical one. In my opinion, God is not finished with His work in a person's life as long as that person is alive. Perhaps there is unfinished business that needs attending to. Who are we to rush that process?"

"In all fairness to your issues, I'm not proposing terminating a life here. I'm just suggesting that we reconsider prolonging the dying process," said Dr. Jeffries.

"I understand that, doctor. I just think we all need more time to discuss the implications of the decision you are proposing," Phil responded.

"That's fine. But here's another consideration," he said, turning once again to Sheila. "Your husband's driver's license indicates he's an organ donor. He'd be a perfect candidate for that, Mrs. Ackerman. He appears to be in good health overall, and donating his organs could save several lives, not to mention the possibility of restoring sight to someone who needs corneal transplants. It's not up to me to determine the timeline for your decision. But you should know that healthy tissue can deteriorate over time in a comatose patient," he added as he gathered up the paperwork on the table and rose from his seat.

Continuing to address his comments primarily to Sheila, he said, "Again, I'm sorry you are facing such a tough decision. And we will honor whatever your family wishes. Your husband's care will not be compromised if you choose our 'no code' recommendation. It will only mean that we will allow your husband to die peacefully if his heart or lungs fail."

Sheila nodded.

"The nurses in the ICU can page me any time if you have any other questions or whenever you arrive at a decision," Dr. Jeffries concluded.

Michelle and her mom sat in a booth sipping coffee in the brightly lit coffee bar just inside the main lobby of the hospital. Phil and Joan were resting on the couches in the ICU, and Tim and Steve had decided to take a walk. John was stable for the time being, and it was time for everyone to take a break and sift through their emotions and options.

"Grandpa and I had a good talk," Michelle began, cupping her hands around the steaming mug in front of her. She'd been having a hard time getting warm ever since that chill in the conference room. Though she felt awkward about it, she wanted to discuss with her mother the spiritual questions that were replaying in her mind.

"What do you think about what Grandpa said to Dr. Jeffries? Do you think God is doing something in Dad's life through all of this?" Michelle asked.

"I really don't know, Mimi. Your grandfather has a strong faith that I've admired for as long as I can remember. He talks to God as if he could see Him face to face," Sheila said, grasping for words.

"What about you, Mom? What do you believe?" Michelle asked in earnest.

Her mother slumped back in her chair. "That's a good question, Michelle. I guess I'd say that I believe there is a God, and I'd like to believe that He really does hear prayers and is able to help us. As far as Him doing a work in your father's life through this mess, it sure would make it easier to bear if I could grasp that."

She sat up and leaned forward. "All I can tell you is this. Ever since I got to this hospital, I've been praying. I mean pleading with God, Michelle. And sometimes I think He's hearing me. Every once in a while, a sense of peace comes over me. I can't really explain it, but it's almost like a part of me knows that everything will be okay. Maybe I'm just in denial or trying to make something up here. I really don't know," she finally concluded vaguely.

"You know, I think Steve's become a Christian," Michelle said.

"I didn't know that, honey. But that's good. I wish your father had something like that to hold onto. If he did, maybe he wouldn't be in this mess now."

"Do you think that Christianity is sort of narrow, Mom?" Michelle asked.

"Narrow? What do you mean?"

"Oh, I don't know. Old-fashioned I guess, or outdated. It just seems too limited."

"I don't think I understand exactly what you mean, Mimi. You should probably be talking to your grandfather about these concerns of yours. I'm not a theologian, you know," she said apologetically, reaching over and squeezing her hand.

"I know, Mom. It just seems like there are so many avenues of spirituality to explore. This guy I know back in Sandy Cove faxed me some articles about healing diseases and injuries with guided imagery. It's like using your imagination to heal your body. I tried to do it with Dad."

"Some of the stuff you have been exploring sounds pretty weird to me, honey. I think your grandparents' faith is more solid than that New Age stuff you're dabbling in," she said gently.

"You're probably right, Mom. When I tried to explain the things I've been learning to Grandpa, they all sounded so strange and kind of unreal. And when I tried to do that positive imaging with Dad, I almost felt silly. I wish I could just be like Grandma and Grandpa and know exactly what I believe and why."

"That's not such an unattainable goal, Michelle. Maybe you should start by spending some time alone praying." She patted her daughter's hand.

Michelle smiled and nodded.

"Well, I'm going to go back and sit with your dad," Sheila said, standing up.

"When Steve gets back from his walk with Tim, tell him I'll be in the chapel," Michelle responded. Her mother smiled and nodded.

CHAPTER TWENTY-NINE

Michelle breathed a silent prayer of gratitude when she found the sun-filled chapel empty. She walked up to the front pew and sat down on the oatmeal cushion, folding her hands in her lap and glancing around the room with its pale yellow walls and scenic watercolors. It was almost as if she was searching for something or someone. Finally her eyes lit on the cross.

She leaned back, closed her eyes, and began to cry. A gentle stream of tears rolled down her cheeks. Her breathing was shaky, as was her hand when she reached up to brush the sorrow from her face.

Where are you, God? her heart anguished.

I'm here, Michelle, a silent voice replied.

A warm blanket of comfort wrapped around her in the stillness. Michelle hugged her shoulders. Her tears were still flowing, but now they were cleansing her instead of swallowing her in sorrow. The presence of God was suddenly so powerful that she was afraid to open her eyes for fear of seeing Jesus Himself standing in front of her. It was as if she had entered another dimension. Her spiritual ears could hear the voice of God speaking.

Come to me, Michelle. I will in no way cast you off. Take my hand and I will walk through this valley with you. I will never leave you nor forsake you.

In that moment, Michelle's heart was pierced with the truth. She knew to the very core of her soul that God

Himself was present with her, and that He had come to meet her at this specific time and place. She sat silently, not moving a muscle, as she soaked in the words He'd spoken to her heart.

Then a thought invaded her mind. *This is not real, Michelle. You are only imagining it. Don't be a fool.*

She shook her head and frowned. Feeling agitated, she arose and walked around the pews. What if she really was just imagining it?

She paced back and forth for a few minutes. Her mind was flooded with so many thoughts—the memories of her grandpa's stories and prayers, the dreams and their interpretations, the tarot cards and the personal evolution classes, Trevor's thoughts and beliefs, her dad's self-sufficiency and pride, Steve's newfound faith in Christ, and her mother's vague but honest view of God.

As these thoughts swam in her head, two voices fought for control. One claimed to be the voice of reason, telling her to be wise and to recognize how much she was growing on her path to enlightenment.

The other simply repeated the call, *Come to me. I am real.*

From the recesses of her memory a song began to find its way to her consciousness—a melody about God's loving kindness and faithfulness in every storm of life.

Michelle smiled gently as she thought about how her grandmother used to sing that song while she washed the dishes. Until this moment, Michelle never really considered the message behind the soothing lyrics. Now she thought aloud, "Maybe you do really understand all my confusion, God."

"He does, Michelle."

Michelle jumped, startled by the familiar voice. She turned and her mouth dropped open with shock and surprise. "Kristin!" was all she could manage.

There stood her best friend since childhood, Kristin McKinley. Michelle could hardly believe her eyes.

Kristin quickly walked over and embraced her. "Sorry I startled you." Her hug brought a new flow of tears, and soon they were both crying—Kristin dabbing her delicate blue eyes with a tissue, her shining blonde hair reflecting the light of the chandelier overhead.

Michelle blew her nose and smiled. "What are you doing here?" she asked, feeling happy and amazed.

"Your husband called me. He thought it might be a good idea for me to come," Kristin replied, giving Michelle another quick squeeze and then holding her at arm's length and looking into her eyes.

"I'm so glad you're here," Michelle responded, her vision blurred by tears.

"Oh, 'Shell," Kristin sighed, holding her close while they both rocked and cried. The bond of friendship between them required no words, and Michelle drew comfort and strength from Kristin's familiar touch. The months and miles melted away, and they were best friends again.

After their tears subsided, Michelle looked Kristin in the eye and asked, "Do you really think He does?"

"Does what?"

"Understand?"

Kristin had a puzzled look on her face. "You lost me somewhere."

"God. Do you think he understands?" Michelle asked.

Her friend's face relaxed into a smile. "Yes, Michelle. He really does." She reached over and put her hand on Michelle's shoulder. "I've learned that God understands us like no one else ever will."

Michelle searched her face. This was the first time she'd heard Kristin talk like this. "How did you learn that?" she asked.

"You got my email about Mark, right?"

Michelle thought for a moment. "Oh yeah. He sounds like a great guy."

"He's taught me a lot about God. It's changed my perspective on everything," she continued.

"So Mark's a Christian?"

"Yeah. He's a youth pastor at the church we're attending."

"No way!" Michelle replied surprised.

"Way!" Kristin smiled.

"I guess we're both ending up with Bible thumpers," responded Michelle.

"Steve?"

"Yep. A friend of his from high school named Ben came to Sandy Cove about a month or so ago. He's a pastor now, too, and he was telling Steve all about his beliefs and sharing scriptures with him. I think they mostly got into talking about the book of Revelation and end times or something. Anyway, Steve's really into it now. He takes his Bible with him everywhere."

"That's great!" Kristin exclaimed. "So how about you? What do you think about God and the Bible?"

Michelle looked away. "I don't know. That was why I came in here. I'm really confused."

"Well, maybe we should pray," Kristin suggested.

Michelle was surprised. "Okay," she agreed. "You pray. I'll listen."

Settling down, side by side, on the pew, Kristin took one of Michelle's hands into both of hers and began.

"Dear Lord, there is so much on our hearts and minds today. Thank you for meeting us here, in this little chapel. First we want to pray for Michelle's dad. Lord, you know how he got to this place. Please help him find his way out."

She paused for a moment then continued, "I pray that you would make yourself real to him, even now as he's lying there in a coma. Be with him, God. Help him sense your presence. Reveal yourself to him in ways that he can receive and understand. I ask that you would use this time to draw him into your family, Lord. That today would be the day of salvation for him. And we ask that you would touch his body. Heal him, God. Bring him back to Michelle and her family."

She squeezed Michelle's hand then added, "And Lord, I pray for my friend, Michelle. She's asking if you are real and if you understand. Please draw her close. Touch her spirit with your love and compassion. Open her eyes to the truth and help her to choose you above anything and everything else. In Jesus' name, amen."

Michelle looked up and hugged Kristin. "Thank you. You are a special friend."

Kristin smiled and brushed the hair from Michelle's face. "God is real, 'Shell. He's reaching out to you right now."

Michelle just nodded. "What do I do, Kristin?"

"Why don't you just let Him in?" she replied.

"But what about all the things I've been learning and studying?" Michelle added.

"Let Him help you sort through them. He'll separate the truth from deception."

"I guess you're right," she agreed.

"Ask Him. Give Him all your questions," Kristin suggested confidently.

"Okay. I'll try. I think I'll just pray here by myself for a few minutes. How about if I meet you back at the ICU?" Michelle suggested.

"Okay. I'll be there," she promised.

"I won't be long," Michelle added. Kristin smiled and nodded. She got up and walked out of the little sanctuary.

Once she was alone, Michelle prayed. "Okay, God. It's just you and me. It looks like you've got me surrounded by Christians. I really want to know if you are real. But I guess the only way is to give you a chance. Please help me. Help me know you. Help me understand what is happening with my dad and why you let it happen. If you really care, if you really understand, please give me some kind of sign. Anything. I'll watch and listen."

Again Michelle felt a warm peace come over her. It was as if she had surrendered something that never really belonged to her. She stood up, looked at the picture of Jesus on the altar, and smiled. As she exited, she noticed another picture—this one of a shepherd guarding his sheep. The shepherd from her dream.

When Michelle walked into the ICU she was immediately met by Kristin, who grabbed her hand and pulled her quickly toward John's cubicle.

"He spoke, Michelle! Your dad just spoke!" she explained hurriedly.

"What? What did he say?"

"He just said 'Jesus'. That's all. Your grandpa was sitting there praying. When he stopped, your dad said 'Jesus'."

Michelle's heart was racing. This was her sign. God really did hear her! She threw her arms around Kristin and started to cry tears of amazement and joy.

They hurried into the cubicle. The nurse was checking John's vital signs and trying to get a response from him, but he was lying still, just as Michelle remembered seeing him an hour earlier.

Her grandfather walked over and put his arm around her. "Let's go find your mother," he said as he guided her out of the small room.

284

"I'll stay here with your father," Kristin said.

Michelle nodded. "Thanks, friend."

As they left to find the rest of the family, Grandpa Phil told her, "I've been thinking about what the doctor said, Michelle, and I've been praying for God to give me wisdom about how to counsel your mother on this 'no code' decision. I guess Kristin told you what happened. Your dad responded to my prayer, Mimi. We can't give up on him."

Michelle nodded in agreement. "What do you think it means, Grandpa? Do you think he understood your prayer?"

"I don't know, sweetheart. Maybe he was seeing Jesus. I can only guess. But I *do* believe it's a sign for us. A way that God is telling us not to give up."

"Oh, Grandpa, I'm so glad we have you here!" Michelle said as she beamed at her grandfather.

"I wouldn't be anywhere else," he replied tenderly. He cocked his head and seemed to study her as if he noticed something different.

"Grandpa," she began

"What is it, Michelle?"

"I'm going to try your way. You know—Jesus."

He beamed at her and drew her into a long embrace, then pulled back and looked into her eyes. "He won't let you down, sweetheart."

A few moments later, they found Joan, Sheila, Tim, and Steve walking back toward the ICU from the coffee shop. As Phil relayed the incident with John and his interpretation, Michelle drifted off into her own thoughts.

Thank you, God. Thank you for answering my prayer and for giving me my sign. Help me learn to know you more, she asked silently.

"So what do you think, Michelle?" Her mother's voice brought her back to the discussion.

"Well, I think Grandpa's right. It's a sign from God, Mom. Forget what the doctor says."

"I agree," said Tim. "It's way too soon to give up on Dad."

Steve nodded, taking Michelle into his arms. She could hardly wait to tell him about her time alone with God. Now they could learn about the Bible together.

As the family huddled together in an embrace, Michelle felt a sense of solidarity and peace that was ignited by hope. Her father faced a formidable foe, but many people were battling on his behalf, and she was not about to see him lose this fight. As she glanced at her grandparents, she saw them look at each other simultaneously and smile, then look up toward heaven. That same feeling of peace she had found in the chapel wrapped around her weary body again.

Turning to look up into Steve's eyes, Michelle felt a tear roll down her cheek.

"It's going to be okay, babe," he said softly, brushing away her tear with his thumb.

She nodded. "We've got to talk," she said softly. Turning to her family, she added, "We'll be back." Then she took Steve by the hand and led him to the chapel.

"Is this where you've been hiding out?" Steve asked as he looked around the peaceful sanctuary.

Michelle nodded. "Steve," she began.

"Yes?"

"Something happened in here a little while ago." She sank down into the pew and pulled him down beside her.

"What happened?"

"I don't know exactly how to explain it, but it was like I had an encounter with God."

"Want to tell me about it?" he asked as he searched her eyes.

"He was here, Steve."

"Who?"

"God. Jesus." Michelle gazed down at their intertwined hands and then looked back up into his eyes. Steve's expression was so tender that her defenses completely melted. "I can't put it into words, but it was almost like He was talking to me. Not like I could hear a voice or anything. Just talking to my mind."

"To your heart."

"Yeah."

He smiled and nodded. Letting out a sigh, he wrapped his arms around her. "I've been praying He would make Himself real to you."

Michelle nestled into his chest. "Guess He answered your prayer," she said in a near whisper.

He gave her a squeeze. "That's great, honey. He was here right when you needed Him most."

She nodded. "It's so weird, Steve. I feel like a different person now. Like a fresh start."

He smiled. "That's just what it is, Michelle."

She returned his smile and continued. "The past few months have been so confusing for me. All the stuff with the dreams and the tarot cards—I thought I had it all figured out. The New Age things Starla and Trevor were teaching me seemed so interesting... so empowering."

She looked down at the floor and shook her head. "Then this thing with Dad. . . well, it made me feel so helpless and confused all over again." She paused, and then continued. "All the stuff Trevor faxed to me seemed so empty. I knew it wasn't the answer I was looking for. It also made me think about how you and I have been going on different paths. It bothered me."

"I know what you mean," he replied.

"Steve?"

"Yeah?"

"I was thinking that maybe I could start joining you in your Bible studies with Ben. I think it would be good for me. Good for us."

"Sounds good to me," Steve agreed.

A silence settled between them for a few moments. Michelle glanced up into Steve's eyes and asked, "What are you thinking about?"

"I was just remembering something Ben said the other day when we were talking about your dad."

"What did he say?"

"He said that God has a way of bringing diamonds out of ashes."

"Sounds like something Grandpa would say." She smiled, her spirit feeling lighter.

"I really believe that God is going to work things out for your dad."

"I know what you mean. Even though I know that logically I should be worried, I keep getting this sense of peace and assurance that comes over me like some kind of promise from God."

Steve smiled and nodded again. "I love you, babe," he said as he pulled her into his arms.

"I love you too."

After they kissed, Michelle said, "We should probably get back to the ICU."

They stood up and walked out of the hospital chapel hand in hand.

As they entered the ICU cubicle a few minutes later, they found Tim sitting close to the bed with both of his hands holding onto his father's hand and his forehead resting on them.

Michelle put her hand on Tim's shoulder.

"Sorry. I didn't hear you come in," he said as he leaned back into his chair.

"How's he doing?" she asked softly.

"The same. He's sleeping, I think."

"Where's Mom?"

"She took Kristin over to the hotel. Kristin's staying with her in our room tonight. I'm going to stay here with Dad."

"Did Grandpa and Grandma go back over there, too?"

"Yep. Everyone was pretty exhausted."

"Do you want me to stay here with you?" Michelle offered.

"No. I'll be fine."

John stirred slightly, and Tim reached out and took his hand again. "It's okay, Dad. I'm still here."

Michelle's heart was moved as she saw the tenderness in Tim's eyes. He suddenly seemed so grown up, so much more mature.

"We'll see you in the morning, Tim. Call my cell if you need anything," Michelle added.

"Okay. Get some rest, 'Shell."

"I'll try. Thanks," Michelle replied as she reached out and squeezed her brother's shoulder again.

She and Steve walked out of the cubicle and down the hall, Michelle leaning against him drawing warmth and strength from his body. *What a day.* She was overcome with exhaustion and yet her heart felt light, hopeful. *Thank you, God. Thank you for all you're doing here for me and my family.*

Then she thought about the future, wondering what would happen to her father. Would he ever fully recover? And what about her mom? How would she manage in the weeks and months ahead? A heaviness tried to invade her spirit again. It seemed like there was just too much to deal with.

As they walked into their hotel room, Steve turned and hugged her tightly. "Michelle," he said softly, his voice shaking slightly.

"Yeah?" Michelle leaned back and looked into his eyes.

"Let's pray together before we go to bed."

"I'd like that," she replied with a smile.

As they sat on the edge of the bed, Steve took her hand in his. They bowed their heads, and as Steve began to pray, Michelle felt that same feeling of peace and hope. After months of wrestling with nightmares, she had a feeling she would sleep better tonight than she had for a long time.

Listening to her husband's voice as he spoke to God, and feeling God's presence in her heart and mind, was a moment she did not want to forget. It felt so perfect and right, like something out of a dream, a very good dream.

In a quiet place in the depth of her spirit, Michelle heard wonderful words of hope. *My peace I give unto you.*

"Amen," Steve said, squeezing her hand again.

"Amen," she replied.

NOTE FROM THE AUTHOR

Dear Readers,

It's been a long journey bringing Michelle's story to life, but I can still vividly remember the day when God shared with me that He was going to redeem the years the locusts ate away. Having spent the first thirty years of my life going my own way on my own strength and wisdom, I wished I could go back and relive them all with Him. Thankfully, as someone once said, nothing is wasted in God's economy. He had a plan for those years of searching, struggling, and dabbling in deception.

As a young girl in junior high school, I first became intrigued by the supernatural. Ouija boards, séances, and tarot cards became a part of every slumber party with my friends. Over time, I began taking my tarot cards to school and would sit on the field and "read the cards" for anyone who had a question or concern. Soon I had people I didn't even know stopping me in the halls to tell me that what I had shared from the cards came to pass in their lives. It was a heady feeling of power to know that I could somehow use those cards to see into the future.

I continued to pursue parapsychology and dabble in what I now know is the occult. I lived my life independent from God, doing what was right in my own eyes and not concerning myself with Him. I became involved in New Age thought and beliefs through some counseling I had for an anxiety disorder in my early 20's.

My therapist, a sweet and caring woman who had traded her relationship with Christ for the "broader" perspective of the New Age movement, taught me to seek my Higher Self, the inner guide who would lead me to all truth.

I began to formulate my own belief system based on what worked best with the type of lifestyle I chose to live. Snippets of Hinduism, Buddhism, and Christianity along with positive thinking and mindless meditation became my new spirituality. I looked down on Bible-believing Christians as narrow-minded and lacking enlightenment.

All of that ended in 1984, when my father chose the desperate act of suicide to escape a financial situation he feared would ruin his life. Rocked to the core of my being, I had nowhere solid to run, no God bigger than myself to help me process this horrific event. Suddenly all my "open-minded" beliefs dissolved like cotton candy. They had no substance to sustain me, no absolute wisdom to offer.

Thankfully, my sister suggested we turn to the Bible and find out what it really taught. We began attending a women's Bible study in the book of Luke, and the truth of God opened our eyes and changed our lives forever.

I believe God gave me this story for two purposes. First, it is to share the seductiveness of the New Age movement, and how easily one can be drawn into its enticing offer to basically become your own god. Second, I believe this story communicates the very real problem of suicide, how it can happen in any family, and how it does not always turn out the way the person committing it expects.

Like Michelle's father, my dad did not die immediately after his self-inflicted bullet wound. While he was lying naked under a sheet in the ICU, attached to a multitude of monitors, we were being told about the possible long-term residual effects of his brain trauma should he survive the ordeal. Partial or complete blindness and paralysis were among those possibilities.

Before my father passed away 36 hours later, my brother, my sister, and I were able to tell him how much we loved him. Tears streamed down his cheeks in response, and I can only imagine the regret and pain he must have felt as he heard those words. I believe that if he could speak today, he would tell anyone facing their own desperate situations that suicide is *never* the answer.

For those of you who have based your beliefs on a god of your own making, I urge you to reconsider the platform of your life. There is a God who has known you since the beginning of time. He loves you with a love you will find nowhere else. And He will see you through any circumstance that crosses your path in this life before taking you safely home to live with Him for eternity. A relationship with Him is only a prayer away. Ask Him to make Himself real to you, and then start studying His Word. Give Jesus' life and teachings serious consideration and decide whether or not you want to become a part of the family of God. He is ready to welcome you with open arms.

I hope you will continue your journey with Michelle in *Through the Tears* and *Into Magnolia* the second and third books in the Sandy Cove Series. You'll find a preview of *Through the Tears* after this letter.

Until then, may God's truth guide you.

With love,

Rosemary Hines

P.S. I would love to hear from you! Please feel free to email me at Rosemary.W.Hines@gmail.com. If you'd just like to be added to my email notification list for future releases or special offers, all you need to say in your email is "Add me!" and I'll be sure you are added to my contacts. You'll be the first to know when I'm about to run a special on one of the books or when a new book is in the works. ☺

You can also visit me on the web at **www.RosemaryHines.com** and keep up with my blogs and news on my Facebook author page: **https://www.facebook.com/RosemaryHinesAuthor Page**

ACKNOWLEDGMENTS

It seems such a small thing to simply make short mention of the many people who have helped bring Michelle's story to life. The experiences God brings to us weave a tapestry of beautiful people who support, encourage, exhort, and instruct us. Each author's tale is flavored by those experiences and people.

The foundation for this book was originally laid by my parents, who always believed in me and taught me to live my dreams. Without their unconditional love and confidence, it's certain I would never have undertaken this journey of writing.

Like Michelle, I had my own season of searching for truth and understanding. My husband, Randy, patiently endured my New Age explorations and my intolerance for traditional beliefs. In God's grace, He brought the two of us to a place of awakening at almost the same time, but through very different means. We had been married for eight years, when we became Christians and were baptized together in the Pacific Ocean.

Several years later, God placed a desire on my heart to write a novel that would share some of the experiences and lessons I had learned on my journey to faith. As I began to tell the tale, He used a number of people to guide me and teach me about this craft of writing. Without these people, I never would have completed this daunting project.

Among those who freely gave of their time, knowledge, encouragement, editing expertise, and instruction are my sister Julie; my friends Sheila, Patti, Nancy, Doris, Misty, and Jan; our pastor, Terry; Bonnie Hanson and Kathi Macias (Orange County Christian Writer's Fellowship); and my children Kristin and Benjamin.

I would be remiss if I did not also mention the almost 2,000 junior high students who called me teacher over the course of fifteen years and who kept after me by asking, "When is your book being published?" Here it is!

BOOKS BY ROSEMARY HINES

Sandy Cove Series Book 1

Out of a Dream

Sandy Cove Series Book 2

Through the Tears

Sandy Cove Series Book 3

Into Magnolia

Sandy Cove Series Book 4

Around the Bend

Sandy Cove Series Book 5

From the Heart

Sandy Cove Series Book 6

Behind Her Smile

Sandy Cove Series Book 7

Above All Else